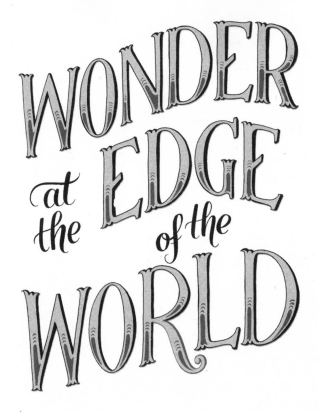

WONDER
at the
EDGE
of the
WORLD

a novel by
NICOLE HELGET

LB
LITTLE, BROWN AND COMPANY
New York · Boston

Text copyright © 2015 by Nicole Helget
Illustrations copyright © 2015 by Marcos Calo

Little, Brown and Company

Hachette Book Group
1290 Avenue of the Americas, New York, NY 10104
Visit us at lb-kids.com

Little, Brown and Company is a division of Hachette Book Group, Inc.
The Little, Brown name and logo are trademarks of Hachette Book Group, Inc.

The publisher is not responsible for websites (or their content) that are not owned by the publisher.

First Edition: April 2015

Library of Congress Cataloging-in-Publication Data

Helget, Nicole Lea, 1976–
    Wonder at the edge of the world / Nicole Helget; illustrations by Marcos Calo. — First edition.
        pages cm
    Summary: Lu Wonder, a bright, curious girl who hopes to be a scientist, sets out from her Kansas home in 1855 with her best friend Eustace, a slave, on a journey to Antarctica to protect a mysterious artifact and hide it from the man responsible for her father's death.
    ISBN 978-0-316-24510-4 (hardcover) — ISBN 978-0-316-24509-8 (ebook) — ISBN 978-0-316-36475-1 (library edition ebook)   [1. Antiquities—Fiction. 2. Supernatural—Fiction.   3. Family life—Kansas—Fiction.   4. Slavery—Fiction. 5. African Americans—Fiction.   6. Voyages and travels—Fiction.   7. Kansas—History—1854–1861—Fiction.]   I. Calo, Marcos, illustrator.   II. Title.
    PZ7.H374085Won 2015
    [Fic]—dc23

                                                                2014024900

10 9 8 7 6 5 4 3 2 1

RRD-C

Printed in the United States of America

✦

To my wonders,
Isabella, Mitchell, Phillip, Violette,
Archibald, and Gordon

✦

✦ CHAPTER 1 ✦

On days such as today, when the wind blows over the flat Kansan plain, I like to amble out to the slow slope of the clover hills and wheat acres to explore and to think.

"Keep an eye on Mother," I say to my sister, Priss.

Mother lifts her head as though she's about to say something. Priss and I both wait and hold our breath, but Mother closes her eyes, rocks in her chair, and returns to her muted world. Priss sighs. She favors our mother, who used to be known as the Beauty of New Bedford, in looks, delicate and fair. I favor Father.

"Make sure she eats something today," I add. Even though Priss is older and more responsible in some ways, I like to tell her what to do every now and then. Surely she doesn't need me to give her anything more to do, though. Priss does all the cooking and the mending, and the cleaning and laundry, too.

"Stay out of town," Priss says. She wrings out an old rag in a bowl of water mixed with vinegar and lemon. She's trying to wipe the soot off the windows, but all she's doing is leaving smears. It's not her fault. Ash from the fires in Tolerone floats on the air always, even though our farm is a couple of miles from town. It settles on the windows. It creeps up beneath the cracks between the floorboards and doors. There's a skim of ash on the surface of the water in our drinking barrel. There's ash on the blade of the bread knife. We drink ash. We eat ash.

I pull the hairpins out of my bun, put them in my mouth, and finger the snarls out of my hair. Ash from my scalp gets under my nails. It's a constant reminder of the tempers in town and in the whole territory of Kansas between the abolitionists and the slave owners.

Earlier this week, an abolitionist set fire to Carson's

livery because Carson's a slave owner. And last week, a slave owner set fire to the schoolhouse because the teacher is an abolitionist. It's summertime, so no one was there and no one got hurt, thank goodness.

Anyway, I don't care if Tolerone ever rebuilds that school. I never learned a thing there. Since Father's been gone, I learn everything on my own, and that's the way I like it. Priss, on the other hand, thinks rebuilding the school is very important. She has designs on being a teacher, I think. As prim and proper as she is, she'd probably make a wonderful teacher.

"Hallelujah Wonder!" Priss says. "Are you listening to me? Stay away from Tolerone."

"I heard you the first time," I say, still holding the pins in my mouth. I try to twist my mop back into a proper bun at the nape of my neck.

Priss wipes the window again. She won't stop until she hears a squeaking sound. "It's dangerous in town with everybody fighting all the time," she says. A squeak. She turns to face me and raises her eyebrows, which means she's serious. "It's *dangerous*."

"I know that," I snap. I don't like her telling me what to do so much, but she can't help that, either. She thinks she's responsible for me because she's older. I tell her all the time that I can take care of myself. I wasn't planning on going into Tolerone in the first place. In the second place, it's none of her business if I *was* planning on going into town.

"All right, then," Priss says. Her eyebrows drop, and she smiles a little bit. "Let me help you." She puts the rag in the bowl and comes to me. She pulls the hairpins from my mouth. With a yank, a turn, and a tuck, she tames my hair into a bun. Then she spins me around to take a look at her handiwork. "Now, that's better," she says. "Go. Enjoy yourself."

Everyone has always said that Priss will make a fine wife and mother someday. To my knowledge, no one has ever said either of those things about me. Lots of ladies in Tolerone are trying to get Priss, who's fifteen, to marry one of their kin. One noteworthy thing about Kansas is that there are two men for every woman.

Before I go, I straighten the blanket over Mother's feet, which are always cold. Mother remains thin-lipped, and she exhales. I know she's thinking about our old home and old life in Massachusetts. I know she's imagining salty air, seagulls, and fish stews. In her gray eyes, I can sometimes see the bay where we used to live. "Poor Mother," I say. She isn't well. She's not sick, though. She's heartbroken, which is just as awful.

Mother rarely says a word. Most of the time, I feel sorry for her. But sometimes, though I don't mean to, I get angry with her for sitting in a chair quiet as the grave. I want her to stand up and talk and do the work that Priss does. Sometimes I want her to be a mother again. When she can't, or won't, I have to get away from her. Once in a while, I'm afraid that if I don't, I might shout at her. Today is one of those days.

I walk outside into the beige-white light of the sun.

"Be back for supper!" Priss calls after me. "And put on your bonnet!"

I don't answer, and I don't put on my bonnet, either. Priss says the sun is the reason my face is so red and why I've got freckles all over my nose and cheeks, but I don't mind. I raise my face to it instead. The smoke has made the big skies strange with colors, like pinks and purples.

I walk for a while. My skirt hem brushes against forbs and shrubs, most blooming with tiny flowers. Wherever I go, bees and grasshoppers scatter. I choose a spot and sit to listen to my own breathing for a bit. In. Out. Whoosh high. Whoosh low. I inhale the hot, dry air. I exhale the hot, dry air.

From somewhere across the plain, a voice seems to be calling to me. It's like that sometimes out here. Ghost calls float on the never-ending wind. More than one Kansas housewife has gone batty chasing the calls of specters. One lady got so lonesome that she started talking to her chickens as though they were people.

I'd never do something silly like that. Not me. I know ghosts aren't real. There's no scientific evidence that supports the existence of ghosts. Still, I think I hear it, a strange call I know I can't be hearing. So I tell my brain to think about something else. One thing I don't want to be is a senseless Kansas lunatic. That wouldn't be very scientific at all.

For a time, I study the ground, until my eyes adjust to the workings of the tiny world of ants. Once I spot one, it's suddenly easy to see them everywhere, scurrying in their efforts to carry grains of dirt out of their burrows to make room for eggs and food.

If it's a new type of ant that I've never before seen, I'll very carefully disable a live one (meaning squish it firmly and then stick it onto a paper) so I can study it again later. Today, all these ants look the same. Instead of ants, I pick up rocks and look underneath them for sow bugs or grubs or worms. I check the rocks for specks of gold or ribbons of copper or maybe even fossils. But there's nothing new to find.

Finally, I lie down in the grass. For a while, I think about Massachusetts, where life was a lot better. I hold my breath until a noise like the swooshing of water fills my ears. Soon I can almost feel the earth rocking beneath me. I pretend I'm on a ship and the sea is dipping and bobbing. If I squint, the thin streaming clouds against the sky are the sails that guide a ship. On the windward side, the waving wheat glistens like gentle waves. On the leeward side, the curve of a rocky limestone outcropping is the breaching of a sperm whale, coming up for air.

I go on this way for as long as I can, trying to beat however long I held my breath yesterday. Eventually, though, I have to breathe again. And with the oxygen filling my lungs comes back reality, comes back Bleeding Kansas, comes back Father, dead and gone, and comes back the great responsibility I have of carrying on the Wonder name.

✦ CHAPTER 2 ✦

One thing you should know about me is that even though my name is Hallelujah, I like to be called Lu. I can hold my breath longer than anyone I know, a full two minutes. And you should know that even though I'm a girl, I'm smart, or as Father used to say, "Lu, you've got a good knot in your skull."

I'm going to be a scientist. As far as I know, that'll make me among the first lady scientists in the whole world, and certainly the first lady scientist in Kansas—maybe the only scientist at all in this sunbaked, thorny-plant, tree-lonely, dirty-water, skinny-animal, dusty-air, grasshopper-happy, God-forsaken place. Have you ever been to Kansas? I wouldn't come if I were you. For one, it's dangerous. For two, there's nothing to do here.

When I'm a scientist, I will sign on with an oceanic expedition and travel to the far reaches of the earth, just like Father did. I'll call myself an oceanist, a person who studies everything in the ocean, from the currents to the largest whales. On my expedition I'll discover new species of birds, fish, and plants. I'll sketch their likenesses and write careful entries in a journal about their behaviors and dwellings. I'll take samples of these specimens and preserve them. That way, people everywhere will be able to enjoy them and imagine what life is like somewhere else, which is a thing everyone is wont to do at least once in a while. I know I do all the time.

One nice thing about Kansas is that it's so boring that nothing is likely to interrupt you when you are imagining about living somewhere else. Lots of times, I just sit and imagine for hours and hours. I imagine what life would be like if our family had stayed in New Bedford, Massachusetts, the most beautiful and interesting city in America. It is the city where Father was born and Mother was born and Priss was born and I was born. Since staying there wasn't possible, sometimes I imagine what life would be like if we had stolen a boat and sailed away from America rather than come here to Tolerone, Kansas, where nothing remarkable or scientific ever happens, except for a cyclone once in a while. I've never seen one yet, even though the folks here talk about them as if they happen all the time. If I did see one, I'd probably run right into it and hope it would fly me away from here. Until then, I guess I'll just have to make do with my imagination.

I imagine what life might be like among the island peoples or the African tribes or in the Orient or the Mediterranean. Sometimes any place in the world seems like it would be better than Kansas. Probably even Antarctica is better, though only whales, seals, and penguins live there. I'm sure it's a very interesting and scientific place, even if no one really knows much about it. One day I'll see that frozen continent. When I'm a scientist, I'll study the hunting behaviors of killer whales and document the migratory routes of sperm whales. I'll feel the spray of their spouts and fluke splashes on my cheek if I have to follow them all the way to Antarctica.

Do you know anyone who has seen Antarctica? I bet not. Well, it was my father who first discovered it, before the British, the French, and everybody else in the seafaring world out looking for it, as though it were lost. My father explained to me that Antarctica is buttressed by an iceberg fortress and barbed with frigid gales and nearly impossible to penetrate.

But my father did it. He was like that. Persistent and brave and strong. And I am, too.

I have to be because I have a secret. I know the where-abouts of a treasured item. My father trusted me to take care of it, and I intend to be persistent and brave and strong enough to do him proud.

✦ CHAPTER 3 ✦

Most girls would fly into a frenzy if a cricket crawled on their leg. But not me. I hold very still so I don't scare it away. Because of the dry weather, the grasshoppers and crickets are thick in Kansas. I let the cricket crawl all the way down into my boot, where I suppose it's looking for a dark place to hide. Then I pick it off my calf, bring it to my eyes, and study it. I hold it gently by the abdomen between my fingers, and its legs kick.

Did you know that the noise crickets make is called

stridulation? Everyone thinks crickets rub their legs together to make that chirping sound, but that isn't true. A cricket uses one wing and rubs the top of it alongside the bottom of the other wing. The wings have ragged edges, kind of like a comb. The friction is what causes the sound. If you could catch one and watch it, you'd see for yourself that I'm telling the truth.

I have dozens of this type of cricket, so I toss it back in the grass. I wonder if there are any crickets in Antarctica. Or any insects at all. Someday I intend to find out. Here in Kansas, no one ever talks about places like Antarctica. Most people just converse about the drought, the fires, and slavery.

The only person in the entire territory of Kansas who is slightly interesting is my pal, Eustace. He's busy a lot of the time, helping his ma and taking care of his animals and whatnot. He can't have an afternoon recess for thinking, exploring, and talking any old time like I can. So I'm alone a lot.

Mostly, I don't mind. But sometimes I do. Sometimes being alone feels like being underwater. Everything looks hazy. Everything sounds muffled. And it feels like my throat is closing, like I can't breathe. That's when I miss my father the most. He knew lots of interesting topics to talk about.

Up in the sky, the moon glows dimly. Have you ever seen the moon in the middle of the day? As I look at it now, it seems like I could jump up and touch it. The moon seems closer than Antarctica. The moon, by the way, is what Antarctica looks like, according to my father.

I imagine I'm on a ship sailing right to the moon. I can feel the air turn cold. I can see my breath. I can hear myself telling the crew we must press on. Though the sun is so strong I can feel my cheeks and nose burning red, I shiver as though I'm really on that ship. I put my bonnet on and a shadow falls over my face as I think about my father, frost-bitten and half starved, climbing up into the slippery rigging of the ship *Vivienne*, many years ago.

The *Vivienne*, a small vessel that had been at sea along with another American vessel, the *Saint Mary*, had meandered through a dangerous field of jagged icebergs in an ocean bay about to freeze and doom my father and the ship's sailors to a glassy tomb. Most of the crew wanted to turn around toward warmer winds and familiar routes. The *Saint Mary*, led by Captain Cornelius Greeney, had already suffered terrible destruction and had to turn back. Captain Greeney had wanted Father's ship to assist the *Saint Mary* back to New Bedford, but Father refused. He was confident that his ship could make it to the frozen continent and claim the discovery for America.

The *Vivienne* pressed on. And after a few more days at the top of the rigging, Father squinted and saw in the distance the shadowy shape of solid land, the continent of Antarctica. On his map, my father wrote WONDER'S LAND to mark his discovery and achievement.

Have you ever looked at a map of the world? If you do, you'll see that the words WONDER'S LAND are right on there, on the continent of Antarctica, which is at the very edge of the world. Whenever I look at a map and see the name "Wonder" down there, pride fills up my chest like a big gust of wind.

One person whose chest did not fill up with pride upon Father's discovery was Captain Greeney. He was very angry with my father.

The same day as Father's important finding, in New Bedford, Massachusetts, after three days of labor and chills, my mother pushed my sister out into the arms of a midwife, who wiped her off, kissed her forehead, and said "Praise Be!" which became her name, but everyone calls her Priss.

My father stayed at sea for two more years, visiting

strange islands and living among the cannibal kings of Fiji and the bare-chested princesses of Tahiti. He collected all kinds of specimens and treasures. When Captain Greeney said to hand them over to the government, Father said "Absolutely not," which made some people mad and got him in a lot of trouble. But he didn't care. He hid the artifacts and returned to sea before anyone, Captain Greeney included, could do anything about it.

Some people might call what Father did stealing. But I don't. He risked his life to get the treasures. He said he was the only one in the world qualified to care for and research them. If you saw the collection, you wouldn't call it stealing, either, probably.

When he returned home to my mother, Priss was almost two years old.

Father stayed only three months, enough time to raise Captain Greeney's ire some more and to plant me in Mother before he raced to sea again. When I was born, the midwife wiped me off, kissed my forehead, and said "Hallelujah!" which is what my name is. But I go by Lu, like I already said.

When Father came home in 1845, he planted in Mother the first of our three little brothers, none of whom survived longer than a few months. With each one, Mother grew more and more watchful. I remember waking up to see her leaning over each of my little brothers in their turn at life, and I remember her putting an ear to their chests to see if they were breathing. But all her attention didn't matter in the end. They died anyway.

You don't have to be a scientist to figure out how the deaths of those boys made Mother feel. Father finally slowed down his world travels and scientific study and stayed home to be with Mother. Captain Greeney was on him like a dog on a pig bone.

Do you know what a court-martial is? I wish I didn't know. I'll just tell you that a court-martial is not good. And in Father's case, it didn't seem fair, either, as he was only doing what he thought was best and protecting his good name and preventing his artifacts from getting into the wrong hands. But it was impossible to convince the court that Captain Greeney, a man dressed in a decorated navy uniform working on behalf of the government, was "the wrong hands."

After the court-martial, we had to sneak away from New Bedford practically in the dead of night.

Now we don't talk about those days much. Though Father was a smart and brave man, he left a lot of loose ends for us to tie up. Mother's too fragile to handle it all, which is why I try to do the things the head of the household would do, as if he were still here.

I lie back and twine my fingers together under my head like a pillow. I stare up at the thin white clouds. Things go hazy. They go muffled. My throat gets thick and I feel like I'm underwater. I close my eyes and drown in the loneliness.

✦ CHAPTER 4 ✦

The wind blows. It sounds like whistling through a cracked window.

Then I hear far-away yelling. "Fob!" On these plains, it's sometimes hard to tell if I'm really hearing what I think I am or if it's just the wind being tricky. I flick an ant off my dress, an old hand-me-down of Priss's. Not that I mind wearing hand-me-downs. I don't like fussy clothes and prefer a dress that I can get dirty without anyone yelling at me about it. Priss will do it once in a while when she tries to act bigger than me. Even though she's older, I can look her right in the eye, my feet are bigger, and I'm still growing. I'm what a lot of ladies call big-boned.

"Fob!" I hear it again. Then: "Get back here!"

It's Eustace yelling for his dog. I sit up. The haze seems to have cleared. Before long, the lankiest, longest-eared specimen of a yellow dog known to man lopes through the grass toward me.

I put out my hand. "Whoa, Fob," I say. He springs at me with his tongue lolling out of his watery maw. He slobbers and licks. Fob walks like the back half of his body wants to be in the front. I'd never tell Eustace this, but when this dog dies, I'd like to cut him open and see whether he's got some nature of crooked spine causing such a strange manner of mobility. Eustace, my best and only friend in this place, walks up. He's picking his way with a long stick.

"Nice to see you, Lu," says Eustace.

"You, too, Eustace!" I say. I stand. I'm happy to see him, but I don't want to go whole hog with excitement. I don't want Eustace to know how lonely I was. "How did you get away today?"

He kicks some grass. A galaxy of grasshoppers and crickets fly in all directions. Fob goes wild chasing them. "Ma wanted me to come over and ask you if you need help this Saturday," he says. "She can spare me, she says to tell you." Eustace snatches a grasshopper off his pant leg and pops it in his mouth. He eats anything.

"Blech," I say. I stick my tongue out.

"They're good," he says. "If you were starving, you'd try it."

"I doubt that."

"Ma says they're as good as eating meat," he says.

Eustace's ma, Ruby, is the house slave of the Millers, who live on the north end of Tolerone. Mrs. Miller and Mother used to be friends before Mother took to her rocking chair. They used to spend long hours paging through their Bibles, looking for passages that approved or disapproved of slavery. They listened to each other and didn't argue the way all the other folks around here do.

Do you know what abolitionists are? Well, they're knotty people who fight for the freedom of slaves, which is good. But some of those abolitionists are making life dangerous around here. They are always riling up the slave owners.

My mother was an abolitionist before Father died, and a quiet, mourning pall fell over her. She was a nice one and didn't condone violence. She certainly didn't start fires everywhere. She preferred to talk with people calmly and try to get them to change their minds and their evil ways. Sometimes her abolition talk bored me. But I'd give about anything to hear her talk again now. I'd also give about anything for people to stop fighting all the time. If they don't quit it pretty soon, the whole country will be at war.

Mrs. Miller is awfully old. About a hundred, probably. She's from Missouri, and slavery has been in her family for years. She talks a lot about white responsibility and guiding black folks as God guides his followers. Her talk is real boring, too. Sometimes I've seen Ruby, Eustace's ma, roll her eyes at Mrs. Miller or groan real loudly when she goes on that way. Mrs. Miller can barely walk and hardly see, so Ruby would always come along to our house to take care of her when she and my mother got together. And Eustace would come with Ruby. That's how he and I became friends.

The Millers inherited Ruby and Eustace, their only two slaves, from a relative who died after getting snake-bit. Eustace was just a baby and doesn't remember, and he doesn't really work for the Millers yet because he's too young. Most of the slaves around here don't go to work until they're fourteen, unless they're girls. Then they can do housework or baby-rocking when they're eleven or twelve, but white girls have to do that, too.

Around here, no matter whether the girl is white, Negro, or Indian, as soon as she's old enough to churn the butter, someone's trying to get her married and make her a mother. The white ladies, especially Mrs. Miller, are the worst culprits. They're always ready to plan weddings and knit baby blankets. If I think about getting married and having babies, I shiver all over.

"You cold?" Eustace asks.

"No," I say. "I'm just thinking about something."

"You've always got interesting things going on in your head. That's for sure."

I smile a little bit. Sometimes Eustace says things that remind me of the way my father used to talk to me. And that makes me happy.

"Hot today," I say. I think about Eustace eating that grasshopper, and suddenly I feel thirsty.

"Surely is." He pulls a hankie from his overalls and wipes his face. Eustace's cheeks have a ruddy tone to them, like he's always blushing.

"I'll ask Priss if she needs work done," I say. "I'm sure she does."

"I saw your sows have gnawed at the fence posts you got on the south end of the sty. I can fix that so they don't run away, which they'll do if you give them the chance."

He shakes his head. "That is the sorriest fence I ever saw. Pigs are real smart. They're going to walk right on out of there one of these days."

Eustace is forever talking about how smart animals are. "I guess they're entitled to their freedom like everyone else." I pick my teeth with a thorn I found in the grass. "If I were going to be an abolitionist, I'd be an animal abolitionist," I say in a way between serious and jest. Eustace knows I'm talking about the collection of animals he keeps in his mother's backyard. He has trapped every species of critter imaginable—raccoon, possum, fox, bobcat, and turkey, to name a few—and keeps them in cages.

"You're not funny," Eustace says. He reaches down and gives Fob a scratch behind the ears. Then he looks out over the plains. His face is stony, like there's something the matter with him. I nearly ask what, but then I remember that Eustace comes and goes, talks and doesn't talk to me in his own time. No use rushing him.

I sit back down in the grass and pat for Fob to sit next to me, which he does. Fob lifts a leg and scratches himself. I giggle a little. I'm hoping that our sitting will encourage Eustace to sit, too, and stay awhile. I don't want him heading back home too quickly. But I know it's not really up to him. Sometimes his ma needs his help getting her work done.

Eustace is on the side of the abolitionists because he's a slave and wants to be a freeman. But for the past couple of years, the abolitionists have been coming here and starting fights that scare everybody. The town is full of threats and agitation. I wish they'd figure out a way to free the slaves without force. Violence doesn't seem like a very scientific solution to the problem.

Eustace says it's the slave owners' own fault the abolitionists have had to get tough with them. He says the slave owners have been stealing, beating, and even killing black people for centuries. It's time for that to stop, even if it takes fires, violence, and war.

I understand what he's saying. But war talk scares me.

Eustace stands there, fidgeting around and staring off.

"Anyway," Eustace says as he finally sits down next to me, "sows and peoples aren't the same.

"Did you discover anything new today?" he wants to know. He's not looking at me, though. I figure he's got something to tell me. One thing about having a true friend is that sometimes you get to a point where you can practically read that friend like a book.

I stay quiet for a minute. I wonder if he'll get to it. When he doesn't, I say, "Nah." I sigh. I pick at my teeth with the thorn some more. "I think I've documented every ant, animal, and plant in this part of Kansas."

"I'm sure you have," says Eustace. We both look out at the nothing all around us, nothing but acres and acres of dirt, rocks, and grass and the huge wide sky above them.

"I have to tell you something, Lu Wonder," he says, "but I don't want you to get upset and commence shouting."

I spit. I'm quite annoyed that he is suggesting I might overreact to whatever he's going to say. "You know me," I say. My heart is already beating fast.

He clears his throat. "Well," he begins. Then he pauses for what feels like several hundred years.

"Tell me," I practically shout. Fob moans. I smack my lips closed.

Eustace clears his throat again.

"When you're ready, I mean," I say.

"Well," he says, "I heard Ma talking with Mrs. Miller, and I think Captain Greeney's coming back here straightaway." He picks up a small rock and throws it. When it lands, a puff of dust rises and blows away.

At the mere mention of the captain's name, my face gets hotter than ever. I close my eyes and wish Eustace had said something else. "Maybe he's just coming to rile up the abolitionists again," I say. Captain Greeney is an abolitionist, too, but he is not nice at all, and happens to be a liar, a cheater, and a murderer. Father used to call him a charlatan, which is a word I don't know the exact meaning of but which sounds right. It sounds like a word that means you've got to look on the inside to see what the person's really like instead of being fooled by what's on the outside.

"Maybe," says Eustace, "but maybe he's gonna keep coming back here until he finds what he's looking for. That thing that you got hidden."

I toss the thorn and pick a grass strand. I chew on its sweetness and try to be calm. The thing that Eustace is talking about—I know exactly where it is. It's safe, for now, and it's my responsibility to keep it that way. "I got it hid good." I feel sweat sliding down my temples.

"I know you do," says Eustace. "But Kansas is too flat. People can see for miles. And Tolerone isn't going to stay a small town." Eustace scratches behind his ear. "The railroad is here. The people are coming. The lumber is coming. The town is spreading out." He waves his hand out over the empty plain. "Your hiding place is going to be in the middle of town pretty quick."

I look out to where he's waving. I don't see anything. "I don't know why anyone would want to come here," I say. "It's not nearly so interesting as Massachusetts."

Eustace hangs his head like he does whenever I get to talking about New Bedford and Massachusetts. "Well," he says, "eventually, someone's going to see you and follow you, and you'll lead that person right to the thing Captain Greeney wants. Maybe *he'll* follow you."

"He doesn't know me," I say. "He doesn't know what I look like." '

Eustace wipes his face with a handkerchief again. "Just seems like you should put it somewhere better, where he can't get it ever."

My whole body feels agitated. "Well, I can't help it that I'm in the most boring place with no good hiding places in the whole territory!" I shout. "Quit meddling."

Eustace kicks at the dirt. I know he hates it when I talk like that to him. I know it makes him think about all the white folks who are likely to be telling him what to do for the rest of his life. I didn't mean it that way. I just meant it as one friend telling another friend to shut his trap.

I reach out and give his arm a friendly slap. He rubs the spot like it hurt real bad, which I know it didn't. "Wanna go swimming in the river?" I ask. Swimming is how Eustace and I spend a good part of our time, but the rainless months have left the river low and muddy and full of slimy weeds and swarms of gnats.

"Nah," he says.

He wipes his face with his hankie again. "Wanna go fishing?" This is something else we do a lot, even though we never catch anything bigger than a pan fish or two, which Priss says are more work to clean and cook than they're worth.

"Nah," I say.

He whistles for Fob, who comes scrambling over, panting heavily. He's full of thistles.

"Wanna go to the cave?" Eustace asks, more quietly than before. He reaches out and gives Fob a pat on the neck and then pulls a prickly cocklebur off his ear. "We could make sure everything is safe and secure."

I'm quiet for a bit, so as not to seem too eager. "Sure," I say. I shrug my shoulder as if going there isn't such an important occasion. "Let's go to the cave. That's a good idea."

"Sure," he says. "And it's nice and cool there."

I look at Eustace sideways. "You're not gonna get scared of the bats or the bugs or the dark, are you?"

"We'll be outta there before dark," says Eustace. "Won't we?"

"By all means," I say. "We can be." He's scared of the dark.

"I'm not scared," says Eustace. "Ma will worry."

"I know," I say. He's also scared of his mother and about as dutiful a son as you'll ever find.

Eustace continues to pat Fob all over, feel for thistles, and yank them out of the fur. "You know it's my birthday next week?" Eustace asks. He shakes a barbed cocklebur off his fingers. It falls onto the dusty ground and Fob steps on it. He holds his paw up and yowls.

Eustace always says that most slaves don't even know how old they are, much less their birthday, so he's particular about celebrating his. "Oh," I say. "Now I remember. I'm not supposed to tell you, but your ma is making you a new pillow." I kneel down to help Eustace free Fob from the mess of prickly weeds.

"I'm getting out of here," he says. "I'm about to be fourteen years old, and it's time I make my own way."

"Out of where?" I ask. Fob licks my face while I pinch burrs off the fur on his belly.

"Kansas," Eustace says.

"What?" I ask, a bit too loudly. "What about your ma? Won't you get lonely for her?"

Eustace sighs real heavily, like he's expelling a great

burden. "I don't know," he says. "But I can't stay here. I'll get sold away from her before too long, anyway. Like we did from Pa. And my brothers."

I purse my lips and hold my breath. Eustace hardly ever talks about his father, and I've never heard him mention any brothers before. I remember the first time I asked him where his father was.

"Gone," Eustace had said.

"At work?" I had asked. This is difficult to admit, but for a smart person, I can ask pretty dumb questions sometimes.

"Ma and me were sold away," Eustace had said. "I haven't seen him since I was small."

"Oh," I had said. I'd tried my best to feel what Eustace must have felt, but I'd said something foolish instead. "My father used to be at sea for months and years at a time."

Eustace had looked at me and chewed his lip. He was thinking that wasn't the same as having been sold away from half your family. He didn't say anything to make me feel stupid, though. I felt stupid enough on my own. And sorry.

I had tried to be extra kind to Eustace for a while. At the time, I couldn't imagine what it felt like to not have a father around. But when my own father died, Eustace and I became closer than ever. Maybe because we had an understanding between us that very few people share.

Now I try to imagine what life in Kansas would be like without Eustace. I get a big knot in my throat. Loneliness is what that knot is made of. Some people don't think white kids and black kids should be friends. Sometimes when Eustace and I are in town together, an old man will say something nasty to Eustace and me if he sees us walking side-by-side. When that happens, Eustace walks head-down to the ground as though he's ashamed. "Never mind him," I always say. Then I give that old man my worst mad face. I'm not always perfectly nice to Eustace, but I won't stand for anyone else hurting him. Though I would never tell him it straight, I need him. He's my best friend, and I won't stand for him leaving me.

"I don't know if that's a good idea, Eustace," I say. "Where is there to go?"

Eustace raises his eyebrows and takes a big breath, as though he's about to launch into a long talk. "All these abolitionists are coming from Massachusetts," he says. "So I figure there must be a lot more like them back east. Maybe I'll go there. You can keep my place here in Kansas, and I'll go take yours in Massachusetts."

"That's the dumbest thing I've ever heard!" I shout.

Fob dashes back into the brambles that caused him all the thistle trouble in the first place. I gesture around at all the flat and boring land. "I don't even want dumb old Kansas. If anyone's going to Massachusetts, it will be me!" I stand up and put my hands on my hips so he knows I'm serious.

Fob runs back and jumps on us. The dust puffs up again and rises into the white sky. I try to remember the blue sky of the East, and it seems harder to do so, as though my memories are becoming fainter and fainter. I turn my back to Eustace and start walking away from him. I close my eyes as I walk. The sun beats on my face. Even my eyelids are burning. I worry sometimes that I'll forget everything about New Bedford or Father.

But suddenly Father's there in my mind, sitting at our table, holding a magnifying glass above two whale teeth, then lifting them each in turn up to the light coming through the window, and inspecting the objects from different angles. He puts them down and makes notes in his journal. "That my life's work could wind up in the ignorant and greedy hands of that scoundrel Greeney makes my skin bristle," Father says without looking up.

I feel like my arms and legs want to go limp and slide off my body and fall onto the ground. I'm shuffling along with my face to the sky and trying not to cry until Eustace grabs me to keep me from tripping into a jackrabbit warren.

"Watch where you're going," he warns.

"Thanks," I say. I'm embarrassed Eustace noticed the warren before I did. I wonder what my father would have said about my inattention. He always told me it was important to pay attention to everything, and I try to do that.

Behind us, Fob falls right in, and his legs go four-up and kicking into the air. A jackrabbit bounds out of the hole and pounces at Fob. Its two ears flit like knives. Fob yowls, surprised and scared, but then rights himself, shakes the dust off his scrubby yellow coat, and slinks away from the rabbit.

"Dumb, cowardly dog," I say.

But it was funny, and Eustace and I both smile.

"That could have been you, upside down like a dummy," Eustace says. "You must have been woolgathering. It's not like you to be clumsy."

I almost get mad at Eustace for using the word "dummy," but I don't. "That sure was feather-brained of me," I say.

Since I'm training be a scientist, it's my duty to notice everything, even things as subtle as slight depressions in the landscape. Usually, when I look across the plain and see a dip in it, I wonder about sinkholes and caves. That's called being curious, which is a different thing than meddling. I'm like that because Father was like that, too.

I scan the horizon. I know this place so well. That tuft of little bluestem grass. The patch of flax. That old cottonwood tree out there all by itself. A hole out yonder where the coyotes go. I know all of them.

And I know exactly where my cave is.

✦ CHAPTER 5 ✦

The cave, of course, is a secret. And even though it's easy to find once you know where it is, it isn't easy to know where it is. You could be practically standing on top of it and not know that right beneath your feet is a cave the size of two covered wagons.

To find it, first we walk as though we're going toward town, a half mile or so. Then we veer off onto the plain. There are no paths, no wagon trails, nothing. Like Eustace, Father used to say that someday every inch of Kansas and the rest of the West would be claimed, but when I look out here, I can't imagine a single body seeing a place he'd want to call his own.

We walk some more. Then I feel myself being propelled forward a tad bit faster, which means we're walking downhill slightly, which means we're close to the cave. I start to look for the ordinary gray rock that marks the entrance.

"How you and your pa ever found this place surely amazes me," says Eustace. "It doesn't look like there's anything out here but dirt and air."

I look ahead and see the rock. I spin all around to make sure no one else is nearby. Fob, as if to help, puts his nose in the air and acts like he's sniffing.

"It sure was a stroke of luck to find this cave," says Eustace.

"It wasn't luck," I correct. "Father knew what he was looking for, and he knew where to find it."

I kneel in the dry brown grass and tamp down some long green strands that grow beside the rock. Believe this or not, but I can smell the cave before I enter it. And I can feel a strange tingly sensation all over my body. A ghostly call seems to be coming from the cave, which, I think, must be the wind.

I start to get excited just thinking about the trove of

treasures down here. My father's collections. My father's life's work. The artifacts and specimens he brought back from all over the world are hidden down here in a little old Kansas cave in the middle of nowhere.

Father said his collection was better than any king's, any sheikh's, any emperor's, and any chief's in the entire world. He said it was the most interesting and diverse collection of scientific and cultural objects on earth. His eyes would get a little squinty and small when he talked about his treasures, and sometimes that would make Mother get a worried look on her face. The sides of her mouth would go down and her cheeks would sink. "A shame," she'd say, "that the citizens can't see what you've collected, my love. Wouldn't it be nice if ordinary folk could see the fruits of your labors?" She'd wring her tiny hands, as though hesitant to say these things to him.

Father would shake his head. He'd hunch over and mumble at the floor, talking to himself more than anyone in the room. "No one understands these things but me. No one else has spent months and years collecting and preserving these specimens." Then, as though he'd been jarred out of a trance, he'd straighten up and say, "Yes, of course. A museum is a marvelous idea. When the time is right. When the specimens are carefully preserved."

Have you ever seen a carefully preserved specimen? A dead thing that looks like it's still alive? I have. Lots of times. I've got lots of them down here. I've even seen an octopus, tentacles covered in suckers that look like buttercup petals, floating in a jar filled with alcohol.

Animals and insects that died a long ways away and a long time ago can be studied elsewhere and forever after if they are stuffed into jars and preserved. Sometimes the skin of the animal peels off a little, and sometimes the eyes disintegrate, but for the most part, the liquid preserves them.

I've also studied a tiny, knobby leg bone of a whale. Did you know that whales used to have legs? Well, Father said they did and that they used to walk on land. But the more time the whales spent in water, the less they needed the leg and the smaller and smaller the leg became, until it disappeared from the outside of the whales' bodies. That's what Father supposed, anyway. No one would listen to him about that, so he went on studying and collecting other things. But you can see for yourself that there are leg bones inside a whale. Sometimes, dead whales simply washed up on the shore in New Bedford, and you could walk right up to them and look at a whole skeleton, if you could stand the smell.

No one around here believes me about whale legs or about whales washing up on shore. It sure does surprise me how so many people forfeit their curiosity just because they're skeptical or stubborn. I like to keep my mind open to new information and ideas.

Eustace taps me on the back, which startles me because it's so unusual. He usually doesn't touch me or any other white person. I guess it's sort of against the rules, but I don't care. "Lu?" he says. "Are you listening?"

"To what?" I ask.

"To me," he says. "I asked if you were ready to go down." He's looking at me sideways.

"Course I'm ready." I push on the rock. It doesn't budge at first. Then Eustace helps me. We push and slowly slide it off a hole in the ground that leads back and diagonally. I can smell the moist air. And I almost think I hear a strange song or chant of some kind.

"Do you hear that?" I ask Eustace.

"Hear what?" he says. He leans his ear toward the opening of the cave. "Oh, that. That's just the fresh air moving through the cave."

"Oh," I say. I swallow. "Let's go in." I lie flat on my stomach on the ground and wriggle my way into the cave like a snake. Getting into it can feel a bit scary, but before

I know it, I'm at the end of the tunnel and dropping down about four feet onto solid ground. Then I can stand up with plenty of room above my head. I hear Eustace slithering in, too.

Caves are the most interesting part of this country, in my opinion. Like I said, Kansas seems a lot more boring than where I'm from, and a person's got to look hard to find interesting things to think about and study. Thank goodness for the caves.

Kansas's caves aren't like the ones a regular person might think of when they first hear the word. Kansas caves are not hollowed out in the sides of mountains or hidden behind hundred-foot waterfalls. Kansas's are mostly underground. You have to get into them by finding holes and sliding down. Most people might be scared to do this, but not me. As a scientist, I have to put my curiosity before my fear.

"You scared?" I ask Eustace.

"No, I'm not scared," he says. "Are you?"

"No," I say.

"I can't believe I lived here my whole life and never discovered a cave on my own," Eustace says. "I can't believe a white girl from Massachusetts had to come and show me one when I been walking over them all this time. I tell you what, it's a little embarrassing."

I'm flattered, but I can't take the credit. "Well, I wouldn't have found out about them without my father," I say. "He discovered them."

I wonder if that makes Eustace wish he had a father who taught him things. He's staring at the cave walls.

"I sure miss your father," says Eustace. "He was an uncommon man."

My throat gets tight. "I miss him, too," I say. "All the time." My lungs huff and puff, and I think I'm about to cry. But I really hate to cry and certainly don't want to in front of Eustace. I start rummaging around all the crates of artifacts and talking instead.

"One day, just after we moved here," I say, "Father and I were in town buying cloth and sugar, when suddenly all the townspeople began buzzing, whispering, and hitching up their wagons and gathering up their youngsters to go out to Stanley Gummand's farm, where, it was said, his herd of cows and pasture just suddenly fell away. As in, one minute the cows were grazing happily and mooing and swishing their tails, and the next minute they weren't."

"Hey!" Eustace says. "I remember that!"

"Hay is for horses," I say to Eustace. "Now, don't interrupt my story, or I won't tell it." Once in a while, I can't

42

keep myself from snapping at him. I've noticed that I do it most when I'm mad at someone or something else.

"Lordy," Eustace says. "Go on, then."

"It was said that the ground gave beneath them and a huge hole opened up and swallowed every one. Some of the townspeople were sure this was a sign from God, and others were sure the abolitionists or the slave owners were digging tunnels and had an accident."

I can tell that Eustace wants to butt in again and say something about the slave owners or the abolitionists, but I stop him by putting my finger to my lips.

"But Father knew better. So while the whole town came to gape open-mouthed and wide-eyed and suspicious-feeling at the big cavity in the ground and tiptoe to the edge to see the mangled cows buried in rocks and gravel, Father and I went out to the plains and poked around.

"He punched his stick at the earth here and there." I pick up a South American staff decorated with paintings of constellations and moon phases and demonstrate with it by poking at the cave floor. "Finally, we came to a place where a natural slope plunged steeper than anywhere else. Father looked around. Then he pointed with his stick to a grassy ridge, which if we were birds would have looked like a huge bowl encircling where we stood.

" 'This is a sinkhole,' he said to me.

" 'Where?' I asked. All I saw was switchgrass, dry weeds, and some thorny thistles.

"He tapped a stick on the ground. 'Right here,' he said. 'This used to be twenty, maybe thirty feet higher. We're standing in it.' Then he began looking around for rocks. He pointed to a purplish-pink outcropping. 'There,' he said. 'Let's look there.'

"Father heaved one more rock to the side. A scent like a wet cellar filled the air. 'Here it is,' he said. He jabbed his stick in to measure. 'This is going to suffice beautifully.'

" 'What will?' I asked.

" 'This cave,' he said. 'Look. Smell it. Rock. Moisture. Ancient air.'

"I looked down. And what looked like a place where an animal slides into his den opened up into a hollow room. I could hear rustling and squeaking inside.

" 'Don't worry,' said Father. 'Just bats. They'll be gone hunting by the time we return.'

"Within a couple of hours, we were moving through the dark with a horse, a lamp, and a cart full of crates tied up with ropes. We worked all night long to fill this place up with Father's treasure."

Eustace and I look around at all the crates. The walls

glisten with flecks of what looks like glass against pink stone. A fine dust floats in the air around us, and it, too, glistens, like fireflies. All around the room sit Father's crates with their descriptions on the sides: ELEPHANT IVORY, EAST AFRICA, 1839; STUFFED KOALA, AUSTRALIA, 1839; SPICES, TIMBUKTU, 1841; SPERM WHALE TOOTH, SOUTH ATLANTIC OCEAN, 1840; and more and more and more.

Eustace puts his palm flat on the cave wall. "These are granite," he says real quiet. "One of the hardest rocks on the planet." Just as I'm about to ask him how he knows that, he turns to me. "Your father told me about granite once while we were collecting stones for your hog fence."

"That's a good memory," I say. I try not to forget a single detail about times with Father. I love those memories. Memory is one kind of treasure. Most people don't recognize that what they already have is treasure, not just gold coins and pearls and rubies and doubloons, and maybe mummies.

I light the two oil lamps we keep in here. I hand one to Eustace even though there's quite a bit of light coming in from the hole.

"Thanks," he says.

"Fob coming down?" I ask. I look up and try to see him. Eustace laughs. "You know the answer to that."

I shake my head. Fob's such a scaredy-cat, scared of the dark and scared of bright light, scared of small places and scared of big places.

Eustace's favorite things to look at in here are the geodes, so the first crate I move toward is the one full of the split rocks resting in straw. Every crate in this cave is secured with a length of rope and a tidy knot on top, tied by me just in case somebody ever finds this place. I can make a simple overhand knot, an oysterman's stopper, a water knot, a fisherman's knot, a bowline loop, an eye splice, a Portuguese bowline, and even a hangman's noose, which I only practice in private and only imagine using on the man responsible for my father's death.

"You all right?" Eustace says to me.

"I suppose," I say. "Why?"

"You got the look in your eye," says Eustace. "The one makes you look like someone stepped on your tail."

I soften the look on my face. Streams of sunlight ignite the walls a deep pink color, but the temperature in the cave is cooler than it is aboveground.

I loosen the knot, a simple fisherman's knot, on top of the crate that says GEODES, AUSTRALIA, 1834, painted in my father's handwriting. The rope ends slip off and onto the rock floor, where they land with a thump. Fine dust flies

46

up, and Eustace sneezes. I pop off the top and swipe away the dust particles that float up from the dry straw inside the crate.

Eustace comes over and pushes aside some straw. He sneezes again. Then he finds his favorite rock and lifts it out.

"Careful," I say.

"I always am," he says, which is true. He turns over what looks like a regular gray-and-brown rock and reveals a hollowed-out inside, which is loaded with purple gems, amethyst. In the center of the geode, where hundreds of crystals converge, the color is deep violet, almost red, like an open wound.

"They're beautiful," Eustace says. He stares at the geode and moves it back and forth to let the light from the entry hit it at different angles. "Someday I'm going to give my mother just a tiny one of these kinds of gems. Where'd they come from again?"

"Australia," I say.

"Then I got to get to Australia and find one of these for myself."

"You can find them anywhere," I say. I bite at a sliver in my thumb. I pinch it between my teeth and spit. "America, even. They're more common than you would imagine."

I think about telling him how geodes are formed, about how rainwater sometimes seeps inside volcanic rock and evaporates and leaves the crystals, but I doubt Eustace is going to be a scientist, so I don't bother.

"Eustace," I ask, "what do you want to be when you grow up?"

As soon as I say it, I realize my mistake and wish I could take it back. Eustace doesn't have any choice in the matter of his future.

He doesn't dwell on that fact, though, and responds quickly, as if he's been thinking about all the possibilities for a long time. "If I could do whatever I want," he says, "I'd be a cowboy. Or a buffalo hunter. Or maybe a soldier or a rancher. Or a train engineer or a sailor. Or an animal doctor." He sighs. "Or a scientist like your father. I don't know. I guess that's foolishness."

I'm surprised. "That's not foolish at all," I say. "My father would have liked that you want to be a scientist, too."

And that's true. Father would have. Whenever Eustace was around, my father just talked to him the same way he talked to me. He liked having students or apprentices. Or maybe he liked having anyone around who would listen to what he was saying.

I try to imagine Eustace and me all grown up. I get sad

when I think that maybe we're not going to be able to see each other much if I'm a scientist doing lots of traveling around the world and making important discoveries and he's stuck here in the most boring place anyone can imagine, doing hard work he doesn't even get paid for.

I've had enough of the geodes, so I turn my back to Eustace and his box of rocks. I shuffle a couple of crates around, pushing aside a small one that contains the long, rolled-up skin of a thirty-foot crocodile that Father got in Africa. I tighten a loose end on a knot around a crate with hundreds of seed envelopes from the plants of East Africa. They are safe in their envelopes but make noises like a dried-up gourd or a rattlesnake tail when I push the box aside to get to the crate I'm after.

When I see it, I say, "Here it is!" and hold it up.

Eustace groans. "Ah. Not that one. That one is creepy."

I slip the rope off the top, pop the cover, and reach in and take hold of a large jar. I lift, very, very carefully.

A fetal shark, with white film where its eyes should be, points nose down in the jar. "Fetal" means it was a baby shark still in its mother's belly when Father collected it.

Eustace, despite his protestations, comes over and looks. "Even if it's only a baby," he says, "it looks like a killer."

I nod. "My father caught the shark's mother off the side of a ship," I tell Eustace, "and then he dissected it in the captain's cabin." My father was a very curious man. He always wanted to know what things looked like, inside and out. I'm like that, too.

"I'll bet the captain didn't like him cutting open a shark in his cabin," Eustace says.

I'd never really considered that some people might not have liked the way my father did things. Except for Captain Greeney, I've never considered that anyone else may not have liked my father.

I decide to change the subject. "Father said that all species of sharks, but especially great whites, follow the Atlantic sailing vessels, expecting the sailors to throw over scraps, or rats, or corpses."

I stop right there, even though there's more to that story. The rest is that sharks are smart, and they learned that by following the slave ships crossing the ocean, they could sometimes get a free meal of the dead people who'd get tossed over. Sharks are smart, if morbid. I don't tell Eustace that part. I don't want him getting sad about being a slave again.

I set the jar on top of a crate. I tap the side of it, almost expecting that the shark will come to life. "I wonder if its mother ever ate any people," I say to Eustace.

"I hope not," Eustace says.

"I wonder if the fetal shark ate its brothers and sisters," I continue. "That's what all fetal sharks do. They eat each other in their mother's womb. The ones that eat all the rest are the ones who get born. Sharks come out of the womb with a murderous past."

Eustace shudders.

One thing about being a scientist is that you are likely to learn things that give you bad dreams or make you shudder. But that didn't bother Father, and it doesn't bother me, either.

But there's one thing down here that *has* awakened me from my sleep a time or two. Some people with less scientific minds might call it wicked or evil or magic. And sometimes I admit I think it's talking to me, even from far away. I don't know why. I don't know how. I wonder if I'm going mad like those Kansas housewives.

I creep to a dark corner of the cave, the coolest area here.

The crate is small. No bigger than a watermelon. Around it, with twine, I have constructed a combination barrel sling, which means the twine goes under and around the crate. On top, I've twisted a butterfly loop, which creates a hook poking up from the knot for easy carrying should I ever need to move the crate in a hurry. In small letters on the side of the crate, Father painted MEDICINE HEAD, OFF COAST OF SOUTH AMERICA, 1835. KEEP COOL. DO NOT DESTROY! I wipe the dust off the top and unravel the butterfly loop until the rope rests on top of the crate, coiled up like a snake, as though protecting the contents.

Eustace shuffles his feet and clears his throat. "Um. Lu?" he says quietly. His voice sounds very nervous.

I don't look at him. "Did you find the thunder eggs all right?" Thunder eggs are rocks, kind of like geodes, but not exactly. Instead of crystals, a melty, swirling pattern of colors is created inside an otherwise ordinary rock.

"Yes," he says. He sneezes. "This one with the swirling white and red and orange and brown colors is my favorite." I turn and look.

"Oh, I know that one," I say. "It's from America, from the western coast near the Columbia River, where Father almost lost his life once. It's a very dangerous river to navigate."

Eustace rubs the thunder egg between his thumb and forefinger. I've done that, too. "This looks like it couldn't be found anywhere on earth. It's too perfect." He puts it up to his face and presses it against his cheek. The smooth, flat surface feels cool, I know.

"Keep it," I say. "Keep that one." Eustace ignores me. He wouldn't keep it. Eustace has real strict ideas about what he owes and what he's owed. He wouldn't take the thunder egg because he feels he hasn't earned it.

I'm worried I might have embarrassed him somehow or hurt his pride. I'm also worried when he asks me, "Are you planning on opening that crate?" He's nodding at the Medicine Head's box.

"You could earn that thunder egg by fixing our pig fence." I smile brightly, trying to distract him from thinking about the crate I want to open.

"Maybe," he says. "I'll consider it." He stares at me for a while, waiting for me to make a move. But I don't. I'm not even breathing. Behind me, I can feel the presence of the Medicine Head. I can feel it so strongly, I swear I can hear it breathing. I put my hands in the air above the crate.

"Lu!" Eustace practically shouts. "I've got to get home. Let's get going."

"Just wait a darn minute, Eustace," I say.

He quietly slumps against a cave wall as I put my lamp down.

I touch the crate that speaks to me, the one that seems alive, the one that Captain Greeney craves, the one that

Father was adamant about protecting. I unknot the rope that holds the lid to the box and slide the twine off the Medicine Head's crate.

I lift off the top and peer down into the crate.

There it is, just the way I left it.

✦ CHAPTER 6 ✦

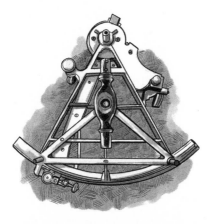

In the glow of the firelight, it looks more haunting than usual. The Medicine Head, an object said to bring power to whoever owns it, faces up. Here, before me, is an object, sacred to its tribe, reputed to remember history and foretell the future. Here is an object said to defy scientific explanation. I remember so well the way Father leaned over it and said these words.

I am disgusted by it. I am mesmerized, too. I have looked at the Medicine Head a dozen times, but I have never held it. Lately, I feel pulled toward it, like an invisible rope draws me close. Even while I'm in bed, in the darkest hour of night, the Medicine Head tugs on my mind. Sometimes, while I'm supposed to be doing my chores, I find myself standing in the yard, looking out over the prairie and daydreaming about the Medicine Head.

From somewhere in the cave, a voice seems to be whispering *Hold me*. Though I can't explain how I know or how it's doing it, the Medicine Head calls to me.

I trap my breath in my mouth and pinch my lips together. My fingers are inches from its skin. I'm so close that I start to worry that I will accidentally touch it before I am ready, so I move my hands back again. Its hairs extend out in every direction, like light off the sun.

I put my hands into the crate again and hold them over the head in the way I've seen lots of Kansas preachers put their hands over sinners. I'm sweating. I can taste salt on my lips.

"It's hot in here," I whisper. Everything else around me quiets and blurs.

I can feel life in the Medicine Head.

My hands shake with strain and restraint. I jerk my hands out of the crate again. "Get ahold of yourself," I say out loud.

Eustace looks up at me. "What?" he asks. He dabs his forehead with a hankie.

I'd almost forgotten he was here. "Not you," I say.

The reason I have never held the Medicine Head is because it is a real head, or rather, *was* a real human head. A shrunken head. In this crate is a *disembodied cranium*.

Do you know what a cranium is? "Cranium" means skull. The skull is where the brain is when a person or animal is alive. "Disembodied" means the head has been removed from the body, usually with a big knife or sword or guillotine. Have you ever seen a real human head detached from its body? Probably not. But you probably didn't have a famous scientific father who traveled to the far reaches of the earth, either.

"What are you doing, Lu?" Eustace wants to know.

"Mind your own business," I say. He turns his back to me while he shakes his head, as though his feelings have been hurt again.

The Medicine Head has a nose, two eyeholes, two lips, hair, ears, and eyebrows. It's been stripped from its skull, boiled, shrunken, tanned, and stuffed with sand, but this head used to be on a body on someone in the world. I have always imagined that it used to be a young man, though it's hard to tell now. Inside this head used to be a brain, a mind thinking thoughts and feeling feelings. Maybe the brain that used to be in this head once looked at the night sky, wondering about the changing constellations or the phases of the moon. Even though its mouth is now stitched closed, words used to flow freely from it. Maybe he fought with his siblings and said things he didn't mean. Maybe he said *I'm sorry*, and maybe he said *I love you*.

I feel breath at my back and I jump.

"I'd favor you putting the cover back over that head," Eustace says.

"I'd favor you not sneaking up on me when I'm not ready," I snap. My heart's thumping. "Aren't you the slightest bit curious about this? Don't you wonder about it?"

"Not really," Eustace says. But he leans over and peers in. "What's in the nostrils?"

"Dried leaves, I think," I say.

"What do you think he smelled last?" Eustace asks.

"Maybe breakfast," I say. "Maybe ordinary things like coffee, eggs, berries with milk."

"Maybe his father's morning tobacco," Eustace adds. "My pa used to smoke in the morning." He exhales loudly.

I hold my breath and wonder whether Eustace will say more about his father. He doesn't. We quietly stare at the head.

This head used to see. Maybe the last thing he saw was a freckle on his sister's face, the blanket his mother made for him, a bird with colorful wings. Maybe not. Maybe it was the ash of a fire, the blur of a hatchet, or his own blood seeping out of a wound.

Sounds used to dance in those ears. Maybe he heard his mother hum a lullaby or his father teach him something about trapping or identifying food. He heard the paws of an animal prowling in the night and the hoot of an owl and the giggle of a baby.

I exhale. I can hear Eustace breathing. Outside, the crickets chirp. A wolf howls somewhere in the distance.

I stretch my hands over the Medicine Head again, my fingers hovering an inch from it, maybe less. I want to pick it up, but I'm scared, so I try to reason. *This is an object,* I tell myself. *It's not real. It won't bite. Its eyelids are skewered shut with wooden needles and won't try to open. Its lips are pierced with a half dozen of those same wooden needles and crisscrossed with some kind of twine, and they won't move, won't shape a howl or a scream. The nose won't suddenly flutter with breathing.*

Then, very deliberately, very slowly, very tentatively, as though I were reaching out to touch a live snake and survive to tell about it, I lower one of my pointer fingers until it is touching the forehead of the Medicine Head.

We are skin to skin.

The forehead is cool, and it gives way against the pressure of my touch, as though I have pressed my finger into wet sand. I gently lower three more fingers of my right hand. My pinkie touches the ear, which feels like an old prune. My middle and ring finger touch the hair, which feels normal, like a live person's hair. I lower my other hand and softly work my fingertips under the head, into the prickly straw that holds it. Then I lift the Medicine Head from the crate and bring it up to my eye level.

What feels like the gale from the front of a thunderstorm hits me in the face. My hair blows back. I take a big breath, the kind you take before you know you're going underwater. Wind rushes past me. A loud whooshing noise fills my head but then is replaced by voices, some familiar and some not, yelling and screaming in my ears. I see flashes of faces—there's Priss! And Mother the way she looked in New Bedford! I see a dock boy from Massachusetts I once liked. I see the fat smiles of my baby brothers, and then I see Father lighting his pipe, his mustache moving up and down as he puffs. Then, the wind, the voices, and the faces stop, and I am back one year.

I know this day. I've replayed it in my daydreams and

nightmares a thousand times. I try to shake my head, to let go of this memory. I try to get out of it. I want to be back in the cave with Eustace. But I can't.

The Medicine Head has put me here, or at least has put my mind here, and it won't free me.

CHAPTER 7

Eustace, Priss, and I are swimming. Then I get a fluttery feeling in my gut, as though something is about to happen.

I am floating on top of the water. But my skirt wraps around my legs, and I can't kick. I start to go under. My skirt swirls completely around my legs until I am wrapped tight like a mummy. I hold my breath, reach down, untangle my legs, and thrust to the surface. I gasp.

Priss is back-floating in absolute calm. She rights

herself and swims vertically. "Lu," she says, "what's the matter?"

I sputter. "I nearly drowned because of this stupid skirt!" I shout. "That's what's the matter!"

Only Eustace's legs appear above the water. His head is in the depths. Then his legs go arrow straight, disappear beneath the surface. His head pops up a few feet from mine.

I have a bad feeling and start paddling for the shore. "Let's go!" I say to Eustace and Priss. "Right now! Let's go!"

"Lu!" says Priss. "We'd never let you drown. We'd save you. Eustace or me."

I climb out onto the muddy bank. Fob is right behind me. "Well," I shout at Priss, "you're the one who gave me this heavy skirt! Almost like you wanted me to get weighted down and killed."

"Lu!" says Priss. "What is the matter with you?"

"I want to go!" I shout. "Right now!" I stand up on the shore and wring out the hem of my skirt. "This is a bad day." I reach for my boots and slip my wet feet into them.

Eustace looks at Priss, and Priss looks at me. She says, "That's silly, dear." But she swims toward the shore, and Eustace follows behind her.

On our walk back home, we see a dust cloud rising up from near our place. I quicken my pace. My wet skirt slaps against my legs.

"Oh no," I say.

"What?" says Priss. "What?" She looks up and sees the dust cloud. "It's only horses." She doesn't understand. But I know the dust from the horses' hooves is connected to my bad feeling.

Eustace squints at the dust and the shapes of horses galloping. "You know those people?" he asks. Fob growls. He knows, too.

The cloud grows, and we can hear the pounding of hooves. I look to my right and left for a good place to hide. There are only grasses and weeds. Tall and thick.

"Get in the grass!" I shout as I push Priss into the brush. "Get down!"

"What's going on?" Priss cries. Her eyes are big as potato slices. Eustace helps me get Priss and Fob down in the brambles and thorns.

"Ow!" moans Priss, and I tell her to be quiet and I press my hand over her mouth hard. I lie down on top of her and cover her body with mine. I'm instantly aware of the rise and fall of her worried breathing.

Within a minute, I can also feel the vibrations of the

horses' hooves. Eustace has got his whole body on top of Fob and his hands around the dog's neck. Fob's eyes are bulged from the pressure of Eustace's hands, but he can breathe a little and can't bark. I'm grateful for Eustace in this second. He's brave and quick and dependable. We catch each other's eyes. He scrunches his eyebrows and then nods in a way that suggests to me that he understands, as I do, that something very serious is occurring.

We wait, we four—a dog, a slave boy, and a couple of girls—as the horses and riders and what I know is death itself thunder past us. As they do, though I know I shouldn't, I raise my head and count them. Eight. I see black, shiny boots like the ones Father wore when he was in the navy.

The last rider gallops more slowly than the rest. We're hidden well, but he's looking at the grasses as though he knows we're there. Even in the shadow of his hat, I can see his blue eyes, which are cold and shallow. Beneath his mustache, it seems to me he's grinning.

He slows his horse. I put my head back down and hold my breath. I am still as a stone until I hear the horse pick up its pace again.

Then there's nothing but a coiling dust cloud and the wind rustling the grass. When we can't hear them anymore, Eustace and I release our holds on Priss and Fob, who spring to life like a couple of prairie dogs out of a flooded hole. Priss slaps my hand away.

"Tell me what's going on!" she demands.

"I don't know exactly!" I shout. "But we've got to get home! Those men were the ones Father's been fearing. I know it."

"They sure seemed in a hurry," says Eustace. "I'm going to get my ma to help." He slaps his hand on his thigh, a signal to Fob to follow. Then they bolt across the flatlands toward Tolerone.

Priss and I stand up, and I start running. I turn to look for Priss, who stands where I left her. *"Come on!"* I scream. She runs, too.

As we get closer, the top of the big cottonwood tree comes into view, black against the afternoon sky. We keep running, even if we don't know what toward. Then the tree, with its full top, thick and sturdy branches, and huge and solid trunk, comes into full view. I see a rope strung from one of the lower branches. It looks like a straight black line cutting the sun behind it. The sun has cast layers of orange, yellow, and pink on the horizon, and the rope intersects those lines perfectly. But the end of the rope leads into the shape of a head, then a neck, and then a body with arms and legs. And the whole thing swings.

At the end of that rope is a man, strangling. I know it's Father. His legs kick and jerk, which means he is alive and struggling. We are a half mile from that tree, and I try to remember how long it takes me to run that distance. Three minutes? Three and a half? I want to yell to him to stop struggling, to be still. I want to shout to him that the more he struggles, the more weight he'll put on the loop around his neck, which will put more tension in the rope, which will tighten the knot. I run faster. Priss is way behind. She can't keep up.

I try to figure out how long it's been since the riders passed us on the road, and I try to calculate how long, exactly, a person can survive without air as I run toward my father, the great scientist, the great voyager, the great discoverer, the great seafarer, the great cartographer, the man who discovered Antarctica, the man who left his name at the edge of the earth, the man I love more than anyone else in the world, who is swinging from the tree by his neck.

We run and run, and only slowly does the tree or the man seem to get any closer.

Then I'm there. His feet dangle at my eye level. I stand beneath him, throw my arms around his legs, and push them up to take tension off the rope.

"Stand up!" I shout at him. "Stand up!" I lift up on his legs, trying to take the pressure off his neck, but it's no use. His legs feel like they weigh a thousand pounds.

He's been dead since before I touched him, and I know it.

I was too slow. He couldn't hold his breath long enough for me to reach him. I was far too slow.

Priss is asking "Why?" and "What do they want?"

The treasure.

They want the artifacts—the Medicine Head, especially. Father knew they'd come.

That's why he hid it all in the cave. I lie over his chest, and I tell him how much I love him. I tell him I won't let him down. I tell him I'll protect the treasure. I stay like that until dark, until Mother, Priss, Eustace, and Ruby pry me away.

Hours later, the owls are hooting and the coyotes calling. Inside our house, just one lamp is lit, casting a gloomy glow in the kitchen. I sit on a chair with my head resting on my arms and my arms resting on the table. My head is too heavy to lift.

"They want the head," Mother says. "That stupid head! I told him a hundred times to destroy it!" She rocks back and forth on her heels. "He wouldn't." She cries and bites on her fist. "He wouldn't give up the head. He told Captain Greeney he had destroyed it." Mother holds her little fists up to her eyes, as if she'd like to block out everything, not see anything. "Then, then..." She trails off, crying.

"Then what?" Ruby asks. She's trying to make sense of everything.

Priss stands behind me and strokes my hair. I can't move.

"Charles," Mother says, "told Captain Greeney that he destroyed the Medicine Head. Then Captain Greeney said, 'Well, there's one way to find out if that's true,' and they dragged him to the tree."

"That doesn't make any sense," I whisper. "What does 'There's one way to find out' mean? They'll be back."

Then I'm released.

I'm back in the cave, face-to-face with the Medicine Head.

✦ CHAPTER 8 ✦

The corners of the pierced and stitched mouth have somehow curled up in the kind of smile one wears after sharing a deep, dark secret.

I toss the Medicine Head back in the crate. It lands in the straw face-down.

"Oh!" I cry. I'm shaking and sweating, and my mouth is dry. I look at it again. I don't know why, but it bothers me that the face is buried in the straw, so I grab the sides of the crate and shake them a bit until the Medicine Head is right-side up again. Now the lips don't seem to be fashioned into a creepy grin. I wonder if I imagined the smile or if, maybe, I imagined the whole thing.

"What?" says Eustace. He puts his hand on my shoulder. "Lu! What happened?"

"Nothing!" I shout. I wipe my hands furiously on my skirt, as if I could rub away the bad feelings, the powerful longing I have to see my father alive again.

I remember all that I saw. How is this possible? How was the Medicine Head able to show, moment for moment, the worst hours of my life? Why did it want me to live them again?

"Shut that crate," Eustace says.

I know he's serious because he never orders me around. But I just stand there, still trying to clean my hands.

He picks up the cover and slaps it back on the crate. The Medicine Head returns to darkness.

"What happened?" he asks again. "You were..." he bumbles. "I couldn't... you were in a trance or something." He turns to me and holds both my shoulders. "What did you see? I was trying to talk to you, but..."

A strained, tight sensation hurts in my chest and throat, like I've swallowed a rock. I know my eyes look watery, and I wonder if Eustace can see me crying.

"You scared me," he says.

I can't respond. My face feels hot and full of pressure. I wipe my eyes. *Be logical,* I tell myself. *Don't cry anymore. Don't cry.* I hold my breath.

Eustace must sense my struggle. He hugs me, which is strange and stiff and awkward at first. But I return the hug, even though it feels strange to hug anyone, much less a boy.

After a few seconds, I blow out a big breath and sigh. Then I pull away from him and kind of laugh.

"What's so funny?" Eustace says.

"Boy, what I'd like to do to that murdering son of a gun!" I shout. My words echo in the cave. Fob moans.

"It's OK, Fob," Eustace yells up to him. "Everything's fine." Then Eustace turns back toward me. "Captain Greeney, you mean? Lu—"

"Don't tell me to calm down!" I shout at him. "Don't! Right now I feel like I could break through the cave wall with my bare hands!"

"Whoa," Eustace says. "Do you need a drink of water or something?"

"I don't understand it," I say. I'm talking to myself, but I'm talking out loud. "I saw my father. I saw Captain Greeney, the noose, you, Priss, me, Fob. I saw the whole terrible scene *again*!" I yell.

Outside, Fob barks.

"It's all right, Fob," Eustace calls up to him again. That Eustace is always worried about animals. "What do you mean, you 'saw' it?" he asks me.

I take a deep breath and sit on the cave floor. I put my hands over my face for a bit. "It was as if I relived it," I say. Remnant images still flash in my mind. The one I hate most, Father dangling at the end of the rope, is always the most difficult to shake. I blink, and I blink again.

"Maybe you were using your imagination or you were dreaming or..." Eustace trails off. "If the Medicine Head can do that, what else can it do? I mean, what else could it show?"

"That is a good question," I say more quietly.

"Sounds like black magic to me," he says. "You shouldn't touch it ever, ever again."

My heartbeat slows, and I don't feel quite so mad anymore. I'm sweating everywhere. The top of my dress is soaked. Eustace looks like he's been dunked in the creek. I breathe regularly. In and out.

"There's no such thing as magic," I say. "Everything is science. One thing about science is that you have to accept limitations. Just because you can't understand how something works right now doesn't mean that it won't be explained someday."

"You mean you think there's a scientific explanation for holding a human head and reliving awful events?" Eustace says. "I don't think so."

"I don't know," I say. "I don't know all the answers, darn you, Eustace. But that doesn't mean that what just happened won't be explained someday. It just means I need more time to study it."

"I think you ought to get rid of it," Eustace says. He's looking toward the cave opening. He probably wants to go home. His ma worries. I wonder then if Priss is worried about me, too. Or Mother. I doubt she's even realized I'm gone.

My heart starts up fast again. My body stings as though I've been shot with lightning. My hands throb as though they've been pumped with thunder. I feel mighty as a summer storm.

"Lu," asks Eustace, "are you all right?" His voice is soft and kind. "Your eyes look funny," he adds. "What are you thinking about? Are you hurt?"

"When did it get so hot in here?" I ask. "This place is usually the coolest spot we know." I've got sweat dripping off me. Sweat beads and runs down Eustace's face, too.

"Could be when we opened the cave," he says. "Moved the stone. I don't know. Could be we let out the cooler air."

"Maybe our body heat made it so hot," I suggest.

"Or maybe the temperature outside rose while we were down here."

"Maybe," I say. "All I know is that the temperature rose, and that thing started...talking to me." I search Eustace's face to determine whether he believes me or not.

He doesn't say anything, but I can tell by his stare and closed lips that he does believe me. I can also see that he's worried.

"You know," I go on, "I never once saw Father bring this into our house to study it." I point at all the other crates. "Every other one of these artifacts has sat on our kitchen table. I would see him turning them over, looking at them, making notes. But not the Medicine Head. Not once."

"Hmm," says Eustace. "That is curious." His eyes have a look that only parents have when they're not sure a kid is telling the truth but they want the kid to keep talking so that they can sort it out.

"I'll bet that's why Father kept it down here," I go on. "To keep it cool. Maybe its power has something to do with temperature." I spin around and glance at the walls,

at the organization of the crates, and at where the Medicine Head was kept, in the darkest, coolest place. I read the instructions on the top of the crate. "Yes," I say quietly.

Now Eustace turns around, too. I can tell he's trying to see what I'm seeing. "Tell me all of it," he says. "Tell me everything you know about the Medicine Head."

I hate to be a know-it-all, but I sure do enjoy sharing what I've got in my brain. "Fine," I say. "But don't come crying to me if what I tell you gives you bad dreams."

✦ CHAPTER 9 ✦

The cave is darkening by the minute. Long, eerie shadows grow on the walls, like ghostly watchmen. The sun must be going down. "Sit here," I say. "I feel worn out. And I don't like you standing over me." I turn up the wick of my lamp a little, but I haven't got much oil left. It's good oil, though, spermaceti, the best illumination oil you can get.

Do you know what spermaceti oil is? Well, if you don't, I'll tell you. Spermaceti oil comes from the gigantic head of a sperm whale. The oil lights up brightly. It doesn't produce a lot of black smoke and soot. Plus, it burns a long time. When we moved here, we brought a whole cask of it, which we keep in our barn. The cask took up a lot of room and was expensive to move, but Father said it would be worth it because there's nothing better in the world than a whale oil lamp to read and write by.

Here in Tolerone, everyone uses the cheap stuff. A lot of people even use tallow candles still, and a good number of people live in houses made of mud blocks. Kansas seems to be about ten years behind everything we had in the East. I guess people here in this sea-empty place don't have access to all the wonderful products humans can make out of whales. Lots of the women here, for instance, don't even wear corsets like Mother and all the women in the East do. Corsets, which cinch a woman's waist real tight, are also made from whales, from their baleen.

Also, since it hardly ever rains, no one in Kansas owns an umbrella. Umbrellas are constructed from baleen, too. And even though the sun glares all the livelong day, none of the women use a parasol to cover their heads like they do in the East. Priss does, though, which is why she doesn't have freckles like I do. I don't mind about the freckles, like

I already said. For one, I'm too busy thinking about my brain to worry about my face. For two, my freckles remind me of a map of islands in the ocean, which reminds me of Father.

"I don't suppose you've ever heard of a place called South America," I say to Eustace.

"Yes, I've heard of South America," says Eustace. "I'm no dolt." I know he's not. Next to me, I think Eustace is the smartest person I know, even though he can't read. He just learns in different ways. He knows everything there is to know about the animals around here, such as when the skunks mate, where to look for fox dens, and how many prairie chicken eggs are all right to take and how many you should leave. Eustace taught me that you can't eat all the prairie chicken eggs, otherwise there won't be enough breeding pairs left. Not many people think about things like that, but he does.

I settle in and get ready to tell my story to him. "Well," I say, "to get to where I'm talking about, you'd have to get in a boat that has been outfitted for a long time at sea. You'd have to have food and water for about a year, because you'd have to set out from New Bedford, which is the shipping center of the whole world, then sail south along the

American coast, past where Columbus landed, through the West Indies and all those little slave ports, along the coast of South America, and keep going all the way down to Patagonia, where penguins will line up to watch you sail by."

Eustace leans his head against the cave wall and stares up at the ceiling. "I want to see a penguin someday," he says. "I heard they don't fly. Like chickens."

I'm annoyed that Eustace is interrupting my story. "Penguins aren't even slightly close to chickens," I say. "Now, shush."

"Sorry," he says.

"On the way, you sail through a tropical area where people live on islands right off the coast of South America. Some of them sacrifice each other and sometimes eat each other and sometimes save the heads of dead people and sometimes worship the head of the victim. That's how far you'd have to go to get to where I'm talking about."

You might be wondering how I know all of that information about sailing routes. If you are, you should know that I pay attention. I think one of the best things a kid can do is be quiet when a smart person is talking. You can learn a lot of interesting and scientific information that way. I listened all the time when Father was talking.

"You sure can talk a long time in one breath," Eustace

says. "It's not easy to believe that head is a *real* head." He shakes his own head.

I grope for the Medicine Head's crate and pull it toward me. It scratches along the floor real eerily.

"That's right," I say.

Eustace chuckles, but it's a fake kind of chuckle, like he's trying to be amused but he's covering up worry. "You're fooling. That head's only the size of a small cantaloupe. No one's head is that small with hair that long and with skin that old. That's just made of leather."

"It is," I say. "Human leather. This is an authentic shrunken head, Eustace."

The flame in our lamp is mostly white and blue, with only a little yellow light licking from the wick. "We better get out of here before the light goes out," Eustace says. He moves his feet like he's heading toward the opening, which is glowing with a strange orange light.

I reach out in the dark and feel for his arm. I grab hold.

"I'm serious, Eustace." I hold on to his arm tight. "I have to tell you something. Please sit back down. I'm going to tell you how Father got the head and what he said the tribesmen said it can do."

Eustace looks at the lamp. I know he's uneasy about getting stuck in here in the dark. He looks into my eyes.

"Please," I say, as nicely as I've ever said anything.

"All right," he says. "All right." He sits down again, and I organize my thoughts.

"My father was commissioned to claim the discovery of the continent of Antarctica for the United States. Along the way, he was supposed to document and map any islands and people he met. Well, as I already told you, he did find Antarctica, and if you look on a map, you can see the Wonder name right on it for yourself."

Eustace scratches his armpit. "You know I can't read, but I believe you. You don't have to keep saying I should look for myself."

"*You* don't have to get ruffled," I say. "It's just the way I like to tell the story." I shift my position and put the Medicine Head's crate on my lap. "A few weeks in," I go on, "one of his crew mates went crazy on board, which sometimes happens when sailors have been at sea too long, and this crazy sailor upended all of the barrels of drinking water and threw some overboard, so the crew had no water to drink."

"I hope they tossed him overboard," says Eustace. "Everybody knows people can't drink salt water or it will dry them up from the inside out." Eustace puts his finger in his mouth and gnaws on the nail.

If I know him, he'll swallow those chewed-up nail bits without a second thought. I scrunch up my nose. "No," I say. "They tied him up to a mast so he couldn't do any more damage, and the captain whipped him until he came back to his senses."

"Slaves get whipped all the time," Eustace says. He puts his hand back down in his lap.

"I know," I say. I should have known better than to use the word "whip." I keep going so he doesn't have a chance to take over my story. "So Father had to find the nearest island and restore the water supply before everyone on board went mad," I say.

"Why would everyone else go crazy?" asks Eustace.

"Well," I say, "as soon as the sailors think they're going to go hungry or thirsty, they get stirred up. They argue and fight with each other over every little scrap of food or tin cup of water. The fear of being hungry or thirsty can drive them to madness."

"I heard of a slave once who ate mud because he was so hungry and thirsty," says Eustace.

I ignore him and continue. "So," I say, "the captain and Father knew they had to hurry before mutiny and murder unfolded on the ship."

"Then what?" asks Eustace.

I pause to build suspense because I know I'm coming to a good part. Eustace's eyes are wide open. "The only island close enough..." I say, "... was one that all the other boats and sailors avoided."

"Why?" Eustace whispers. I can hear him gulp.

"Because it was inhabited by cannibals," I say.

Eustace lowers his eyebrows and squints.

"If you don't know what cannibals are," I say, "I can tell you. Cannibals are people who eat other people."

Eustace opens his mouth in surprise. "I would never eat another human being," he says. "It's against nature. Pigs will eat each other, though."

I think about all the things I've seen Eustace eat: insects, moss off trees, and the tender ends of pinecones, and I'm about to tell him not to make hasty predictions about what he would or would not eat, but I don't.

"Lots of species in the wild eat their own kind," I correct. "Anyway, the captain of the ship and Father rowed to the shore in hopes of securing fresh water for the crew. Within a few hours, they were both caged up by natives and watching as the natives built a huge, roaring fire on which to cook them. That's when Father used science to make them think he was a powerful sorcerer."

"What's a sorcerer?" asks Eustace.

"Everybody knows what a sorcerer is," I say. "Like a magician or witch doctor."

"Hmm," says Eustace. He crosses his legs and leans forward. "Well, what did he do?"

"Father told the natives that the moon was going to grow dark with anger at their mistreatment of the sailors looking for water," I say. "And it did."

"What?" Eustace grimaces. "How did he do that?" I can tell by the tone of his voice that he doesn't believe me. "They didn't speak English, did they?"

"One of them did," I say. Truthfully, I'm not sure if any of the cannibals spoke English or not. I don't see why they would have, but when Father told me the story, he just said he explained it to them. I've always wondered myself if that could be true, but I never got a chance to ask him before he died.

One thing about getting older and wiser is that a girl starts to see her mother and father in new ways. When I was small, I thought both my mother and father were always exactly right, especially Father. Now that I'm older, I know that parents aren't always exactly right. Still, I don't want Eustace suggesting that my father was a liar.

"Anyway," I say to Eustace, "never mind that. Father told them the moon would grow dark with anger. But what the tribe didn't know was that the largest penumbral lunar eclipse ever recorded was going to happen that night. Father, being a scientist, already knew about the eclipse."

Eustace tightens the muscles in his neck. "'Penumbral lunar eclipse' sounds like a bad disease no one would want to get," he says.

I get mad at Eustace for that comment. But I don't snap at him. "It's when the earth's shadow blacks out part of a full moon, making it look like a giant has chomped a bite out of it."

"And then the eclipse happened?" he says, and before I can answer, he adds, "I'll bet those cannibals were impressed."

"You'd best believe it." I tap the top of the Medicine Head's crate. "They thought Father was some kind of a witch doctor, and to honor him, they let him and the captain go and gave Father the most powerful tool in a witch doctor's supply, which is the Medicine Head."

"Did your father get the water?"

"Yes," I say. "He got the water, too."

"That's good," says Eustace. "I was getting worried, thinking about all those sailors going crazy with thirst."

"Father accepted the Medicine Head, and he thought it was going to be just another interesting addition to his scientific discoveries, but when he held it, he had a vision."

"What was that?"

"When he first held the Medicine Head, he saw himself discovering Antarctica."

Eustace gives me a puzzled look. "You mean he saw himself doing it before he actually did it?"

"Yes," I say. "That's why he was confident he could do it. That's why he couldn't turn back with Captain Greeney and his ship before he made the discovery."

"Wow," says Eustace.

"There's more," I say. "He saw his name in newspapers and books and saw himself being pinned with medals and receiving accolades. He saw his name on maps and globes. He saw the United States of America remembering his achievement forever. He saw the whole world honoring the Wonder name."

"And all of that came true," Eustace says. "For a while, anyway."

"Yes," I say. "Until Captain Greeney ruined it. And ruined Father."

"Well," says Eustace, "why didn't the Medicine Head predict that part?"

I do not know the answer to that question. Right at

that moment, the lamp goes out. Eustace gasps and so do I. Being in complete and total blackness feels a bit like being underwater. It feels as though I should hold my breath. My heart is thumping hard. It feels like the pressure of all the universe is on my head. Thick. Upside down. Like I haven't yet been born. It feels lonely. It feels warm, not cold. I breathe slowly, and I control my fear. My heart slows.

Then I can hear what sounds like far-away shouting, which must be coming from Tolerone. Maybe someone's horses got loose, or maybe there's fighting again. Eustace is right, I think. The town is growing and spreading out. Pretty soon settlers will be sticking up a barn right where this cave is.

I listen harder. More shouting. Screaming. Then I remember that Captain Greeney is in town, and wherever he goes, calamity comes, too.

"I can't let Captain Greeney get it," I whisper. "He's a bad man and would only use it for evil. Father died rather than let him have it." That whisper flits like a bat in the pitch.

"Let's get out of here," Eustace says. And this time, I agree. I put the Medicine Head's crate firmly under my arm, determined not to let it out of my sight.

✦ CHAPTER 10 ✦

𝓔𝓊𝓈𝓉𝒶𝒸𝑒 𝒶𝓃𝒹 𝓙 𝒸𝓁𝒾𝓂𝒷 𝑜𝓊𝓉 of the cave on all fours. The distant shouting becomes clearer. I carefully hold the Medicine Head's crate against my chest, and Eustace carries the lamp, though it's gone dark and cold. I hear Fob stand and shake his fur coat. Then an acrid smoke smell hits my nose. I look in the direction of Tolerone. An orange glow floats above the town.

"Something's burning again," I say. We start walking in the direction of town. I know Eustace is scared of the dark, the story, the situation, and that he feels safe close to me even if I am carrying the Medicine Head. The eerie light hovering above Tolerone stretches far into the heavens. "Lordy," I say. "It looks like the whole town's on fire."

Though we can't see, we jog along. I run with one hand out in front of me, feeling for anything that might be in my way. Fob prances next to us, so close that he brushes against my leg now and again. I fall once, trip into a gopher or rabbit hole, and Eustace stumbles next to me. The Medicine Head's crate hits the ground.

"Oh no!" I say.

"Is it out?" Eustace wants to know.

I feel all around the crate, and it seems to be in good shape, nothing broken, nothing spilled. "No. Let's keep going."

This time Eustace leads the way, and I hold on to the back of his overalls. Once we reach the train tracks, we can hear the grunting of pigs and the rattling of bells around the necks of cows that have escaped from the fire and have wandered out here. There's a fierce wind blowing at us in hot gusts. No wonder the cave felt so hot.

We stand on the tracks and gape. The sight is terrible. Everything in Tolerone is burning. The general store, the lumber yard, the granary, the houses. Everything but the church is shooting flames. The fire roars and spits, crackles and churns. Licks of fire spit into the sky like tongues of devils. It's loud. Very loud. But the screams from the people and occasional explosions of lamps and casks of oil rise above the noise of the fire.

"Ma," whispers Eustace.

I groan.

Eustace sprints past me in a way I remember doing myself when I saw those men on horses ride past us on the road. I have a sick feeling in my gut. What if Ruby is hurt? Or worse? What if Eustace won't have a father or a mother? He's dashing toward the fire, which seems like a rash thing to do.

"Hey!" I yell. "Don't go there! Don't go toward the fire!" But he's not listening, and I don't blame him. Eustace is running for his ma. The power of the sun and the stars and the moon couldn't keep him from going to her. "Cover your mouth with your hankie!" I shout after him. "Or you'll—" But I don't finish my sentence because he's long gone. Fob stands at my side, whimpering, as though he doesn't know what to do: follow his master into danger or stay with me where it's safe. Fob takes a couple of steps forward. Then sits down. Then he stands up again. His back legs walk forward even though his front paws stay put and brace the rest of his body against the force of the back legs trying to go forward. The poor dog's torn. All at once, though, his entire body springs into forward motion and he runs off, barking after Eustace.

I decide I'd better go, too, to make sure Eustace's ma is all right, Eustace doesn't get hurt, and Fob doesn't get himself into trouble. After a minute or two of running, I can feel a full, wavy wind of heat coming from the fire, and even though I'm a good half mile away from town, it blows back my hair and my skirt. This fire is powerful and big. It doesn't take a scientist to figure out that people will die tonight, that people are dying right now.

I keep running, and Fob keeps running ahead of me. Soon I can't see him anymore. The air is smoky and very thin. It's difficult to breathe, and all my instincts tell me to turn back. My feet hesitate at each step. But my heart pushes on. Father must have felt this way in his final push to Antarctica, as though his freezing body wanted to turn toward warmer air but his heart's desire was stronger. Did you know that freezing to death feels hot, like your skin's on fire? It's true. That's why frozen people have half their clothes off when other people find them dead in the ice or snow. They felt hot and tossed their coats, boots, and hats off. People easily confuse extreme hot and cold.

I look toward Tolerone and hope no one is suffering. Unless it's Captain Greeney, of course. He could suffer all day and I wouldn't mind one bit, I don't think.

I keep moving toward town, half of which is engulfed in flames. People run around, screaming "Have you seen my Abby?" or "Where is little Harold?" or "Have you seen my mother?" or "I can't find Grandpa!" or "Someone get the doctor!" I say a little prayer, which I almost never do, asking that those lost people, if they must die, go painlessly of smoke poisoning.

I have to stop running and walk carefully now because fiery bits of wood and cloth smolder all over the ground, and I have to watch where I step. It's like the ground is a field of hot, glowing flowers. I clutch the Medicine Head's crate close to my chest. I wonder, if I had held it longer, whether it would have predicted this inferno. The Medicine Head seems to whisper *Hold me.* I know there's no logical explanation, but I hear it. I remember the woman and her chickens. I worry I might be losing my mind.

What would happen if I just threw it into one of the burning buildings and let it get destroyed? I wonder why Father didn't do that. Then I think there must be a reason he wrote DO NOT DESTROY! on the crate. I've got to figure out what Father would want me to do with it.

Then I see someone walking by, waving and pointing this way and that way, mumbling something I don't understand. He's got a big gash on his forehead and looks disoriented, which I have to admit to myself that I am, too. I look around and try to figure out where I am. All the landmarks, Mutch's Lumber Yard, the general store, the church, are on fire or fallen, misshapen, gone.

"Sir," I say. "What happened?"

He looks at me, blinks, and smiles strangely, as though he's not in his right mind. Black soot is smeary over his teeth. He sighs. "Ahh," he says, and then he coughs up a laugh or sob. I can't tell which one. "Um. Greeney came into town today. Got a bunch of Bleecher's men riled up. Bleecher's men pulled the Jessups from their house and butchered them in the street." The man makes a hacking motion with his arm. "Yes. There was...um...b-b-blood all over. Um." He turns around and spins some more, as though he's trying to make sense of what he's seeing. "Then Jessup's men went to the downtown and they, um, started the fire at the little church for the black folk. Ahh. And the Negro lane on fire. After that...um...I don't know. The whole town just went up." He puts a handkerchief up to his mouth and starts to cry. "It's been so dry this year. Ahh. I can't find my wife," he says. "She's, um, expecting a child, and I can't find her anywhere. We don't have any slaves. Ahh. We don't want any slaves. We didn't want anything to do with any of this." He grabs me by my arm. "Help me, um, find Lenora."

I jerk my arm from his hand and back away. The Negro lane. That's where Eustace lives! *Oh, Ruby.*

I run. Even though I'm wearing good leather boots with wooden soles, my feet feel like they're burning. The fires have roasted the hard gravel ground, and the heat is transferring to the soles of my boots, then to my feet. I keep running toward where I think the Negro lane is, and trying not to breathe so I don't inhale poison into my lungs. My feet are burning up, and I'm on the lookout for a barrel of water to soak my boots in when suddenly, out of the dark, the smoke, the confusion, the rippling air, a black dog leaps on me and laps at my face.

"Hey!" I say. I'm about to push the dog away, but then I get a good look and see that it's Fob, his yellow coat full of ash. "Fob! Fob! Hey, boy! Where's Eustace?" Some dogs are real smart and can understand what a human is saying and help that human out. Fob is not. He just keeps jumping up on me and whimpering. He's scared.

"It's OK," I tell him. "Down. Down!" He stays down, but he tries to nose himself into my skirt and hide his face from what's happening. Poor Fob. I pet him and kind of push his head away from my legs so I can walk. He stands beside me and presses his body against my leg.

"Let's go, boy," I say to him. I start walking and he jogs alongside me, leaning into my knees and whimpering and trembling. I keep my hand on his head as we proceed. I keep walking toward where I think Ruby and Eustace's house is. No one pays me any mind at all. It's like I've walked into the end of the world.

Finally, I see it. Almost every house in the lane is on fire somewhere. People are everywhere. Some stop and ask me questions they don't really expect me to answer, like "I wonder if you've seen the saucer that goes with this tea-cup?" or "I told Janey to run to the church. Do you think she made it?" Some stand still, staring at the scene, like they are in shock and can't believe what their eyes are seeing. Little kids are crying, but a few others are playing and laughing, like it hasn't occurred to them that the whole town is on fire and they should run to safety. I get kind of mad at their parents for not telling them what to do until I remember that a few of them probably don't have parents anymore.

"Get out of town!" I yell at all those kids. "Go to the river and wait there!"

They look at me like they don't know whether or not to listen to me. One thing about kids is that, usually, they don't like being told what to do, especially if it comes from a person they haven't been told they have to mind. But when Armageddon is practically falling around their feet, kids are hoping for someone trustworthy to tell them what to do. I shout, *"Move it!"* They scatter like apples rolled on the floor.

Finally, I see Eustace's house. I run, and Fob walks alongside me, getting tangled up in my legs and blocking my path. We fall, and I scrape my hands and knees on hot gravel.

"Darn," I cuss. I look around and wonder if anyone has heard me or will scold me, but everyone is too busy with his own crisis. "Darn!" I say again. I upright the Medicine Head. Fob tilts his head and moans at me. "I know, boy," I say to him. I touch his back. He's trembling and lifting his feet up, alternating them every few seconds. The ground must be too hot for the pads of his paws.

I get up, wipe my hands on my apron, and loop my arm through the rope of the Medicine Head's crate to carry it like a handbag. Then I lean down and scoop Fob up. I hold him with his belly to my chest, with his head over my shoulder like you might carry a toddler. He doesn't kick or scratch or resist in the slightest way.

It's hard to see, it's still dark, and the smoke is thick, but I know when I get to Ruby and Eustace's house because all Eustace's animals are hopping, slithering, loping, and skulking around, confused about where to go. Fob kicks and scratches to get down. Even through the fire and smoke, he knows he's home. He jumps down and runs under a tree, where there's a soft patch of grass. And then, in a break from the smoke and by the light of the fires, I can see Eustace's porch and house.

"Eustace!" I shout. "Ruby!" I cough.

I step up onto the porch and try to look inside. The door is wide open, but it's too dark to see anything. I yell for them again. But I don't hear anyone. Fob squirms around and yaps. One of Eustace's cats hisses and runs up and scratches Fob on the neck. Eustace has some fierce cats.

Beneath the tree, the cat is swiping at Fob with its claws, and its hair is on end and its tail whips back and forth like a snake striking. Then I hear, "Queenie! Stop that. Leave that dog alone!"

It's Eustace shouting, and it's coming from the shadows at the side of the house. I can just make out his shape in the flickering light from the flames. Fob runs to him and curls around his feet.

"Eustace!" I shout.

"Back here!" he says. I see his arm waving me back. The heat is so intense that his arm looks like it's rippling in the wind. Some people who see this get confused or think it's a kind of ghostly trick, but because I'm going to be a scientist, I know that his arm isn't really cock-eyed and rippling like water. I know that the heat from the fire creates a mirage. I probably look ripply to Eustace, too. "I gotta let these critters out," he says, "so they at least have a chance."

"I'll help," I say.

The Medicine Head is calling again. I set the crate down. I slide my eyes to it and then to Eustace, wondering if he hears it. I look around, curious whether there's anyone else nearby, curious about who the head is whining for. But there's no one else. Then I remember why I'm here. "Where's your ma?" I bark at Eustace. "We've got to get her out before the house falls down!"

"Back here," he says. He darts about, unlatching doors. "These cages will be ovens if I don't open them up."

I go around the side of the house with Eustace, who carries Fob like a baby.

Along with the crackling and rumbling of the fire, the houses themselves seem to be groaning and whining. The wind is wicked. Great wafts of heat sometimes blow so hard that I have to stop walking and fight to remain upright.

99

"We'd better hurry and get out of here!" I say. "This whole lane's going to burn."

"I know," says Eustace. "But Ma won't move! She's scared and stubborn."

In the back of the house, most of the animal crates and gates have been opened. A couple of billy goats are chewing on some shirts they've pulled from the clothesline.

"What am I gonna do?" moans Ruby. She's crying. She's got her apron up to her mouth and is weeping into it. "Those are the Millers' shirts. All smoky and now eaten by goats."

Tolerone's burning, and she's worried about shirts? She's not making sense. "Ruby," I say. "It's me, Lu. Let's go to my house where it's safe, OK?"

"Oh, Lordy," she says. "Is your mother and sister safe?" Then she starts howling again. "Who would do such a thing?"

Eustace opens the last of the cages and kennels. A couple of pheasants take flight, and a turkey waddles out. I touch Ruby on the elbow and then grab a firm hold and try to lift. She's a heavy woman, and her joints pain her. Eustace puts Fob under his one arm, like a sack of potatoes, and he goes to Ruby's other side and lifts her arm. Together, we get Ruby to her feet.

"Come on now, Ma," says Eustace. "Let's go where it's safe."

Ruby makes some protestations about how we should leave her and only worry about ourselves. We ignore her and lead her to the front of the house.

"Just a minute," I say, and neither Ruby nor Eustace objects. I go and grab the crate. Though it's slow and dangerous, we walk all the way out of town. Eustace and I don't talk at all. He's got his jaw set firmly. Ruby moans and cries nearly the whole time.

"Don't you think we ought to check on the Millers?" she asks. Eustace and I look at each other, but we keep walking. The end of town where the Millers live is completely engulfed. My eyes hurt with biting smoke, and I keep moving forward, toward my house. Eustace comes along, too, and ignores Ruby's worry.

And then the Medicine Head screeches like an eagle.

✦ CHAPTER 11 ✦

Out of the flames and smoke and chaos, a hand grabs my arm firmly. I yank it away and brace the Medicine Head's crate against my side.

"Don't do that!" I yell at whoever grabbed me.

I look up and find a tall man standing before me. My eyes glide from his chest to his face. His blue eyes study me.

I know those eyes.

I hold my breath and hear my heart pounding in my chest. Instinctively, I clutch the crate even tighter to me until it presses into my hip bone. I back away from the man. My skirt hem blows around my ankles from the winds of the fire.

"Girl!" the man with blue eyes yells. "A smart child would get out of this town." His voice is crisp somehow, even above the howling of the fires.

I'm speechless, as though my voice wouldn't work even if I had the right words to say. Those eyes know me. For years, I have been imagining the revengeful words and deeds I would heap upon this man, but in this second, I am caught totally unprepared and I am scared inside and out. All I do is stare and hold tight to Father's possession.

More loudly than before, undeniably, the Medicine Head is saying *Hold me. Hold me.* The man tilts his head and turns his ear toward me, or toward the Medicine Head. He shakes his head, like he's trying to rid himself of some idea.

"Girl!" he yells at me. "Are you stupid? Get out of town!" He bends to my face and gazes deep into my eyes.

I see a flash of recognition. He grabs my arm again, but this time it's the one that's holding the Medicine Head. I turn as though I'm going to do as he says and get out of town.

He pulls me closer. "Wait," he says. He looks me over

again. "I wonder if we haven't met before." He's staring at the crate now, turning his ear to it as though he can hear it.

The ends of his mustache are coiled and singed. His face is blackened with soot, but this is without a doubt the last rider of the posse that hanged my father. And what I knew then, what I've known all along, comes to me surely: This is the man responsible for my father's death. I feel sick in my stomach. My mouth tastes like iron and is full of saliva.

"I," he booms, "am Captain Cornelius Greeney." He lowers his head closer to the Medicine Head's crate. He's listening, and he smiles as though he has just read my mind. He lifts his quirt and uses it to point at the box. "Do you hear something?" he asks.

Just then a rider on a horse shouts out, "Captain! We need your counsel on the north end of town. The insurgents are regrouping, sir." The horse rears and kicks up dust and whinnies.

Captain Greeney faces the rider and says, "Get me a fresh horse."

Even if he didn't see me that day hiding in the grass, which I think he did, I worry that I look every bit the image of Father. I can't think of what to do or say. I hold my breath and I try to swallow all of the saliva in my mouth.

But when I do, my stomach lurches it back up. With the smoke, the heat, the fires, the worry, the whole world seems hazy. I can't see. My ears ring. The ground beneath my feet is unsteady.

"Girl," Captain Greeney demands, "what is in that box?"

Eustace comes forward. I put my arm up in front of his chest, to stop him. But he gently puts it back down.

"Sir," Eustace says, "you might want to step away. That's my pet rattlesnake she's got in there. Keeping it safe for me, she is."

Captain Greeney backs away from me. Eustace is clever and quick. I'm grateful for him right now.

"I hate snakes," Captain Greeney hisses. He leans back and slits his eyes. "You look very familiar to me." He tilts his head as though a slightly different angle will determine whether he recognizes me or not. "I think," he sneers at me, "we've met before, but I just can't place you." He smiles a strange smile. His eyeteeth are longer than most people's. They make him seem serpentine.

Captain Greeney jerks his quirt against his leg. "Your eyes remind me of…" He touches his mustache and grimaces.

The fires reflect in his eyes. I can't look away. I'm mute.

How long will this go on? Could I die of fear? Could I hold my own breath to death? Is that possible? My mouth is full of a bitter bile. I have to spit. But I can't. I shouldn't.

He goes on. "Yes, yes." He tilts his head one way and then the other. "The long nose. The eyes that seem squinty from peering at small things." He leans in so close to my face that I can smell his breath. He reaches out again and moves a strand of hair away from my forehead. His fingernails are long and scratch against my skin.

The rider from before gallops up again, this time holding the reins of another horse. "Captain!" he shouts. "Your horse is ready, sir."

Captain Greeney's evil eyes glare at me and then at the crate.

"Ahem," interrupts the rider. "Sir! The fire!"

Captain Greeney ignores him. "Kill that thing. I don't like snakes." He strokes his mustache. "You will be seeing me again, girl. Count on it."

My stomach churns in revulsion. I have to get the disgusting taste out. I can't keep it in for one more second. I lean over and spit right on the toe of Captain Greeney's boot. My spittle slides from the top of his foot to the parched ground, leaving a wet and shiny streak.

He looks at his boot. He makes a sound like "Wha!"

He shakes his boot as though he's trying to shake the slaver off. "You little..." he begins to say.

"Captain!" shouts the rider. "We need your orders, sir!"

Captain Greeney raises his hand to the rider. Then he straightens his coat, turns, and mounts his horse, even as flames shoot all around us. He looks like the king of Hell. "Oh, duty, duty! You call for me again and again!" He takes off his hat and waves it in the air. "Let it burn!" he shouts. "Let the whole town burn!" Then he whips his horse and shouts, "Yah!" and rides toward the north end.

The rider gives me a sympathetic look, soft and kind. "I don't know who you are, young lady, but you'd best get yourself out of Tolerone." Then he rides away.

The Medicine Head is screeching now, like a hawk over a Kansas sky. I drop it. I press my palms against my ears. The swirling flames and curling smoke and dizzying smells overwhelm me. "Stop!" I shout. "Quiet!" I pinch my eyes closed. I wish the whole world would go away.

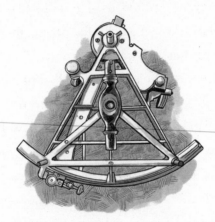

CHAPTER 12

I open my stinging eyes. Ruby fans me with her apron. She's talking to me, too. "Hallelujah Wonder. Who was that man? That's a bad man, I think."

"Come on, Lu," Eustace says. "I'll help you." He hands me his hankie. "Here. Take deep breaths into this."

I take it and cover my mouth. I inhale a few times. Even with the hankie, the air is thick with smoke. But I begin to feel a bit better. I look around for my crate, but I can't see it on the ground. "Where is it?" I ask Eustace.

Ruby bends over and leans into my face. "I got it," she says, and points at the ground near her feet. "It's right here. I got it safe for you, but I didn't want to hold a snake crate." Then she looks from me to Eustace, like she's suddenly realizing something. "But it isn't a snake in there, is it?"

I look at her; then I look at Eustace, who shakes his head at me, which tells me not to tell his ma. I grab the crate.

✦ ✦ ✦

From Tolerone to my house is only two miles, but with Ruby and me, and with Fob acting like a baby again, we move very slowly. The Medicine Head is thrumming a mellow call to me. I feel like I am constantly adjusting the crate under my arm.

Ruby stops and looks back at the town every few feet. People scream. Horses whinny. We hear crying and anguish. We also hear shouts of good people trying to help other people, things like "Here! Get in my wagon." And "I've found her!" But in between those kindnesses are mostly crashing and rumbling and black smoke, gray ash, and red embers. I never liked much about Tolerone, but I sure feel sad about that now. When Ruby stops, I stop, too. I look back and nearly want to run and maybe help somebody—even the Millers. Maybe help anyone. Eustace tugs at us.

"Don't ever run at a fire," he says, as if reading my mind.

"You did," I say quietly.

Ruby whacks Eustace on the back of the head.

"Ouch!" Eustace says. He rubs his skull furiously. "What was that for?"

"For running into a fire!" Ruby says. She tucks stray hair back up into the cloth she always wears wrapped around her head. Ruby's hair is nearly all gray and white. I'm struck again by how old she is. "I'd have gotten myself out," she insists. "You could have gotten yourself killed."

"All right, Ma," says Eustace. He rubs his head again. Fob barks as though in agreement.

My lungs hurt. My feet are burned. We're all of us, head to toe, ashes. I should be exhausted, but the events of the night and the mere fact that I survived them, the Medicine Head, the fire, Captain Greeney, make me feel full up with verve. I look up into the sky and try to breathe deeply.

"Oh," moans Ruby. "I am tired." She keeps moving, though, one foot in front of the other. She looks back at Tolerone and shakes her head. "All those poor souls," she says. "I hope they don't suffer."

I recall a story Father told me about a fire. Once, when he worked on a whaling ship, he survived a fire that burned up the whole thing in the middle of the ocean. The whalers were boiling whale blubber in cauldrons inside an enormous brick oven. The flames didn't stay in the oven, though.

One of the sailors was tarring the deck too close to the oven, and he and the bucket burst into flames. So did the deck, the side of the ship, then the sails, then the rigging, and eventually the whole ship. My father and the rest of the crew, including the burned sailor, were able to escape by lowering the small whaleboats into the ocean.

Father said the burned man suffered awfully for the three days it took for a ship to come find them. The top half of his body was totally burned. His hair was gone and his scalp was burned down to white membrane with red spots all over. His ears had melted completely off. One of his eyes was fine, but the other eyelid sagged over the eyeball. Father said his eyelid looked like a clump of wax on a candle. Father was good at describing things, especially awful things, so that you could really see them in your mind. Father said the man's burned hands had no skin and had curled into claws. Whenever anything touched him, he screamed in agony.

The burned man from my father's story was in such pain that he begged someone to shoot him, and they would have done it if they'd had a gun, but no one did. So they tried to keep him as comfortable as possible and gave him every last drop of rum they had. He lived long enough to be lifted onto the rescue ship; then he finally died after a few more days. His last words were "Oh, good."

"I hope they don't suffer, too," I say to Ruby about the people of Tolerone, though I know better.

"Come on, Ma," says Eustace. "You're doing fine."

Good old Eustace keeps us all going. And the farther we get away from the fire, the quieter the Medicine Head gets.

I hold on to Ruby's arm. It's bare. Her blouse's been burned or torn. I've never seen her arm before, and now I can see why. White scars run up and down the entire length of it. They look like wrinkled worms.

"What are these?" I ask. "All these marks?"

Ruby shuffles along and breathes heavily. I suppose her lungs hurt, too. "Miss Wonder, you don't want to know about that."

Eustace looks straight ahead and picks up the pace.

"Yes, I do," I say. "What did you do?"

"She didn't do those to herself," Eustace says. He

shakes his head like I'm a big dummy. I'm too tired to get mad at him. "Tell her, Ma," he says.

"I was younger than you," Ruby says. "It was a long time ago. I don't like to think about those days."

"Did someone hit you?" I ask.

"Oh, yes," Ruby says. "Someone hit me all the time. And tied me up and hit me some more."

"For what?" I ask.

"For *what*?" she repeats. "For nothing. That's what. I was just a child. If I looked at a body wrong, I got tied up and hit with a spoon or a lash or a fire iron. My missus was a madwoman."

"Why didn't your mother stop her?" I ask.

"My mother?" she says. "I never saw my mother but a half dozen times. She died or got sold." Ruby shrugs. "Truth is, I don't even know what happened to her. I was too young, and then it wasn't proper to ask. I got raised by an elderly house slave. She was a good woman, but she couldn't protect me from the white missus."

Ruby has the kind of face that makes it easy to imagine her as a little girl. Some people do, in case you haven't noticed it before. The image of a mean lady whipping poor little Ruby stiffens my back and arms, as though I'm bracing to receive those blows myself.

In the past, when I listened to Eustace go on about slavery, I would chuck away his talk sometimes. I guess I thought his life appeared sufferable. No one smacked him or whipped him or chained him. In a lot of ways, he seemed just like me—young and at the mercy of adults' choices. But after listening to Ruby, I'm realizing Eustace's life is a lot more troublesome than I thought. "Why would anyone do that to a little girl?" I ask.

"Well, the whole territory is asking that very question," says Ruby. "You're a smart girl, Hallelujah Wonder, but you got to look up once in a while. You keep studying the small things, rocks and seeds, but you also got to study what's happening all around you." She stops and turns back toward Tolerone. "Don't let that town burn down for nothing," she says. "Probably not much going to change while I'm alive, but you kids got a chance to improve. You can change all of this." She waves toward the black sky.

I can't remember the last time I had so little to say. I can't remember the last time I was interested in anything an adult had to say.

"You understand?" Ruby asks.

I nod.

I don't like it that some people, like Ruby's missus and Captain Greeney, seem to be protected by the law or by title. I don't like how the world can be completely upside down. Captain Greeney's the one who should have been punished. Not my father. Ruby's missus is the one who should have been punished. Not sweet Ruby.

The fire winds lap at my hair and lift strands of it. By morning, everyone in the territory will know what happened here tonight.

"You all right, Miss Hallelujah?" Ruby asks.

"I think so," I say. I touch Ruby's scars and stroke them softly. She doesn't mind. "Ruby?" I gulp. "Does that mean you won't be sad if the Millers...are dead? Because then you won't be owned anymore?"

Ruby pats my arm. We keep walking. After a while she says, "Of course I'll be sad. I don't want anyone to suffer. I've had my share of miserable owners, but the Millers weren't evil. Did you know Mrs. Miller nursed me through pneumonia a couple years back? Saved my life with her nursing. That was a good deed. But the owning of another human being was a bad deed, a real bad deed. And she ought to have recognized it and set it right! It takes folks a long time to change their minds and their ways sometimes. Good people do bad things all the time." She shuffles along. "But that doesn't mean I'm not angry at them. I am. And I deserve to be!"

"Do you think bad people sometimes do good deeds?" I ask.

"Well, I don't know," she says. "I don't know what you mean."

"I do," says Eustace. "'Yes' is the answer to that. Just because Captain Greeney is an abolitionist doesn't mean he's a good person. He's a bad person, Lu. And just because he's an abolitionist doesn't mean abolitionists are bad."

"People are complicated, Lu," Ruby says. "Truth is, they all got good and bad mixed up in them. Some got more of one. Some got more of the other."

She groans a little, and she looks a bit teary. "I don't wish no harm to the Millers," she says. "That's for sure. But it sure is a complicated feeling I have in my heart. I'm worried about my boy, mostly."

I wonder what the deaths of the Millers might mean for Ruby and Eustace. They might get to be free. But more than likely, some relative of the Millers would come and claim them. Ruby and Eustace are property, according to some laws.

My brain and my whole body want rest. I'm weary. On one arm, I've got Ruby and all the troubles of Tolerone. On the other arm, I've got the Medicine Head and all the troubles of keeping it away from Captain Greeney.

I'm bothered by how close I allowed Captain Greeney to get to the Medicine Head. I know I have Eustace to thank for his quick thinking. I am very disappointed in myself. I'm even a little bit ashamed. And embarrassed that Eustace witnessed my cowardice. I've got to be braver. I've got to be more prepared. I've got to be the girl with "the good knot in her skull," as Father always said I was.

As we walk, I remember the lengths to which Father went to keep the head from Greeney. And now it's my job to keep it from Greeney. Suddenly, the Medicine Head feels like a thousand pounds of pressure. I worry that I'm not smart enough, that I'm not brave enough, that I'm not a good enough person.

"Thank you, Eustace," I say. "You did some quick thinking back there."

He keeps walking, holding his mother's arm with one hand and carrying Fob tucked under his other arm. He's got a queer, far-away expression on his face. I can't tell whether it's happy or sad. Or worried or intent.

"Why do you have that look on your face?" I ask.

Eustace's eyes meet mine; then he glances at the Medicine Head's crate and turns his face forward again. "I'm thinking," he says.

He's thinking about my problem. That's what he's

doing. That's what kind of a friend Eustace Miller is. His house just burned up. His animals are scattered all around the town. He's a slave whose masters might be dead, which might mean he'll have to have new masters, maybe mean ones. And he's thinking about how to solve my problem. I start thinking of what to do, too. I also try to think of a good solution for Eustace so he doesn't have to be a slave anymore.

What am I going to do with the Medicine Head? I know for certain I can't let Captain Greeney have it. I also can't keep it hidden or give it to anyone else. I can't destroy it. Who knows what might happen if I did? Would it unleash some kind of evil force out into the world? Would I be personally cursed? I don't know. But I trust that if destruction were the right choice, Father would have done it himself.

Then the Medicine Head seems to thrum or moan like it's being hurt.

"Do you hear that?" I ask Ruby and Eustace.

"Hear what, Miss Wonder?" says Ruby.

Eustace glances at the crate. But he shakes his head.

✦ CHAPTER 13 ✦

We're nearly to my place. It's that time between night and morning when the sky is the color of the circles under Mother's eyes. I've never been out so late, gone so long, and I'll bet Priss is worried and upset. The fire has stirred up the air, and even this far out, the branches of the trees sway in the swift, ropy wind. When we get near enough, I see Priss waiting at the cottonwood tree. We can see her skirt and the straps of her bonnet flapping in the wind from a long ways back. She looks like Mother must have in her younger days. She must have been watching for me. One thing about Priss is that she has a way about her that makes a body happy and scared to see her at the same time.

She begins to walk toward us, and when we finally meet, she doesn't hug me or make a show of being upset or worried. She uses a dish towel to wipe the ash from my eyes. She takes my place at Ruby's arm and says, "You must be awfully tired, Ruby." Then Priss looks at the crate and bunches her eyebrows together like crochet needles, but she doesn't make mention of the Medicine Head, though I know she knows what it is and is wondering why I've brought it back to the house.

Priss is a proper lady. She would never start an argument or engage in a disagreeable conversation in front of company. She knows exactly what to do and how to behave in almost every situation. Some girls might cry uncontrollably and make a tense situation even worse. Not Priss. She's like Mother used to be. I tend to get upset and shout. Like Father.

The closer we get to our house, the less timid Fob gets. He hops and skips around and noses on the ground for gophers and mice. He snaps his jaws at them, but he never catches anything. In the light, I can see now that Fob has patches of singed fur and burns. Across his back, he's got one long scorch mark, where a burning plank must've fallen on him. I reach down and pat his head. No wonder he was so scared.

"Ah, thank the Lord," says Ruby once we pass the pigpen and the barn and see the house. "I've got to have a nice long sit and a drink of water."

"Mother's going to be so happy to see you," says Priss.

I help her get Ruby set up in the sitting room next to Mother, and those two share a nice smile and a nod. They don't talk. They don't have to. You can be that way with some people when you're comfortable enough with them. That's how it is between Ruby and Mother.

I run upstairs and put the Medicine Head beneath my bed. When I come back down, Ruby and Mother both have their eyes closed. Priss is at the stove. I don't quite know what to tell her or how to tell her about all I've seen and heard. Instead, I do something normal.

"You need help?" I ask her.

She's putting water on for tea, and she's got a mound of bread dough on a table. I look around to see if there's anything to eat. I'm starving, I realize.

Priss pulls a dish towel off a pie tin and pulls a spoon from a jar. She passes both of them to me. "Mince-meat," she says. "You need to eat."

I dig in. "Where are Eustace and Fob?" I ask.

"Taking a rest in the barn," she says. "Everyone's worn out. You've been gone all night, in town, I guess. You could have been killed."

"I wasn't," I say.

"I was worried," she says. Her voice sounds shaky.

"I'm sorry," I whisper. "I'm sorry."

She puts her hand on my arm. "I was so worried, but I trusted in you, too."

Her eyes are red all the way around, so I know she's been worried and crying probably all night. She does something strange. She comes to me and pulls me into a skinny-armed hug. And then I do something strange, too. I hug her right back with my own big bones. I'm hugging her, and it feels so good, I lift her off the floor a little and squeeze her until she says, "Lu! I can't breathe." Then I put her down. That's two hugs in two days for me. That must be a record. I like it, and I tell myself I'm going to hug people more often.

"I was worried, but I wasn't too worried because I remembered what Father always said about you," she says.

"What's that?" I ask.

"Lu, you've got a good knot in your skull."

I remember, too. I wonder if my eyes are starting to get red around the outside like Priss's, because I'm feeling like crying just a little bit. I'm not sure why. I'm halfway relieved and halfway scared.

"How bad is it?" she asks. She nods in the direction of Tolerone. "In town?"

I exhale real long. I shake my head, as though I'm shaking away the bad sights and smells and sounds. "Real bad," I say. "The whole Negro lane is gone. The north end, too, looked like."

Priss nods. Her eyes get misty. "The Millers?" she asks, her voice soft and trembling.

I shrug. "I didn't see them," I say. "But that end of town was engulfed."

She puts her hand to her mouth. "Oh no," she says.

And then we stand there staring at the floor, quiet for a minute or two. We're both thinking about losing people. We're both thinking about death. We're both thinking about grief.

"Once in a while," she whispers, "I wake up and am happy."

I nod. I know what she's going to say next.

She puts her hand to her throat. "But then I remember all that's happened." She rubs her neck. "I remember Father dying. I remember his face. I remember that I have to get up and take care of Mother." She looks up at me. Her eyes are full of tears. "I remember that hole in the ground out there, doomed to bring us trouble over and over again. Sometimes I'm afraid I'll never be happy again."

I nod. "I understand," I say.

"I know you do," she says. "I tell myself every day that it's all right to be happy. I tell myself that I should try to be happy."

I pick the skin around my fingernail. "But we have to take care of some things first."

Priss fidgets her feet on the wood floor. "I know you're up to something," she says. "I guess that's why you've brought that awful head into our home." She crosses her arms in front of her chest. "I trust that you know what you're doing."

I nod again. "Captain Greeney's back in Tolerone. I saw him." I take a quick look behind me to make sure nobody's around and lower my voice. "He saw me. I'm not certain he knows who I am, but he'll figure it out sooner or later."

"Oh no," she says. "What will we do?" She stares out the window. "Why don't we just destroy it? Why haven't we already destroyed it?" Priss swallows so hard that I can hear it.

"We can't do that," I say. "If that were the answer, Father would have done it."

In the distance, I hear the train whistle.

Priss lifts her eyes to me. She perks her ears to the train, too. Then she runs her finger over her lips, a thing she does when she's got cooking grease on her fingertips. "I'll tend to Fob's wounds and put Ruby to bed." She throws back her shoulders and looks out the window toward the black fog hanging above Tolerone. "And I've got to see about the Millers." Her voice sounds shaky. "I've got to know."

I want to tell her not to go. I want to tell her she won't like what she'll see. But I don't. One thing about me, and probably about Priss, too, is that we've got to see things with our own eyes to believe them all the way. Even though I hate those last images of my dead father, I know that without them, I would probably have a difficult time believing he's gone. "All right," I say. "But be careful."

"You, too," she says, "with whatever you're up to." Then she looks out the window. "You need some rest."

"I'm too riled up," I say.

The same window she washed until it was squeaky clean is caked with ash again. She points at the pigpen. "I wish you'd help Eustace fix that sow fence before you do anything else."

"Sure," I say. "I can do that. But first I need to take a walk. I need to think."

"Stay away from town," she says. "And wear your bonnet."

I shake my head. That Priss. She never gives up wanting to be the boss of me.

I avoid Mother and Ruby and Fob and Eustace. I step out. The brown grasses crinkle and crack.

The sky blooms with purples and pinks and creams, a bit like the geode Eustace likes so well. My legs lead me toward the cave. As I walk, I hear men in the distance. I get down on my belly and slither closer to see who it is and what they are up to. I hold my breath and peer through the long, crunchy grasses. They set up a telescope, and one man is studying what must be a compass. A surveying crew is what they are. Already. The fires aren't even out in Tolerone, and these men are making plans for the town's steady growth. I scoot back again until I'm sure they won't see me.

Eustace was right. Tolerone is growing, and pretty soon my cave is going to be in the center of it.

I stand, but then I crouch over and run to my cave. I move the stone, and I slip down inside. I breathe heavy. I stand in the cave's center. It's cool again down here. Smoke and ash are now deep inside me. I cough. The noise echoes off the granite.

Do you ever wonder what you'd save from your house if it was on fire and you only had one minute to grab your most important possessions? I do. Tolerone feels like my house right now. I've got to save the Medicine Head. And I've got to help Eustace. Everyone and everything else will have to either save itself or burn. It's hard to make decisions like that. There's only one other thing down here that I've got to have. I shuffle the crates around until I find it. In my palm it feels like a ball of fresh, clean snow.

I climb back out, look around, and dash back to the farm road. I don't stop running until I'm sure the survey crew can't see me.

I pick up a stick and walk along, scratching with it in the dirt, leaving long trails behind me. I notice what looks like a pale-colored bone in the rocks on the side of the road just a foot or two from where I'm standing. It's a timber rattlesnake, but it's not moving. Its long body is coiled around itself like a rope on a ship deck. But the front part of it is face-up, revealing a white, vulnerable skin to the sky. I almost stepped on it without even seeing it. I see flies creeping in and out of its mouth. The scales of its skin lie still. Thank God it's dead.

"Looks like you croaked," I say to it. I pick up a stick.

It doesn't move. I know it's dead, but I imagine it

leaping to life and striking me in the face with its fangs. I poke it hard, once, just to be sure. The whole body moves a little, but only from the force of my prod.

I take a breath. I'm immediately sorry I did, because I can smell decay from where I moved the snake. I laugh to myself. *Settle down, Lu.* Then I walk over, reach for the end of its tail, and hold it up. Though it is beginning to puff up with the gases of decay, the snake is not yet stiff with death. Its head remains on the ground. Stretched out, the snake is taller than me by at least a foot.

"Boy," I say out loud. "You were a big snake. I think I'll take you home to show Eustace." I start walking, dragging the snake along the ground.

Even though I know our farm is just over the next hill, when I look out across the plain, I feel a long way from anyone or anything. I start to feel a little lonely for some company, so I hum, which makes me feel not quite so alone somehow. I start to get a funny feeling, like something is about to happen again.

The sun is getting stronger and hotter. Even though it's far away, I think I can hear the Medicine Head calling to me, *Hold me.* I begin to worry that maybe I shouldn't have left it at home.

Maybe I should take it with me everywhere. Maybe I

should just hold it and let it reveal all its secrets to me. Maybe I should be the one to harness its powers. Maybe I could use it to secure a good life for my family. Maybe I could use it to get rid of all the bad things in Tolerone. Maybe I could use it to destroy all the bad people. Maybe I could use it to kill Captain Greeney.

My anger is rising up in me again, and I feel so mad I could scream or punch a tree, if there were one in sight.

Then I worry that maybe someone has taken the Medicine Head. Maybe Priss has taken it. Maybe Eustace has taken it. I imagine them holding it, and I get even madder. *It's mine*, I want to yell. Then I pick up the hem of my skirt and move my feet faster. Then faster. It seems like the crickets chirp faster and like the wind has picked up, too, as if we're all suddenly in a big hurry. The snake whips behind me.

As soon as I see the farm, I shout, "Priss! Priss?" I keep going, past the pigpen, where the sows poke their noses at me. I stop and use both hands to heave the snake into the pen. The sows descend upon it fast and rip it up and chew on pieces of its body.

I run past the barn, where our only horse shakes its mane and swishes its tail. Everything looks normal. "Priss?" I call as I enter the house.

No one answers. I run upstairs and open each bedroom door. Ruby is asleep in Priss's room. Mother is asleep in hers. Where's Priss? I charge to my bedroom door. Maybe she's in there right now, holding the Medicine Head. I'm so angry, I feel like I might slap her.

I throw open the door.

There's no one there.

Then I remember that Priss went to town.

I hear a faint whispering at once. It's the Medicine Head whining at me. "Stop it," I say. "Stop doing that." But it continues to taunt me.

It's warm in my room, and sweat gathers again on my forehead. I go to the window and force it open. A breeze rushes in. I go to the other window and open it, too. Even though the air is smoky, I keep the windows wide.

My room cools down. I stop sweating. The Medicine Head stops tempting.

I collapse face-down on my bed and close my eyes. A hundred ideas race in my mind. I've got to keep the Medicine Head cool. That's why Father must have kept it in the cave. But I can't keep it in the cave forever. I can't even take it back there now. What if Captain Greeney is already watching for me?

I think about the destruction from the fire. He'll be

busy awhile longer. The dead will have to be collected, identified, and buried. The injured will require medical attention. Clean food and water and shelter will be needed. Captain Greeney will be consumed with his duties for a little longer, but not forever. I know I've got to take advantage of this time. I need a plan to keep the Medicine Head away from him.

Then I hear the racket of rocks knocking against each other. I rise and from my window see Eustace working on our fence. *Good old Eustace. His whole life is upside down, and he's fixing our fence.* I stretch and decide to go down to help him. I leave the windows open but close my bedroom door. I stand in the hallway and listen for a moment. The Medicine Head is quiet.

I walk into the yard and head straight to the rock pile. I select a square of granite and haul it over to where Eustace is working and set it carefully in the dirt.

"Here's a good one," I say. "It could be a cornerstone."

Somehow, building a fence to keep the pigs from getting out seems like the best thing to do right now. I yell at the sows to "get the heck back," and it feels good to yell and get my nerves out that way. Eustace laughs at me. We work, finding stones that seem to fit together, and then stack them up.

"I'll mortar it later," he says. "But this'll keep those hogs from wandering for now." He tilts his head toward a piece of snakeskin. "You feeding these pigs snake? Makes them crazy if you do that," he adds matter-of-factly, as though it were a fact and not an old wives' tale. "They'll turn vicious on you if you let them eat venomous serpents."

I nod. "Just one—a big rattler I found." Then I add, "These hogs'll eat anything."

He shakes his head. "I know it. You got to be careful around them. They'll eat *you* if you're not minding your backside."

I search the snouts and eyes of our sows and put my hand up to the slats of the fence. A couple of the sows come grunting up and sniff my fingers.

"You'd better get someone to snip their tails for you, too, or they'll bite each other's tails off."

"I don't even like pigs," I say. "I don't know why Father ever thought he should be a hog farmer."

When Captain Greeney had Father dismissed from the navy, Father assured us he'd have no trouble finding employment on a whaling ship or at a college or anywhere. But then the order for the return of the entire treasure trove came. Father refused. To be honest, I don't remember a lot of these events. I remember what Father told me about them instead. Also, I was just a kid, and even though I was a smart kid, everything was very complicated.

One thing that always bothered me was when Father or Mother would say "It's complicated" to every blasted question I'd ask.

"But, Mother," I'd say, "why do we have to leave New Bedford?"

"It's complicated, Hallelujah," she'd say.

"But, Father," I'd say, "why does the government want to take your collection?"

"It's complicated, Hallelujah," he'd say.

I don't know about you, but I don't like that answer. One thing I intend to do if I ever have children is to tell them the answers to the questions they ask instead of simply saying "It's complicated." I, for one, can recognize a complicated situation myself. What I want to know is why and how it's complicated.

Anyway, refusing to give the collection to the government meant my father had to run. To be honest, I don't know if he was justified or not, which is a difficult thing to admit when you love your father as much as I love mine. The older and smarter I get, the more I realize that my father was an extremely intelligent person, but not a perfect one.

So we had to steal away and come west. We found land in Kansas, and Father found a nice hiding place for his things. "When Greeney gives up," Father always said, "we'll make a museum out here. The first one!" But instead of giving up, Captain Greeney persisted. And instead of building a museum, Father built a pigsty, a shoddy one.

"Well," says Eustace, "maybe your father ought to have learned more about them first because pigs are very smart animals, and there's good money in them if you know what you're doing."

I know I should defend Father, but Eustace has a point. Father had no head for farming.

"This one," says Eustace, pointing to a pig with a weary face, "has a rotten tooth. We ought to get it out of him, or he could get poisoned all the way through."

"We'd better get the fence fixed first, or the pigs will crash through it," I say.

"Good idea," says Eustace.

We work quietly for a minute or two. I don't know if there's a sound more satisfying in the whole world than the clacking of stones together. I have always liked that clean, low, pleasant sound. I remember running around as a child in New Bedford clapping the flat rocks from the beach together. Eustace and I work in turns. He places a rock, then I place one.

"Well," he says finally. "What are we going to do?"

I drop a rock onto another rock. I don't look at him, but I say, "I've got to hide the Medicine Head somewhere no one will ever find it."

He drops a rock on top of the one I just dropped. "Where's that?"

I fit another rock on top of that one. "I don't know."

All the sounds of the day fade away.

Eustace steps over the fence and goes to the pig with the toothache. The pig stands in a shady corner of the sty, leans against it, looks miserable. Eustace bends over the hurt pig and presses on his backside. The pig lies down. Eustace puts his hands above the pig and says "Stay," real calmly, and the pig stays put. Eustace catches a cricket and feeds it to the resting pig. The pig chews on it as though it's a real satisfying treat.

"Boy," says Eustace. "That tooth is infected something terrible. Look how that pig's whole jaw looks swollen and oozy."

I look. "Yes," I say. "It sure has festered."

"We need some cold water to rinse it and calm the wound," Eustace say. "Or ice, if you have it."

Cold water. Ice. Yes. Those are good for calming angry wounds.

The pig looks a picture of misery. The eye on the side of his rotten tooth is red, with a puffy lid.

"You pull his tooth while I hold on to him," Eustace says.

"No sirree," I say. "I'll hold on to him while you pull his tooth."

"Suit yourself," Eustace says. "Hold him tight."

I put my arms around the pig's middle and brace my legs in the dirt and my backside against the fence. "All right," I say. "I've got him."

Eustace closes in on the pig and grabs his head. He wiggles the pliers into the pig's mouth and then clamps down on the bad tooth. "You got him?" he shouts back at me.

"Yes!" I say. "I already said so, didn't I?"

Then Eustace starts pulling, and the pig jerks and hops and stomps like he's been hit with lightning. I hang on for dear life. When Eustace finally holds the pliers with the tooth up in the air, I let go. Just as I do, the pig rears up and kicks me in the legs. I fall into a fresh pile of manure.

"You did that on purpose!" I shout at Eustace. The anger in my body feels like a lightning storm. My fingers and toes feel sharp and mean.

"Did what on purpose?" he says. He reaches out a hand and pulls me to standing.

"You wanted me to fall down!" I accuse.

Eustace uses his hands to help wipe me off. "You know that's not true, Hallelujah Wonder. You know it's not." Then he turns from me and walks away.

The pig scrambles to his feet. Blood drips from his mouth.

"Why don't you go get a cold drink of water and sit down in the shade," Eustace says. "You need to cool down."

"Maybe I will!" I shout at him. My tongue is thick. My neck muscles tighten. I step out of the sty and start walking toward the drinking barrel. I kick a couple of stones, I look up in the sky as I walk. There's the moon out in the middle of the day. I get to the drinking barrel. The water looks black and quiet. Patches of ash float on the surface. I yank the dipper from the side of the barrel and slap it onto the water's surface. Water sprays in every direction. I lift the dipper to my mouth. The water rushes over my teeth and tongue, and I swallow. A calm flows down my throat and to the center of my body. I take another drink. My neck relaxes. The water ripples gently. The black surface reflects the moon.

Cold.

Calm.

The moon.

I stare into that barrel for a good while, just looking at the moon on the surface of the water. It seems peaceful.

Landing on Antarctica is like stepping on the moon, Father said.

"Hey," I whisper. No one hears me. I lower the dipper again to collect cold water to rinse the pig's wound. I turn back toward the sty and toward Eustace. "Hey!" I shout as I go across the yard.

Eustace looks up at me. "Hay is for horses," he says.

"Hey!" I shout again. I'm running along, sloshing water. "I know what to do! I know what to do!"

Eustace tilts his head.

I hand him the water dipper. He goes to the pig and pours the water over his jaw. "There you go, pig," he says. "You'll feel better now."

"I've noticed something about the Medicine Head." I wait and see if Eustace will ask me what, but he doesn't. "It seems to become more powerful the hotter it is. And it seems to quiet down the colder it is."

Eustace rubs the snout of the pig and pats him on the head.

"Are you listening?" I ask Eustace. He looks up at me. I widen my eyes at him. "So?" I say. "Are you?"

"What?" he says. He cocks his head. "What have you noticed?"

"So," I say, "the Medicine Head needs to be kept cool."

Eustace smiles with one corner of his mouth. "Well, it says that right on the crate you read to me. To keep it cool."

"Eustace!" I snap. "I know that."

"All right," he says. "Go on, then."

"So," I say, "where's the coldest place in the world?" I cross my arms and wait.

His eyes go up to the sky and then off to the horizon. He bites his lip. Then he nods and closes his eyes. "I can't think of a colder place than Antarctica," he says.

"Right," I say. "Antarctica."

"Antarctica," Eustace repeats. He doesn't have the slightest bit of disbelief in his tone. He just says it matter-of-fact-like, and that's another reason I like Eustace.

"Antarctica," I say, "is a place Captain Greeney couldn't get to. He tried and failed when Father succeeded."

"That's right," says Eustace. "He had to turn back."

"Right," I say. "He wasn't as brave and persistent and smart as Father." I sigh. "But I think I am."

"Hm-mm," says Eustace. "But how are you going to get it to Antarctica?"

"There's only one way," I say. "There's only one port in the world that has ships good enough to get to Antarctica."

"Hm-mm," says Eustace again. "New Bedford, Massachusetts."

"That's right," I say. "New Bedford, Massachusetts."

Eustace slaps his hands on his thighs. Then he points at me. "I'm going with you," he says.

"Well, I don't know why you wouldn't," I say. "You don't have anything else to do worthwhile around here. You've just been sitting around on your bottom your whole life, not doing anything." I say it kind of mean, and I even know it's a lie, but Eustace knows I'm not mad at him. He knows that's just the way I talk sometimes when I'm excited and teasing.

"We'd better finish this fence for Priss first," says Eustace.

We build in silence but for the rhythmic collisions of rock against rock and the music of crickets.

140

✦ CHAPTER 14 ✦

It's getting hot again, and the work on the fence and the pig has made me sweaty. I go to the house to wash up a bit. When I lift my head from the washbasin, I'm surprised to see Mother standing there behind me. I hadn't even heard her. She doesn't speak to me, but her eyes are wide and expressive.

"What is it, Mother?" I ask. "Are you all right?"

Her lips tighten, turn whitish pink. She's clutching a satchel to her chest. I recognize the scent of it before I recognize the shape of it. It's Father's satchel, an old black leather case that he took everywhere. Sometimes, he said, he used it as a pillow. Aside from his collection, this satchel was his most prized possession. It was where he kept all of his notes, research, and important papers.

I reach for it.

Mother steps away from me, just a little bit.

"I don't understand," I say. Why won't she just talk? I know she can. I remember when she did. It's not that hard. I do it all the time.

She steps back toward me and presses the satchel into my arms. I take it. She shuffles to her rocking chair, sits down, and closes her eyes to return to her silence.

I touch the top of the satchel. I remember my father pulling papers out of it and shoving papers into it. I lift it to my nose and sniff. There he is, tobacco and dust.

"Thank you, Mother," I say. I'm glad I didn't shout at her.

✦ ✦ ✦

Memory after memory floods me. After long, frustrating days in the field or with the pigs, Father would pull out his satchel, sit down at the table, and pore over his studies. He'd be happy again. Farm work did not make my father happy.

You can ask anybody about that. Especially Eustace. Lots of times, when Eustace would come to see what Father was doing in the field, planting beans in rows rather than in between corn plants, for instance, Eustace would take off his hat and scratch his head and say, "Well, I've never seen it done like that before."

Father would try to explain. "This is the newest method, Eustace."

Eustace would nod, but he'd also say something like, "Don't need to use as much soil or space the old way."

I leave the kitchen and dash up the stairs to my room. I toss the satchel onto my bed and stare at it for a while. I've always wanted it. I've always wanted to look inside and read my father's handwriting, his thoughts, his notes. But at this moment, I'm afraid to open it. My room feels airless and heavy with heat. The Medicine Head seems to be whispering again. I lie down on the floor and peek under the bed. It's still there, right where I left it.

"Be quiet," I say to it. "I'm not listening." But I am. I'm sweating. Bad, cloudy thoughts and bad, mealy feelings mix around inside me. Sadness. And anger. And fear. My mind flip-flops like flapjacks these days.

I unbuckle the satchel and lift open the top to reveal papers set carefully on the satin lining. Father's papers.

I touch them delicately, and I select a newspaper. I tenderly unfold a *New Bedford Times* with the headline "Local Man's Discoveries Discredited" and read:

Captain Charles Wonder was charged today with falsifying records and theft of United States property. Captain Wonder will face a Naval Court-Martial to strip him of his rank, return him to civilian status, and hasten the return of a priceless cache of items collected on several voyages at sea. Captain Wonder was chief scientist, naturalist, mineralogist, botanist, map-maker, and taxidermist aboard the ship Vivienne, *part of the United States Exploring Expedition between the years 1835 and 1842, which resulted in the discovery of the continent of Antarctica for the United States.*

According to Captain Cornelius H. Greeney, who also was a member of the United States Exploring Expedition as the captain of the ship Saint Mary, *"Mr. Wonder has behaved in ways unbecoming a representative of the United States Navy, has claimed to have discovered lands I, myself, discovered a full week before his ship reached the continent of Antarctica, and has kept for himself artifacts and jewels and gold, which are rightly owned by the United States. I will not rest until this man is revealed as the charlatan he is and I have in my hands the objects, worth millions, that should rightly be in my charge." Captain Greeney has taken over the responsibilities of Captain Wonder. He is a member of the Seaman's Bethel Chapel and is a prominent member of the abolitionist movement to eradicate slavery from the nation.*

Captain Wonder is married to the former Clare Seton, the daughter of Horace Seton and a pillar of the New Bedford community and leader in the abolitionist movement.

Have you ever read something bad about someone you love in a newspaper? Probably not. Well, I'll tell you. It doesn't feel too good.

I put it down, on top of another paper with the head-line "Captain Wonder Dishonorably Discharged Amid Scandal." The creases of the newspaper are almost worn through, which means Father opened and reopened these articles again and again.

To tell you the truth, I don't know why Father kept the artifacts, why he didn't ask someone to help him, why he allowed Captain Greeney to destroy his reputation. I do know he said that Captain Greeney intended to sell them off to the highest bidders, who would put them in private collections in dark and dirty smoking rooms in their gothic mansions. I suppose Father couldn't stand the thought of his stuffed caracal cat, his thunder eggs, his mounted piranhas, his Egyptian pharaoh's headdress, and, particularly, his Medicine Head sitting in places where he couldn't study and learn from them. But I don't know for sure. Maybe he simply wanted to keep them for himself. Though he told me and taught me a lot, he didn't have time to teach me everything or tell me all I needed to know.

I feel sad when I think about him sitting and reading all these nasty half-truths and lies about himself, but then my stomach clenches and a gush of bitter bile comes up my throat. I swallow it back down, leaving a sour taste in my mouth. I think of the man responsible for this misery, for Father's death, and I clench my fists and promise Father that I will get revenge.

I know that in most families, a son is responsible for upholding the family name and for carrying on the knowledge and trade and work and wealth or property or herds or acres of the father. But since Father had no sons who lived through childhood, it's my responsibility instead. It's usually the daughter's duty to find a suitable husband and make a suitable home and have clever children for her parents to be fond of, and then take care of her aging parents in their waning years, but I'm certain those things can wait until after I've avenged Father. And in any case, I haven't seen a single boy or man around these parts whose attention I'd like more than I like my scientific pursuits. All the boys around here look too much like Kansas: stringy, dusty, and boring.

I touch the newspapers one more time, and I'm about to close the satchel when I notice the corner of a folded piece of paper sticking out between all the old newspapers. It seems strangely clean, when all the others are yellowed and brittle. I pull on it carefully. I unfold it and am surprised to see my own name at the top.

It's a letter, addressed to me.

I catch my breath and read:

Dearest Hallelujah,

One of these days, I fear, Captain Greeney will come for the treasures and come for me. I hope I am prepared, but this letter is for you in case I am caught unaware.

I have spent my life traveling the world. It is a marvelous world to behold. From the smallest insects of the plains to the behemoths of the oceans, from the frigid floating ice islands to the volcanic sandy beaches even now being born in the seas, the world is ripe for discovery and appreciation. Every element of nature, the moon's phases, the sun, the winds, the clouds, the seas, the animals, and the mountains and valleys, functions in concert. It has been a great blessing to be able to see and study so many wondrous things. I think, child, that you, too, are destined for this kind of life, one of curiosity and toil and learning.

I write now to warn you of one mystery I have yet to understand, and, I must admit, one that I fear. It is the artifact that truly interests Captain Greeney and is the one he must not find. I am afraid he could, frankly, exploit its tremendous power and destroy our family. What else the artifact is capable of, I am not sure. For it prevents careful study. I am too weak to handle it much. It calls to me in wicked ways. It conjures enormous anger and thoughts of revenge in me. It begs me to hold it. I don't know what I might do if I entertained it for long. But I fear the worst.

For now, I know it magnifies negative feelings, evokes difficult memories and terrible prophecies, and that it is best kept in a cool place. Heat seems to galvanize its power. And it is magic. Or, rather, the source of its power is unknown, undiscovered by me. For all my years of learning and logic, I must admit that some phenomena cannot be explained. I also know, based on anecdotes I have heard but can hardly believe, that the artifact must not be destroyed. *DO NOT ATTEMPT TO DESTROY IT.* If the stories are true, the consequences of its destruction are as terrible as anything I can imagine. The item I write of is the Medicine Head. It calls to me. It calls to *others. Not everyone. I do not know how it selects, but it does. I have seen you attracted to it, too, Hallelujah. I have seen you stand near it with your ears alert. Be careful, but be courageous.*

Kansas, with its heat, is not a safe place for the artifact. If it is ever safe for me to return to New Bedford, there is a good man there who will help me take it to the coldest place on earth, the place that bears my name. His name is Captain Abbot, and as the world's best whaling captain, he is familiar with the iciest and most treacherous seas. He is a frightening man, full of wild tales and bad spirits. But he is the only one, I believe, who could make the journey. No one else on earth is as familiar with that deadly region of the sea. No one else on earth has as little to lose as Captain Abbot.

I write this now as though my time is short. Perhaps I will be able to dispose of the Medicine Head myself, and I will rip this letter to shreds. If not, I will sign off now, entrusting you with this great responsibility. I love you, your sister, and your mother very much. You are the brightest stars in my universe. And you, Hallelujah Wonder, have enormous intellect and heart. Where I have failed, I trust you will succeed. Your greatest gift is your everlasting curiosity about the world. Keep it, my darling daughter.

Your devoted father,
Charles Wonder

My eyes grow bleary and hot. And then I cry like a baby all over the letter. I hold it to my chest. I sob. I'm loud and shaky. I miss Father so much.

He'd be so disappointed in me if he could see me now, bawling and frightened and not at all like the girl with the enormous intellect and heart he hoped for. I let it all out, and after a while, a long while in which I try to cry out every bad thing that's ever happened to my family—my brothers dying, my mother fading into herself, my father's trial, my father's murder, Captain Greeney hunting us, the fire—I finally calm down and fold the letter.

I was correct about what to do with the Medicine Head. I figured it out on my own. I discovered its sensitivity to heat and cold all by myself. I didn't need anyone to tell me or guide me. I was smart enough to use my own observation and mind. I think maybe Father would be proud about that. Maybe he would be proud that I thought of Antarctica, too, before I read the letter.

I think maybe I do have a good knot in my skull.

Maybe I can do this.

✦ CHAPTER 15 ✦

Priss is back. Her face is sooty and sad. There are clean streaks where tears have run down her cheeks. I suppose she's got bad news about the Millers. She's preparing a supper of beet soup, bread, and a bit of cheese. We all eat together at the table, and even though so many bad things have happened, it's nice to look around at all the people I love right here in one room. Even Fob sits there, nose poised on the corner of the table.

We finish, and Eustace settles Ruby into Father's old

study, which Priss has converted into a place for Ruby to stay. I talk to Priss.

"The Millers were killed last night," she says. "Burned in their beds." Priss stares off. "They were found like that, together, as if they had simply fallen asleep."

I cross my arms over my chest and squeeze myself. "Thank goodness," I say, "they were probably killed by the smoke before the flames got them."

"Thank the Lord," says Priss.

She's always saying things like that, about God. Mother was that way, too, before she stopped talking. I'm not sure if Priss means she's thankful to God or if she simply uses it as an expression. One nice thing about religion is that it can help a girl deal with bad things, like death. If you believe in a religion, you might feel like you'll get to see all those dead people again someday. Father never subscribed to religion, and I don't, either. I trust in science. But even I have to admit that the science of death, the idea that death is forever, is difficult to believe all the way. I sure would like it if science had a way to prove that I could see my father again someday. But there's no evidence to suggest that I'll ever see him or the Millers again.

But then I'm startled by a thought. "Are Ruby and Eustace going to be free, then?"

"No," Priss says. "Probably not. I heard that the Jessups have already sent word to Mr. Miller's brother in Missouri to come and collect his property."

"What?" My face flushes with anger and fear. I can't let my best friend get moved away from me to go and be a slave somewhere else. "So Eustace is going to have to go to Missouri?"

"I'm not sure," says Priss. "But that is the way slavery works, Lu."

"Did you see Captain Greeney?" I ask.

"No," she says. "I don't think so, I mean. There were a lot of men putting out fires and collecting the dead for burial. It'll take a day or two, probably."

Urgency hits me. "We can't sit here and wait for the Missourians to come get Eustace. And we can't sit here and wait for Captain Greeney to come back for the Medicine Head." I'm prepared for her to change her mind and to turn motherly like she sometimes does when she remembers she's older than me, but she doesn't.

"I agree" is what she says. "I can tell you've got a plan, Hallelujah. And I'm not going to stop you." She folds a napkin in her lap. Then she looks up at me. Her eyes are wet but soft. "How long will you be gone, and what should I do if Greeney comes back before you do?"

I look to Father's rifle above the mantel. Priss knows what I am thinking. But I know Priss would never hurt anyone.

"I'm not sure how long I'll be away," I say. "A long time. Remember Father's voyages to the Southern Ocean?"

She nods.

"Long as that, I guess," I say. "As for Captain Greeney, I don't think he'll come here. I think he'll be after me." I remember the way Captain Greeney knew the Medicine Head was in that crate during the fire. It calls to him, too.

Just then Ruby comes in, and Eustace and Fob follow behind her. Eustace has a guilty, low-eyed look about him. He told his mother everything, it seems. I know he's embarrassed about it, as though he thinks I'll think he's a big tattletale or a big baby. I do often think those things, but tonight I don't care.

"I'll take care of business here, Hallelujah Wonder," Ruby says. "I know what's going on, and I'm not gonna let anyone hurt Mrs. Wonder or Priss long as I'm here."

Knowing there's an adult here to help with Mother makes me feel better about leaving Priss.

"And I know those Missouri folks you're talking about," she adds, "and I'm not letting my boy go there." She sits down at the table and groans in pain. She slides the rising bread dough to her and kneads her hands into it. She pulls and hits and folds it.

"You two go on," she says. "Get him out of this crazy place with all these crazy people running around, killing each other, and burning everything down. Don't worry about us." She beats the bread. Her eyes get squinty, and I can see they are full of tears. The tears that have been shed today could water all the crops in Kansas.

"Ruby?" I say. "Are you sure?"

"Yes, Ma," says Eustace, "are you sure? Will you be all right?"

"Eustace could get killed here," Ruby says. "Or he could be sold away from me tomorrow or the next day. I know these people of the Millers. I know what they're like." She pounds the dough, then pulls it, then folds it. "They're not like the dead masters. They don't have a kind bone in their body." She flours the table and slaps the dough on top of the flour. She shakes more flour on top of the dough. "I'll be fine," she says. "They won't want me. I'm too old. Knees don't work. Eyes going bad. Eat like a horse. I'd be more trouble to them than I'm worth. But my Eustace? My big, strong, good boy, Eustace?" Her top lip starts to curl up and her breaths get shorter. "They'd take Eustace and work him to death or make it so I never hear of him again, like my other boys." Then she heaves and cries full on. Mother emerges from the other room, stands in the doorway, and leans against it. She's been up and listening. Her eyes are glossy and her cheeks are splotched with red, the way they used to get when she'd cry.

Ruby looks at Mother in the doorway. "All those sweet sons," Ruby says, "the child one and the half-grown one and the grown one. All gone." She moans and wails for herself and for Mother, too. She goes back to pounding the dough.

Mother shuffles toward Ruby very slowly with one arm reached out before her and the other at her chest with a closed fist, the way she used to hold it when her own boys passed, in a way that seems to put a weight on the place where the baby boys once rested their heads. Then Mother puts a frail, skeletal hand on Ruby's shoulder and squeezes.

Ruby keeps beating the bread dough but chokes and sobs like no one's watching. I can't look away.

✦ CHAPTER 16 ✦

In Tolerone, I never wake up to a bird chirp or a rooster crow. I have not awakened to the gentle lapping of waves against the sides of ships or to the scents of a baker baking bread or women making coffee, like I did in New Bedford. No, I awake to the clanks and rings of hammers. I awake to dynamite blowing away rough swaths of land. I awake to the scent of metal grinding against metal. For the past year, railroad owners have been tossing down and hammering train tracks across the

West. Father used to say that trains would open up the West for settlement and exploration, and that interest in the West would destroy people's interest in the sea.

I don't like the trains.

I have never been on one. I have sat and watched the railroad workers dig up the earth, hammer the slats, pound down the rails, and connect Tolerone to the great cities of the East. I have watched the churning, whistling monster engines with their lines of freight cars scream across the barren land and screech into Tolerone. I have waved to the engineers, the coal shovelers, the porters, the tramps riding on the top, and the passengers inside the passenger cars. I have even skipped down the tracks and practiced my balance on the rails. But the truth is, I am afraid of trains.

When we moved here, Father brought us by horse and wagon, and he paid two of his most trusted mates from his days aboard the *Vivienne* to bring his things in a separate wagon. But today, if Eustace and I want out of Tolerone in a hurry and without detection, there's only one option. We don't have tickets, and we can't go into town because Captain Greeney might see us. Or maybe by now the Jessups are thinking they should lock up Eustace until the Millers of Missouri get here to claim him.

So we must stow away aboard the Western Railroad. We are about to jump a train, like bandits. Doing such a thing doesn't feel like a very scientific approach to traveling, but I guess I'll just have to make do with the circumstances provided.

I don a pair of Father's pants, his suspenders, and his old coat. Everyone knows you can't jump a train in a dress. I pack a satchel with an extra set of clothes, a purse full of coins (earned from selling a couple of hogs) that Priss makes me take, and some food for the first few days. After that, Eustace and I are going to have to figure out how to get food on our own.

That, too, seems impossible right now. It also makes me realize how dependable Priss has been and how much like a mother she really is. I can't remember the last time I worried about what I was going to eat. I never had to. For his part, Eustace isn't worried at all about finding food. He says his ma has had him out foraging for food since he was in diapers. I decide to count on him. If I'm going to trust him about hopping on a train, I may as well trust him about eating acorns, mushrooms, and dandelion leaves.

I pick up my satchel, and I carefully place the Medicine Head's crate inside. When I come downstairs, I see Eustace waiting for me with nothing but Fob.

"Aren't you going to pack anything?" I ask.

"I don't need anything," he says. Fob whimpers. "Except my dog."

I look at Fob, and he tilts his head at me and makes a soft moan, almost as if he knows he's going on an adventure and is scared.

Now, don't get me wrong. I like Fob. But I don't want that timid, crooked-walking canine to mess up this journey. "I don't want this cowardly dog holding us back," I say. "What's he good for?"

Eustace grimaces and leans down to cover Fob's ears. "Don't talk about my dog that way," he says.

One thing about Eustace is that he's real sensitive about his dog. I look at Fob again. "Well," I say, "I guess maybe he'd make a good pillow." I nod to Eustace to show him it's all right with me if Fob comes along. "For on the train, I mean," I add.

I kiss Mother good-bye and hug Priss tight. I can tell we understand each other.

"Be careful," she says. Her voice is quivering now. She's trying to be strong and brave.

"I will," I say. "Don't get married off to the first boy who shows an interest before I get back here to give my blessing."

Priss smiles. I hear Ruby guffaw and mumble something about not letting any no-good boy around. I feel better knowing she's here to help. Then I really look at Ruby hard. I feel sad for her and for Eustace because I wonder if she'll ever see him again. This moment might be it. Whereas I might be gone a year, Eustace might be gone forever.

Priss seems to read my mind. She goes to Ruby and holds her hand. "And, Eustace, don't you worry about your ma." She pats Ruby's hand. "We'll love her and protect her with our lives."

Everyone looks at Eustace. He nods, but he doesn't speak. I don't think he can. I know that feeling. The one where it feels like a big hot rock is stuck in your neck. I say something to stop everyone from staring at him so he doesn't have to worry about the whole world seeing him get teary and get embarrassed about it.

Then Eustace goes to his ma and wraps his arms around her tightly. He shows no shame over his indulgent embrace, and I wonder why our family isn't always affectionate like theirs. Ruby lifts him up and hugs him, then holds his hand in her hands. She says "I love you, son" over and over. She says, "I love you so much I have to let you go and have yourself a life." She says, "I did my best, and I hope you remember that." He promises he will. He says he loves her, too, and that he's going to see the world and make a big life for himself. And then Eustace, Fob, and I are out the door of my Kansas home and into the blackest and hottest night I can remember on the plains.

Immediately, the Medicine Head begins whispering to me.

"You don't hear that, huh?" I ask Eustace.

"I hear nothing but dry grass and gravel," he responds. "But I get worried every time you ask me that when you're carrying that thing. I can't wait to get rid of it."

We walk in silence the rest of the way. The air is hot. Sweltering. The Medicine Head howls like a wolf.

Eustace and I wait in the dark a mile or so outside of town. Fob horses around behind us. Sporadic fires still burn in Tolerone, and many of the buildings are reduced to blackened, skeletal frames, but the trains are running. We're waiting on the ten-thirty p.m., the train that usually brings in lumber, then takes out the wheat, the cattle, and the mail of the people here.

"When it gets here," says Eustace, "it should still be moving slow enough to hop." Fob whines like he doesn't believe it. Eustace pats him. "Don't worry, boy."

"You toss on Fob, hop on yourself, and I'll hand you the Medicine Head," I say. "Then I'll hop on, too."

"That's the plan," says Eustace. He rubs his palms on his trouser legs.

"What time is it?" I ask.

"Don't know," he says. But we can hear the warning whistles, which means the train's about to leave the station.

"You ready?" I ask.

"Yes," he says. "I hope Mother will be all right without me."

"Priss'll watch her."

Then we hear the train's workings lurch into movement and the telltale *chug-chug* coming closer. But there's something else, too.

The silhouette of a horse and rider is pounding toward us from town.

"What's that?" I ask. I point at the form.

Eustace squints. "Oh no."

"What is it?" I ask. "Who is it?" But I already know.

"Come on," Eustace says. "Come on. Come on!"

We dive out of our hiding place and head toward the berm on which the tracks lie. It's rocky and gravelly and a bit slippery. I hadn't thought about having to climb a hill and then jump onto a moving train.

It's dark and breezy, and as the train gets closer, noisy. But above that noise is the screeching of the Medicine Head. It's enough to drive me mad.

"Be quiet!" I say to it.

Eustace tips his head at me like I've lost my mind.

"Not you," I say. I have a bad feeling in my gut. I don't think the Medicine Head is calling to me right now. I think it's wailing to someone else, to Captain Greeney. And I have a notion that Greeney is listening and coming for it. Does the Medicine Head know what I've got planned for it? Is that possible? Is it angry? Does it want to be with someone who will use it?

"OK!" shouts Eustace. "I see it! When I spot a car that's open, I'll point and then start runnin'. Just follow me." He picks up Fob and gets into a crouching stance. The train roars toward us. So does Captain Greeney. I'm sure I can hear him shouting "Yah! Yah!" at his horse.

"Go!" Eustace yells, and he starts running up the berm. I follow him. Rocks and gravel slide down, and I lose my footing, but I get up again and keep climbing. At the top, Eustace is standing a few inches from the rushing cars. I fear he'll get hurt, fall underneath, or get hit by a car, but it's hard to tell if the doors are open or not unless he gets really close. Next thing I know, I hear Fob yelp as he flies through the air and into a dark car, and I see Eustace running and reaching for that same car's door handle.

"Come *on!*" he yells back at me. I start running.

Ahead, Eustace grabs hold of the door and pulls himself up. He turns back toward me. The train is building speed, and the *chug-chug* is getting faster. I look behind. Captain Greeney is coming. He's getting closer and closer.

"Lu!" shouts Eustace. "Look at me! Don't look back!" I run harder and push the satchel out in front of me. Eustace takes it and sets it inside the car; then he reaches his hand back for me. I'm getting tired, but I'm still moving my legs as fast as the stumpy things will go.

I hear Captain Greeney shouting, "Halt! Halt! Do not get on that train!" I sprint. My lungs feel like they may explode. I've only run this hard one time before, and that time I was too slow.

"Go!" Eustace yells. Fob's barking, too. I pick up my legs and will my feet to move faster. I reach out my hand, and then I can feel Eustace's fingertips touching mine. He's leaning way out from the car, barely holding on to the door to give himself enough reach to hold on to my hand.

I finally get close enough that he can grab it. Now he's pulling, pulling me toward him, but the train's traveling too fast for me, too fast for anyone to run alongside it.

"I won't drop you!" Eustace says. And then my feet give way beneath me, and I'm being dragged.

I think I'm going to die.

My feet swing behind me. I can feel them get close to the undercarriage and running wheels and gears of the train. There's so much heat coming off them, and I can feel the speed of the train increasing and my legs being sucked under.

"Hold on!" Eustace yells.

"Stop!" Captain Greeney shouts. "Drop her!" he orders.

Fob is howling and pacing back and forth in the car like he's upset he can't help. Eustace pulls on me harder than ever, and with the strength of two grown men, he heaves me into the train car.

My stomach scrapes along metal, and my head hits a hard floor. When the rest of my body lands with a thump, I begin to cry. "Lordy," I whimper. I roll onto my back. It's very dark in the train car, but I know Eustace is there.

I touch my arms, my legs, my face. *I'm not dead*, I tell myself. *I'm not hurt.* I look out the door and as the train speeds up, Captain Greeney falls behind. He pulls the reins on his horse, and it slows and then stops. But he watches us. And I watch him until he's nothing but a dot on the horizon. The farther we get from Greeney, the quieter the Medicine Head becomes, until it's silent.

I breathe deeply. I'm glad he's behind us, but he won't wait to follow. I know he'll come after us as soon as the next train leaves Tolerone. I'm persistent, like I already said. But maybe so is Captain Greeney.

CHAPTER 17

My boots burn. They've been close to fire or the heat of grinding gears. "Eustace," I say, "how did you do that? How did you get me up? I thought I was going to die."

I hear a voice that does not belong to Eustace say "*¡Tontos!*" and then a string of things I do not understand.

"Who's there?" I ask. I try to sit up, but I just curl up on my side. "Who said that?" Whoever it is keeps talking, keeps repeating that word *tontos*, which doesn't sound like a compliment.

"Eustace?" I say. My eyes are adjusting now, and I can see Eustace and Fob sitting up against the wall of the car, near the door where we flew in. Both their chests rise and fall in exaggerated breathing. I can see my Medicine Head resting there, too, safe and sound. There is a tall man standing close to them. He's wearing a railroad worker's uniform, a smart one with a black coat and white shirt. He's the one talking.

"He's calling us fools," Eustace says, "and he wants to know what we're doing here." Fob makes a groaning sound, like he wants to know what we're doing here, too.

I'm worried the man's going to stop the train and kick us off. He's pointing at Fob and shaking his head, then pointing at us and shaking his head some more. He's flailing his arms and saying "*Dios mio.*"

"Is he Spanish?" I ask. I finally feel oriented enough to sit up, which I do. My head pounds. I put my hand to it and discover a huge bump near my hairline.

"He's speaking Spanish, yes," says Eustace.

"I didn't know you spoke Spanish, Eustace," I say.

"A little," he says. "My ma speaks some. My old man was half Mexican."

For a moment, I consider asking Eustace all the questions I ever wanted to know about his father, but then I decide this probably isn't the right time. The tall man continues to rant, wave his arms, and slap one hand against the other like he's a stern schoolmaster. I'm not scared of him, though. He doesn't seem mean, only wound up by having two kids and a cowardly animal heaved up into his train car. With my objective, scientific mind, I am able to understand that this reaction is completely reasonable.

"Well," I ask, "what else is he saying?" I peer at the man.

Eustace is scratching his head, trying to decipher it. "I think something about how crazy we are and how we almost got ourselves killed," he says. "Plus something about the dog having more sense than both of us."

"Well," I say. "That's not very nice."

"Phew," says Eustace. "That was close, Lu. Greeney was right on your tail. And you almost got sucked under." The movement of the train grows louder and smoother. "This man saved your life."

I shake my head. "*You* saved my life."

"Some," he says. "But I wouldn't have been able to pull you up without him pulling me."

I think about that for a few seconds. The man is still rambling. I understand one word: *idiota*. He walks back and forth in the train car. Then I understand another word.

The man says "Greeney," and then he says *"muy malo"* and draws his finger across his neck.

Seems like this man knows Captain Greeney. And even though he might be mad at us for hopping on this train, he seems like he might even help us. Sometimes I just get a good feeling from people, and I've got a good feeling about this man. I know that's not a very scientific way of thinking, but you probably know what I mean anyway.

Mother used to call this type of phenomenon "women's intuition." She said that at the exact moment Father discovered Antarctica and she was in labor, she felt a freezing jolt lurch her body. She intuitively knew that Father had made the discovery. Priss probably has women's intuition, too. She seems to know every time I'm up to something I don't want her to know about. I wonder if that feeling is the same one I get before something is about to happen, like when I found the dead snake. I wonder if that means I'm developing women's intuition.

"Idiota," the man says again.

"I knew you were going to say that," I say to him.

Then I close my eyes. I don't care if he calls me an idiot for hours. I'm very tired. I just have to rest for a minute. I wrap my arms around my knees and place my head on them. I take in air and blow it out slowly as I replay all the events of the past two days: the cave, the Medicine Head, the fire, Captain Greeney, the articles, the letter, the train, Captain Greeney again. I wonder how dangerous this journey will be, since I almost just got myself killed and we aren't even out of Tolerone yet. I wonder if Captain Greeney will be on the next train.

Of course he will.

Do you know what a theory is? Well, it's an educated position based on facts. Based on all the facts I have so far, including the ones where Captain Greeney chased Father across the country, killed him, and came back to Tolerone again, I'd say it's safe to theorize that Captain Greeney will be on my tail quick.

I sigh.

The Spanish-speaking man comes to me, kneels down, takes my hand, and pats it. Then he drops it, sits, and puts his head on his knees like me. I don't know a thing in the world about him except that he saved my life and then called me an idiot, but somehow I feel safe around him. I don't have a scientific explanation for how you can sometimes tell if a person is good or bad after only a couple of minutes, but I hypothesize that this man is a nice one.

I suppose now you're wondering what a hypothesis is.

One thing I try to remember is that not everyone, hardly anyone, was lucky enough to have a famous scientist for a father to teach him or her everything there is to know about the world. A hypothesis is an educated guess.

I smile at the man. He smiles back and shakes his head like he can't believe his eyes. Then he puts his hands together, as though in prayer, and rests them against his cheek. He closes his eyes. He's telling me to sleep.

After a while, I do.

✦ ✦ ✦

When I wake, Eustace and the man are sitting on the edge of the car with their feet dangling over the side as the train moves. Eustace slices an apple and gives half to the man. They act chummy as old friends. They laugh together, and they take turns petting Fob. I watch them for a while, and I can see that the man is not as old as I first thought. He is maybe only eighteen or nineteen. He has fascinating hair, black, glossy, and curled over like a plowed furrow of earth. He has very dark brown eyes and thick eyebrows. He has excellent posture.

I sit up, and then I realize that sometime during the night he covered me with his wool coat. He is already providing me with lots of evidence to prove my hypothesis, and that makes me smile a little. I take the coat off and fold it over neatly.

"Well, look who finally decided to wake up," says Eustace. The man stands up and makes a slight bow.

"*Perdon, niña,*" he says. "*¿Cómo dormiste?*"

"Huh?" I say. I look at Eustace.

"He wants to know if you slept OK?" Eustace translates.

"*Sí,*" says the man. He closes his eyes and pretends to rest his head on his pressed-together hands.

"Uh...uh," I stammer. I look outside, at the land rushing past. I see cows in pastures, birds in the sky, huge full clouds against a blue sky. "I think so. How long have I been sleeping?"

"All night," says Eustace. "And most of the morning."

"Wow," I say. "I was tired."

"You were snoring," says Eustace. He snorts like a snore. The man looks at him and smiles and then says something to me. I look at Eustace.

"He says you purr like raindrops when you sleep," says Eustace.

I blush. "Are you sure you translated that correctly?" I ask.

"Not really," says Eustace. "My Spanish is rusty."

I hand the coat to the man, and I look deep into his eyes, which are quite pretty and fringed with very long black lashes. Even though they are very different in color, the mood they express reminds me of someone. Priss.

"What's his name?" I say.

The man must understand because he answers, "Lopez de Santa Anna-Carson." He takes his coat from me and bows again. It occurs to me that he is quite handsome and also debonair, not at all like most of the boys I know. I think I'd like for Priss to meet him someday.

For the rest of the ride, Eustace asks Lopez my questions and then tries to translate the answers back to me. Lopez asks me questions, too. I tell him all about New Bedford, Tolerone, and Priss. He asks lots of questions about Priss. I tell him about how boys sometimes try to come and ask her out for walks and sometimes even bring her flowers from the prairie. Lopez is very curious about this. He raises an eyebrow quizzically.

So I make Eustace act it out with me.

Eustace bends over, pretends to pick flowers from the train car floor. Then he pretends to arrange them in a bouquet. And I have to admit that Eustace is a very good thespian. Finally, he brings the pretend flowers over to me, bends down on one knee, and reaches them toward me. I put my hand on my chest and pretend I'm surprised, because that's what Priss does. I open my eyes and mouth really wide. I say, "Oh, for me?" Then I pretend to take the flowers, clutch them to my chest, and raise the back of my hand to my forehead, as though I feel faint.

Lopez laughs and laughs. He applauds and says, "Bravo. Bravo!"

I don't know what language that word is, but I know what it means.

I don't understand anything Lopez says, but I like him a lot and decide I wouldn't mind one bit if he came to court Priss someday. It turns out he's a porter on the railroad, which is why he's dressed in that dapper black coat and creased trousers. He's in charge of the passengers' baggage that doesn't fit in the passenger cars.

Riding on a train makes my stomach lunge and lurch, flip and flop. Once in a while, despite how warm it is in the car, I break out in a cold sweat and think I might vomit. Most of the time, I sit with the Medicine Head's crate on my lap and think. So it's nice when Lopez takes a break from his work to talk with us. Sometimes, for a little while anyway, he helps me forget all the bad. But the bad always comes back.

Lopez points to my crate and asks Eustace a question. Eustace looks at me and shakes his head.

"What?" I ask. "What did he say?"

"He wants to know what's in the crate," says Eustace. He raises his palms. "What should I tell him?"

I hug the crate to me. "Don't tell him anything," I say. "Tell him nothing. Tell him it's none of his business. In fact, tell him to mind his own business."

Eustace doesn't say any of that. He shakes his head at Lopez.

Lopez lifts his shoulders, gesturing *Why?*

I wag my finger back and forth. I wonder why Lopez is so interested. Does he know what's in the crate already? Maybe he's heard of the Medicine Head. Maybe he wants it for himself. Maybe he's been hired by Captain Greeney to take it from me and is just pretending to be nice to us.

I point to the crate and use both my hands to simulate a great big explosion. I make a noise like *Boom!*

Lopez raises his eyebrows. "Boom?" he repeats.

"Big, big boom," I say with a nod. Lopez looks at Eustace, who shrugs.

"OK, OK," Lopez says. "Big boom."

✦ CHAPTER 18 ✦

That night, Lopez has to leave us to check on the other cars and make sure there aren't any stowaways hiding among the packages. He tells Eustace and me to stay away from the door. Well, he uses a combination of talking and gesturing to tell us these things. He warns us that the train will stop in the morning, and that the conductor will make his rounds, peeking into each car to make sure everything is as it should be.

While Lopez is out, Eustace and I work on moving

boxes and crates to create a small cubby in which we can hide when the time comes.

It's hot in the car with the door closed, and the Medicine Head is whispering to me again. My palms sweat. "Why does he think it's any of his business what's in my crate?" I ask crossly. I've got the bad feelings, the angry ones that make me want to walk hard and talk sharply.

Eustace sighs. "He doesn't," he says. "He's being as curious as any other normal person would be. Don't be distrustful."

I think about this for a minute as I inspect the cubby from all angles to make sure we won't be seen. "Maybe you're right," I say. I pick up the Medicine Head's crate, weasel my way into the cubby, and push it back behind other boxes.

"What are we going to do about Fob when the conductor comes?" asks Eustace.

"I don't know," I say. "Can't he sit and be quiet?"

"Not reliably," says Eustace. "Can you, Fob?"

Fob barks. For the next hour, Eustace tries to teach him the difference between "speak" and "be quiet." As evening comes, the train car becomes cooler and more comfortable. The light from the moon and stars creates a very dim glow in the car, but I wouldn't be scared even if there were

179

no light because I'm used to being in small dark places. I wonder if Eustace is afraid, and I'm about to ask him when I see that he and Fob have fallen asleep together, Eustace curled up and Fob resting his head on Eustace's legs.

I'm just about to doze off, too. I close my eyes and see the things that I miss: Mother and Priss...and even Kansas, a little bit. I scoot a bit closer to Eustace and Fob.

In the morning, the train pulls into Chicago, Illinois, and Lopez bursts in from the small door at the end of the car and tells us to hide. Eustace, Fob, and I squeeze into the small place we've created behind the boxes, and Eustace tries to keep Fob quiet. Lopez leaves again through that small door and crosses a platform into another car.

We wait for what feels like forever for our big door to slide open.

When it does, the car is flooded with light, and we can feel the cool air circulate. Fob starts to get excited, like he wants to go outside and run around. Eustace shoves a piece of dried meat into his mouth. I peer through a couple of cracks between the boxes.

A man in a sharp uniform is talking as he runs a cane along the floor of the car. He looks up and down and side to side and then shouts, "All clear! Lock it up." Then I see Lopez, who is walking behind him, look directly at me as he slides the big door closed again. We're safe, but we have to stay quiet while the train is in the station.

For hours, we sit with our ears pressed against the sides of the train car or our heads leaned back against them. The inside steams with heat. Eustace paces back and forth, casting furtive glances at me and the Medicine Head. From the confines of its crate, it starts up its call again. This time, it sounds pleading.

"Be quiet," I say.

"Who are you talking to?" Eustace asks. He frowns at the crate.

"Never mind," I say. Eustace is really getting on my nerves. Even Fob bothers me. The way he walks, the way he skulks around, the way he whines and cries. All of it works on my last bit of patience. I press my ear to the train car's wall again.

I can hear a husband and wife having an argument about how the husband squandered the wife's father's money. Another person says he has to find an outhouse. Somebody else remarks that this town smells like cow manure. I sit quietly and listen to the noises and arguments and confusions of the people.

The Medicine Head continues.

What if I just opened the crate but didn't hold it?

181

Maybe that would cool it down a bit. Maybe it would stop taunting me then. I pry my fingers between the ropes of the knot on top. I make a little wiggle room. When Eustace has his back to me, I loosen the whole thing and the rope falls to my lap.

Eustace spins around. "What are you doing?" he asks.

"Nothing," I say. "Just sitting here roasting to death, like you."

Then another train pulls into the station. Its gears grind and squeal to a halt. I peer between the slats of the wood. It's difficult to see, but I recognize the train, with its leaf-green engine, as one that comes in and out of Tolerone.

I wave Eustace over. "Eustace!" I say. "Is that a train that comes through Tolerone?"

"Sure looks like it," he says. "Think Greeney's on it?"

"Certainly," I say. My stomach flops, and saliva collects on my tongue.

Eustace and I watch for a long while. We're both quiet. But the Medicine Head keeps up its taunt.

I spit on the floor. I shuffle my feet. I clear my throat. The Medicine Head whispers *Hold me.* I wonder if it means me or Captain Greeney. "You don't hear it?" I ask Eustace. He ignores me. I don't blame him.

We wait for what seems like another long while. My

stomach rumbles with what I think is hunger, but it could be from the long train ride or my nerves. I've felt stomach-sick since I got on this thing. I try to remember the last time I ate or did anything normal. That all seems like a lifetime ago. I curl over my stomach. Eustace sees me do this and pulls a hard biscuit from his pocket.

"Thanks," I say, and bite into it. It's dry, but at once I feel its nourishing effects on me. My head gets clearer. My muscles strengthen. I don't feel so tired anymore. But I get that strange tingly feeling, like something is about to happen.

I listen. There are voices right on the other side of the train car's wall.

"I don't know what it is or does," one voice says, "but Greeney wants it, and that's all there's to it. No sense asking questions because you're not gonna get no answers."

Immediately, I suck in my breath and hold it there.

"It's some kind of magic ball he wants," says a gruff voice. "If we don't bring him that Medicine Head, he'll have our tails."

Fob shuffles his back legs, as though he's nervous. Eustace puts his hand on Fob's neck. I put my finger up to my lips.

"If you'd a gotten it the last time, we wouldn't have to be out here in the middle of nowhere," says another man.

"We'll just see how good you are at finding it," says the first man. "We done everything we could to get its where-abouts last time. If Wonder had just told us where it was, he'd still be walking the earth. It's his own fault." Then he adds, "Must be a mighty powerful thing Greeney wants."

"Sounds like hocus-pocus to me," says the third man. "But I hate to be the one who crosses Greeney."

✦ CHAPTER 19 ✦

As the day wears on, the temperature rises. There's not much to do besides be hot and be sleepy in this dark place. I doze off once in a while, and my dreams are filled with wild images, some of my father's dead face, some of Captain Greeney slipping a rope around my neck. When I wake, my throat hurts, as though I've been strangled in my sleep. All the while, the Medicine Head's crate sits on my lap, or right beside me.

I'm more worried than ever that someone, anyone, is

going to try to take it from me. I loosen the ropes on top of the crate and dismantle the knot, then retie it, making a sheet bend. I loosen them again and make a double sheet bend, loosen, then a water knot, loosen, then a square knot, loosen, and a double fisherman's knot. Finally, I stop and let the rope hang loose on my lap.

This train car smells like damp straw, unwashed feet, and wet coats. Hardly any light gets in. Even though we've been at a standstill for nearly a day, my stomach hasn't settled. It wants to empty whatever's in it, which isn't much.

I never felt stomach-sick while walking around on the flat, stay-steady ground.

I think for a while that we should go back. Is Captain Greeney too powerful for us to outwit? He's got the authority of the whole United States Navy behind him, for goodness' sake, and all I've got is a smart Negro friend who is breaking just about all the laws in the nation even if the laws are not right, a crooked dog with a fearful nature, and a porter who can't even speak English.

Eustace and Fob fall asleep in a heap. I can't sleep because the Medicine Head won't quit. It moans and whines and whispers to me relentlessly. The noise of it, along with the heat, makes me want to bust open the door and jump off the train. But I can't do that. I can only wish it would be quiet. I touch the rough wood of the crate, and I don't even care when I get a splinter in my finger.

Do you know what sirens are? Well, they're not real, so don't worry if you've never heard of one. Sometimes the sailors aboard ships would think they heard women singing off in the far distances of the ocean. Sailors can be on ships a long time, even years away from their wives and mothers, and they get lonely for womenfolk. So the lonely ones who don't know any better steer the ships right toward the music. Then they crash directly into rocks and wreck the vessels. The music they heard was only the wind whistling through those rocks and not women singing them lovely songs. Like I already said when I told you that story about the woman and her chicken, people do some illogical things when they're lonely. They forget all about science and let their imaginations run wild. Not me, though. I definitely don't want to do that.

Yet I hear it.

Almost like a whispered lullaby or the faint humming of a far-away child. I thrum my fingers on the top of the crate.

I want to touch the Medicine Head. It wants me to. It begs me to.

I slip my fingertips between the lid and the crate. I ease the lid off.

A scent like dry leather and dust and brittle hair hits my nose. It's so powerful, I look up to where Eustace and Fob lie asleep to see if they've noticed, but they sleep on.

The Medicine Head sits askew in its straw. If nothing else, I should get it upright again. Without another thought, I hold my breath and reach in and put my hands on it.

Instantly, my hair blows back, and I feel like I'm on a train, but a much faster train than this one.

Clouds race in the sky. Ocean waves crash violently, and I hear what sounds like all the voices of everyone I've ever known talking at once. The images slow down, and I'm standing at the prow of a ship, freezing. It hurts to breathe the ice-cold air. My toes ache from the chill and from being cramped in tight boots.

I see nothing but gray-and-white ice.

"Note the time, Jenkins," I hear a very familiar voice say. I try to turn and look, but I'm frozen where I stand.

"Yes, Captain," I hear Jenkins reply.

"The continent of Antarctica. There she is, boys." My father's voice causes my heart to rush. A warmth runs through my veins.

I am with him on his discovery. I squint and try to see

where he is, but I can't. I see dark forms of men, but I can't make out Father. I look out to where Antarctica should be and see dark mountainous shapes, white mist, and gray sky.

"We made it," Father says. "Only the bravest, wisest crew could have managed it. Our names will go down in the history books, boys."

I try to move my mouth, my lips, and my tongue. I try to tell him, *I'm here! Father, I'm here, too!* But my mouth doesn't work. It's frozen. My legs are frozen, too. I listen for him to say more, but I only hear the groaning of ice, the crunching of ice, and the squeaking of ice.

This is as close as the Medicine Head will allow me to get to Father.

And suddenly, I'm released.

I let go of the Medicine Head, and I am back in the train car, dark and dingy and hot. I'm sweating.

I exhale and look around. It's still dim. Eustace and Fob are still sleeping. I'm panting, but my stomach doesn't feel sick anymore. My heart is full. I got to hear Father. If the Medicine Head is a dangerous and evil artifact, why would it give me a vision so good, so delightful? Why would it give me just what I need? If all of its gifts were like that one, I could hold the Medicine Head all day, every day, for the rest of my life.

I want to hear him again. The Medicine Head rests in the straw, face-up. It has no expression. It's not calling to me or begging me to hold it. But I want to.

I decide to touch the head again.

I hold my breath and let the wind come. The clouds, the waves, and the voices pass, just like before. When they slow, I'm back in my Kansas kitchen.

There's Priss, looking pretty as ever but older. She's wearing a new dress, a white one with blue cornflowers all over it. She's not wearing an apron like she usually does. Mother is at the kitchen table, quiet but smiling a small smile. She's wearing an old dress, a nice green frock she used to wear in New Bedford. Ruby is standing at a table frosting a round cake.

"You'll make a fine wife, Miss Priss," Ruby says. "Yes, ma'am."

Priss is getting married? Who? Is this happening now? No. It can't be. Priss wouldn't get married without me. Is this the future? I turn around and around but don't see anyone else there. But then I spot a train porter's coat hanging over a chair. It looks just like the one Lopez wears.

I turn around again, looking for Eustace and Fob, but I don't see them anywhere. Where could they be? I look out the window to the pigsty, and they're not there, either. I try to call, *Eustace? Eustace!* But again, my mouth doesn't work.

Out the window, I can see a cloud of dust rising from the road, rolling into the sky like a dark, ominous ghoul. I try to shout *Hide! Hide!* to all the people in my house. *Captain Greeney is coming again!* But it stays trapped in my mouth. Everyone continues with wedding preparations. They can't hear me. And then Captain Greeney is in the yard, dismounting from his horse and yanking a long rope from his saddle. At the end of it is a hangman's noose. *Hide! Hide!* I scream to Priss, to Mother, to Ruby. No one hears a thing.

And then I drop the Medicine Head.

I am back in the hot dark train car.

Moments later, before I can even catch my breath and shake the terrible images from my mind, the car door flies open.

Lopez leaps in. His eyes are big as buttons. He's speaking loudly and quickly and pointing at me and the crate, where the Medicine Head lies for everyone to see. Eustace and Fob scramble to their feet.

"Slow down!" Eustace says. "I can't understand you." Then he sees me, sees the open crate, and his face gets mad, too. Even Fob barks as though he's mad at me. I slap the lid on the crate.

Lopez continues to talk, but a bit more slowly. Eustace is listening and nodding.

"He wants to know what that is," Eustace tells me. "He says Captain Greeney's searching the train looking for a girl from Kansas who has stolen a government artifact." Lopez looks at me with lowered brows and a pinched mouth.

"Captain Greeney is evil!" I shout. "Tell him, Eustace. Tell him Captain Greeney is evil. Tell him he killed my father!"

Eustace translates to Lopez, who is listening and nodding, but his eyes are skeptical, squinted. He exhales loudly.

"Greeney," Lopez says, "*muy malo.*"

"*Sí,*" I say. I look him straight in the face. "I've got to keep this scientific artifact away from Captain Greeney." Lopez is staring into my eyes now, and he nods, as if he's understood every word I've said. "I have to take it somewhere safe."

"*Sí,*" he says. He straightens his porter's coat. I remember how I saw that same coat hanging over my own kitchen chair. "*Muy importante*," he adds as he points to the Medicine Head's crate and grimaces.

"*Muy, muy importante.*" I shake the crate a little. "Antarctica."

He rolls his eyes like I've lost my wits. "*Ay, yi, yi,*" he says. I know exactly what that means without anyone translating it for me. Lopez stands there for a moment staring at the head. Even over the noise of the other trains, shouting and crashing in the next car can be heard.

"*Rápido,*" Lopez urges. "Hide," he says in English.

Eustace and I get behind the crates again. Eustace waves and calls for Fob, but he won't come. He's taken a liking to Lopez, who has brought him scraps from the dinner cars for the past few days. Fob sits on his hind end right at Lopez's feet.

Lopez pats Fob on the rump and motions for us to get our heads down. My heart's racing fast, like horse hooves. The door bursts open, and the car is awash in light.

"But, sir, this isn't a passenger car," a man says. I see him between the slits of the crates, and he's wearing a uniform like Lopez's, but even fancier.

"I want every car searched thoroughly," another man says. When he steps in, the light from outside is blocked, and the car grows dim again. He lifts a lantern up to his face, casting a hot glow on one temple, cheek, eye. Captain Greeney looks like a madman. I glance down at the Medicine Head, and it looks like it's pursing its lips at me, sneering.

Lopez steps forward and speaks urgently at the two. He gestures to the crates and then spreads out his arms high and wildly.

"What's he saying?" Captain Greeney asks the other train worker.

"Something about dynamite, I think," the train worker says. "I don't know. He's just a porter."

Greeney eyes the train car from corner to corner and floor to ceiling. He spots Fob.

"What's that dog doing in here?" he demands.

Lopez sniffs and then points to the crates again. He speaks slowly to the train worker, who looks afraid. His eyes widen, and he tiptoes away from the crates. He takes off his hat and wipes his forehead. He's very, very nervous.

"Sir, the porter says the crates carry nitroglycerine," he says to Captain Greeney. "The chemical being tested as a blasting agent. The dog can smell a leak that could potentially create a big explosion and kill us all, sir. That's what he said." The train worker clears his throat and eagerly eyes the door.

I don't suppose you've ever heard of nitroglycerine. Well, to be honest, I don't know much about it myself. But I do know it's highly combustible, which means explosive. I have to admit I am very impressed that Lopez knows more about something than I do. But I intend to study up on it first chance I get. I don't like anyone getting ahead of me in scientific advancements.

Then the train worker adds, "The porter says he's seen no sign of a runaway girl with a stolen artifact, sir."

Captain Greeney raises his head and seems to be smelling the air. "Is that so?" Captain Greeney reaches the lantern toward Fob, who barks loud and snaps at him. Captain Greeney recoils. "All right, porter." He eyes the crates, but he's careful not to put the lantern near them. I suppose he's wondering if they're really filled with nitroglycerine.

Captain Greeney walks toward the door, but then he stops. He puts his hand on his chest and begins to shout into the train car. "I would simply like to say that with this missing girl there may be a runaway slave, property of the Millers from Missouri. I would like it known that should this runaway slave come forward and provide the whereabouts of the missing girl, he would be granted his everlasting freedom and my personal protection."

I suck in a gulp of air fast and then slap my hand over my mouth because I feel a cough coming. Eustace gets close to my face and puts his hands over my mouth, too. He's shaking his head *no, no, no,* and I don't know if he means "No, don't cough" or "No, I don't believe a word he says." I'm hoping it's both. The seconds go by, and while it feels like a week has passed, it's only been half a minute.

Captain Greeney waits, I suppose, for Eustace to come forward, take his freedom, and give me and the Medicine Head up. But none of that happens because Eustace Miller is the truest friend a girl like me could ever have.

"Very well," says Captain Greeney, "continue with your brave duties, porter. Protecting the train from a fiery doom and whatnot." And then they turn and walk out the door. Lopez shuts it, and the car is dim again. Within an hour, the train is moving east toward New Bedford and the last leg of my journey.

Lopez watches over us all night, so I try to sleep because I know once I get to New Bedford, I'll have a lot of work to do. But I keep seeing Lopez standing up to Captain

Greeney, coming up with that clever tale, and saving me and the Medicine Head. I think about Eustace, who was promised his freedom in exchange for me but chose to stay with me on this journey instead. I even think about Fob, who barked and snapped at Captain Greeney, when he's usually timid as a mouse. What have I done to deserve such brave, smart, and loyal friends?

I can't think of much.

CHAPTER 20

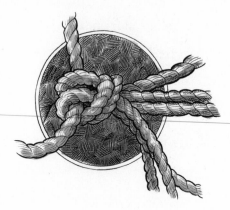

For days, we lurch forward in the train car. Every minute of the ride, I worry that Captain Greeney will come back. I worry that the Medicine Head will call to him so loudly that we'll be found. But it doesn't.

Then, on the fifth day, I smell a new scent that's old at the same time, a smell that fills my head with hope. It's the ocean. We've made it to New Bedford, Massachusetts. The most beautiful city in the entire United States. My home.

The cool breeze off the ocean lifts the haze of the train car. It feels lighter in here, as though a thick veil has been blown away. The Medicine Head remains quiet. Maybe it's because of the cold wind. When the train squeals to a stop, I'm ready to hop out and get moving. "We've got to get to the port. I've got to find Captain Abbot and his whaling ship."

"I'm hungry," says Eustace.

"Yes," I say. "We can find something to eat."

Lopez says to us, "Good luck, *amigos*." He has watery eyes and pulls us into a hug. He goes on in stilted English. "Good luck of secret science in box. Good luck of Fob. Good luck of Eustace. Good luck of Hallelujah Wonder." Those two words, "good luck," have meaning that bests any others. Even though Lopez can't say them, I think I know all the words he wants them to mean.

He kneels down and grabs Fob, scratches behind his ears until Fob groans with pleasure. Then Lopez stands and reaches into the pocket of his porter's coat.

He says something to Eustace.

Eustace nods, then shakes Lopez's hand. "He says to find him when our journey's complete. He says he'll get you back to Kansas safely."

I usually like to think that I can do everything myself.

But it sure is nice when a girl's got some reliable friends to help her.

Lopez wraps his arms around me and hugs me tight. He lifts me off the floor. I hug him back. "*Gracias*, Lopez." And then it's time to go.

Eustace, Fob, and I step out of the train car and jump down onto the ground of New Bedford, where I took my first breaths and my first steps as a babe. I've got my satchel and crate, and Eustace has Fob. My legs shake. The ground beneath me seems unsteady, but I know it's only because I've been on a moving train for so long.

Eustace, on the other hand, walks sure-footed as I've ever seen him. His eyes are wide at the swarms of people. "You could get lost in a crowd here," he says. "I've never seen so many people in one place before."

He's right about that. Old people, young people, children—all bustle back and forth. Trains steam in and out. I know Greeney will soon be on my trail, but I feel somehow protected here. There are tall buildings and lots of alleyways and backstreets. There are lots of places to hide. Not at all like Kansas, where everyone knows every-one else, knows when and if people go to church or school, knows if they sleep with their lamps lit or windows open, knows if they sneeze or blow their nose.

"What if this captain won't let us on his ship?" Eustace asks.

"Why wouldn't he let us on?" I say. "Ships always need crew. There are signs up about it all the time. Everywhere."

"Yes," he says. "But I'm a Negro, in case you haven't noticed."

"You're more ruddy-colored," I say. "But don't worry. Lots of Negro men work on the whaling ships. Lots." I'm fairly certain this is true, but not absolutely. I can't see why it *wouldn't* be true. "And I'm good at tying knots," I say. "They'll hire me for that. And Father knew this man. He'll understand. He'll want to help us."

Eustace raises an eyebrow at me, and Fob seems to do the same.

"I've never heard of a woman, much less a girl, on a whaling ship," he says.

I worry a little that I might not be able to get on the ship. But I've come so far already. I have to. I have to get the Medicine Head to Antarctica. I'll do whatever it takes. I'm not turning back now. I'm not giving up.

"You could just give the darn thing to me," Eustace says. "If what you say about Negro men is true, then Captain Abbot will hire me on. I'm strong. I'm a good worker." He bites his lip. "I could take the Medicine Head to Antarctica, and you could go home to your family. You could go home and help take care of Ma."

I watch him. Is he sincere? I think he is. But maybe he wants the Medicine Head for himself. I shake my head to get that thought out of my mind, and I also shake it to tell him *no*. "Thanks, Eustace. But I've got to do this. The entire way. The whole journey."

He nods. "I thought you'd say that. But I would do it for you, Lu. I would."

"I know, Eustace." I look away so he doesn't see my lip quiver. Sometimes Eustace and his goodness make me want to cry.

I take a deep breath and exhale slowly. "But I promise when this is all over, I'll go home and tend to Ruby. I promise you that, Eustace." I stare off toward the ocean and don't look at him. I don't want him to see that my eyes might be watery.

✦ CHAPTER 21 ✦

New Bedford isn't quite the same as I remember it. For instance, I don't remember quite as much smoke hovering in the air or soot blackening every building as there is now. I don't remember so many grimy people walking around with moldy coats and missing teeth. I certainly don't remember this many untended dogs with matted hair and missing limbs. The fish smell seems familiar, but it was more appetizing than the scent now wafting from the crates of rotting fish carcasses sitting in the middle of the lanes. My stomach flips again.

Eustace puts his hand in front of his nose to block out the smells. "This is the New Bedford you've been crowing about all these years?" he says.

I don't say anything. I keep walking, holding the Medicine Head's crate close to my heart, looking for places I remember and moving toward the port.

"Smells bad here," Eustace says. "Like everything's been dumped on with old kitchen water and then left to fester in a chicken coop."

He might be right, but I tell him, "That is not true, Eustace!" I walk and clutch the Medicine Head to my chest. I wish New Bedford looked and smelled a little better. "You're not used to it yet," I say. "Kansas smells bad, too. Like smoke all the time!"

Eustace pauses in his walking, which causes Fob to nearly trip him. When Eustace steadies his footing, he says, "That's only recent. Because of the fighting."

I know he's right about that, too. One good thing about Kansas is that even if it was the most boring place in the world, you could always get a good-smelling breath of clean air, before the fires started. I don't tell Eustace I think that, though.

Eustace points to the sky. "Look at those," he says. Seagulls are circling and cawing. "What are they?" he says.

I can hardly believe Eustace has never seen a seagull. I laugh. I can't help it. "Don't you know a seagull when you see one?" I say. "They're everywhere. The sailors always know they're close to home when they see a seagull."

"Kinda look like the pigeons we got back in Kansas," Eustace says.

"They do not," I say. "A seagull is a much more digni-fied animal than a silly old pigeon. Seagulls are a hundred times more interesting than those dumb old Kansas birds."

As we walk, Fob runs ahead of us, and he scatters a flock of seagulls, which were fighting over the carcass of a stinking black eel.

"Don't seem more dignified to me," Eustace says.

I don't say anything. Fob comes back to us. The eel was too smelly for him to investigate.

Men of every kind—black, Indian, Japanese, and Portuguese—clog the lanes. The whaling ships aren't par-ticular when hiring people to sign on to be at sea for months and years at a time. They need people who are strong and courageous. They don't care what color you are. No one gives a second glance at me, who must look like a scrubby piece of riff-raff, or at Eustace, who is a runaway slave from a burned-up town in Kansas.

Eustace is walking funny. He moves through the lanes of New Bedford with a confidence I never saw in him at home. Sometimes in Tolerone, when I was walking with Eustace, some white people would say to us that it wasn't proper "for a white girl to be consorting with a darkie," or something like that. I never cared what those Kansas people thought, but I know Eustace sometimes got his feelings hurt. I bet if he lived here, he'd never have to walk crouched over or ashamed ever again. And here, he'd get a whole lot of eager listeners who like to hear about abolition.

On the corner stands a man reading aloud from a newspaper. He reads to a group of people, white, black, men, and women. "We must act on this blow to liberty!" he shouts. "We must stand with our Negro brothers in the Kansas Territory, which is now burning with the wrath of God!"

I nudge Eustace. "He's talking about Tolerone," I say.

"Shh," says Eustace. "I want to hear."

The reader goes on. "The North must not cower under the yoke of the slave masters of the South. The North must now take a stand for the freedom outlined in the

Declaration of Independence. Let the fires of Tolerone be a call to action against tyranny and injustice."

I pull on Eustace's arm. "Let's go," I say.

He shuffles along with me but looks back now and again.

New Bedford has churches on every corner, and many of the congregations are involved in the movement to free the slaves. I see a familiar lane, the one that leads to the church we used to go to when I was small. "Let's go up here," I say to Eustace. "I want to show you something." We walk up the cobblestones to a simple white chapel. "I remember this place," I tell him. I think back to the times when I was small, when Mother, Priss, and sometimes even Father would come here and sit together.

"Do you want to go in?" Eustace asks. He stares up at the spire going into the sky. Then he points to the sign above the door. "What's that say?" he asks.

"Seaman's Bethel," I tell him. I sigh.

Mother was a member of Seaman's Bethel Chapel, and the members there wrote letters to all the country's newspapers about the evils of slavery. They collected money to donate to free black men to help them get places to live. They helped them find employment.

Practically every member of this church was connected

to the whaling industry in some way. Sailors and sailors' wives. Captains and captains' wives. It was the sailors' and captains' wives who started the abolitionist movement at this church.

Father didn't come with us to services often. He didn't give much clout to religion. Superstition, he called it. "Science is where the real truth lies," he would say. And Mother would shake her head and warn him not to make "such conceited and hasty pronouncements." You might find it difficult to believe that Mother once spoke articulate and beautiful words, but she did. She was considered, in her time, to be quite a catch, smart and well bred. As well as beautiful, like I already said.

While Father rarely attended services at Seaman's Bethel, Captain Greeney attended all the time. Even though I was little, I remember seeing him here, before everything went so bad. Sometimes he delivered lectures from the pulpit. Before my father swept my mother off her feet, Captain Greeney even courted her and wanted to marry her. Lots of men did, her being the Beauty of New Bedford and all. Sometimes I wonder if all Captain Greeney's plotting to destroy my father comes from an old grudge over Mother. People sometimes lose their heads over what they think is love.

"Yes," I say. "Let's go in."

We go to the door, and I open it to let Eustace step in. He hesitates, as though he's not sure he's allowed. "Go on," I tell him. "Things are different here in New Bedford."

Eustace points to Fob. "What about him?" he asks.

"Oh, he can come, too," I say. "These people aren't particular about dogs going to church."

Then Eustace nods to the Medicine Head's crate. "That thing, too? You think it's right bringing it inside a church?"

I clutch it to me. "Well, I'm not leaving it. All this religion stuff is just superstition, anyway." The truth is, I don't know about that. But Father said it was, so I'll believe him until I find out for myself what I think about the matter.

We step in. The chapel is bright white and cool. Every window is open. The breeze blows in off the ocean. Somehow, all the bad smells have been filtered out, so nothing but sweet, salty air blesses my nose. I breathe in deep and exhale slowly. I spy an open pew in the back and lead Eustace and Fob to it. Fob's nails clack on the floorboards. A few heads turn around to look at us, but none of the faces gives us a second look. We look as welcome and normal here as everyone else. There are women dressed in the black garb of the widow. There are young women surrounded by small children, the families of sailors, probably. There are old seamen, white-bearded and red-faced. There's a whole row of Wampanoag whalers up front. Maybe you didn't know this, but before Europeans ever got to the Americas, Indian people lived here first. And they were whaling before any Europeans thought it up.

Eustace twists his head one way and then another, taking in all the sights of the chapel. I don't tell him to sit still. I let him look around. I imagine it makes him happy to see white folks, black folks, brown folks, red folks, young folks, old folks, tattooed folks, scarred folks, scantily clad folks, and rich-looking folks all in one place. He relaxes and eases into the pew.

Then the pastor takes his place at the pulpit, which is interesting and unusual because it's shaped like the bow of a ship.

"For them that don't know me," he begins, "I am Father Captain Mahogany." He gestures with his right hand to his missing left arm. The coat sleeve on that side is pinned up. Then he gestures to his peg leg, which he lifts for the congregation to view. His head is massive, and he's fully bearded. "'Aye,' says them everywhere's I goes. 'Aye, Father Cap'n Mahogany, 'tis true the sea monster took yeer left-side appendages, but yeer faith makes you full strong as any man about.'"

Eustace elbows me. "What's that supposed to mean?" he whispers. "What's he saying?"

I shrug. *I don't know.*

Eustace says, "Huh?"

"Shh," I tell him. Eustace has never gone to school, so I guess he doesn't know that sometimes a kid is supposed to listen and be quiet when a grown-up is talking even if the kid has no idea what the grown-up is talking about.

"You talk funny, too, to them," I whisper. "Now be quiet."

Father Captain Mahogany goes on. "'Aye,' says I. 'Me arm and leg been scuppered clean off by a mighty fish, 'tis true, endin' me days prematurely as a nautical man. But dids this sink me spirit? Dids it keelhaul me heart? Nay. Nay." He wipes his face with a handkerchief, then stuffs it inside his tattered vest, the buttons of which strain to hold the vest together. He's so big, he looks like he's swallowed a whale.

"And now I shall stir the congregation with a whopper

of a tale from the gospels." Father Captain Mahogany clears his throat. He uses his coat sleeve to wipe his nose. "Followin' a lengthy bit of sermonizin' one mornin' into the late afternoon," he says, "Jesus the Christ escapes the throngs by takin' onto a boat for a bit of a rest. Now, not many of ye likely consider Jesus the Christ much of a seafarin' chap, but I likes to imagine Jesus the Christ supremely squared away afloat on a vessel."

"Oh," says Eustace. "I know this story!"

I elbow him in the gut hard. I clench my lips together until it hurts my teeth. Fob whimpers.

Father Captain Mahogany continues like he doesn't even hear Eustace interrupting all the time. "So when the men accepts Jesus the Christ onto their boat and asks him wherest he'd be happiest to venture, Jesus the Christ says, 'Oh, hither and yon, my brothers. It matters not.' For Jesus the Christ was weary to the bone and in need of the kind of respite only the cradling of the sea may provide.

"So the nautical fellows takes up the oars as nautical fellows are wont to do, and no sooner have they dipped ten times than has their blessed passenger Jesus the Christ fallen into a mighty snooze. Bamboozled by sleep, he was, fairly awash in a great restorative slumber, rocked as he was by the tender roll of the sea. Imagine him now, if ye can, and let the smile play upon yeer own lips at the thought of his heavenly snooze. Holy calm.

"But then a tyrant of a storm rips the peace to ribbons, and the boat is tossed like a seed on the swells. The sailors brace up and batten down the hatches, but it's rogue wave left and right, and the sea has their vessel in her clutches.

"So the storm has the paltry boat in her clutches, and what is Jesus the Christ up to? To the sailors' disbelief, he sleeps. Aye, like a babe in his mother's womb he sleeps. And the sailors, lashed by wind and walloped by wave, are in complete disbelief at the sight of the sleeping fellow. And try as they might to wake him, asleep he stays.

"Finally the clattering reaches such an unholy din that Jesus the Christ awakens, rubbing sleep from his eyes with a princely yawn. And the careening sailors immediately accost his ears with fearful complaints, such as 'What the blast'll become of us?' and 'How the blaze'll we avoid the deep slumber in this bluster?' and 'Today we'll surely die! Help!'

"And what does Jesus the Christ say? Peaceful as a fluff of cloud, he intonates, 'O ye of little faith, be still.' And at his voice's command, the whirling sea goes calm, and the sailors follow suit.

"What will ye glean from this tale? May it be the same

gleaned I when me port side was in a whale jaw's clench: faith. Faith so strong it can move a mountain. Faith. When your harpoon's dashed and the ship's on its ear and your friends are a-swim or bubbling under and your left side's in the crunch—avast, worry! Avast, doubt! Avast, fear! Faith. Faith. Faith." Father Captain Mahogany shakes his one good fist in the air and then pounds it down on the pulpit. He steps back and down the steps and disappears to the back of the chapel.

We leave the chapel and walk back to the main lane.

"Boy, that was some sermon," Eustace says.

"I don't understand it," I say. "Faith in what? Faith can't move mountains. There's no evidence to support that. Sounds like thin logic to me."

"I get it," Eustace says. "I understand it in every way." He looks up into the air and puffs up his chest almost like he's floating. Even Fob is walking in a lighter manner.

I think Eustace is pretending to understand the sermon. He must be, because the sermon didn't make sense. What is faith? A person can't just believe something and expect that it's true. "You do not," I say. "You're just saying that."

"I am not," says Eustace.

"Well, what's it mean, then?" I ask.

"Uh—er," he stammers. "It means you've got to believe."

"Believe in what?" I ask. "What, exactly?"

"Um," says Eustace. "You know...believe in faith and power and things."

"That doesn't make sense," I say. I shake my head at his simplicity. "To believe in something, you have to have evidence, Eustace. You have to have a scientific basis for belief. It wasn't too long ago that every dummy thought the sun revolved around the earth, you know. Those dummies *believed* that. They had *faith* in that. But it was hocus-pocus and false."

"Well, what about you?" he asks. "You believe that Medicine Head is talking to you, don't you?"

I breathe quick, and my face feels hot. "You be quiet about that!" I snap at him.

But he doesn't stay quiet. "There isn't a lick of evidence that says that head can talk or do anything else you think it can," Eustace says, "yet here we are. Away from home. Getting chased by a madman. Thinking about getting on a ship to the most far-away, freezing place on the earth. If that isn't faith, I don't know what is."

I'm so angry at Eustace I could smack him. "It's not the same!" I shout. "We're doing research right now. We are conducting a scientific study! Just because I can't under-stand how the head works doesn't mean it doesn't have a perfectly rational explanation. I know it does!" Then I curl up my hand into a fist, and I punch Eustace right in the arm.

He rubs his arm. Then he smacks the back of my head with the palm of his hand. My ears ring. I'm so surprised, I nearly drop the Medicine Head. I stop and clutch it close to me.

"You *believe* it has a rational explanation, you mean," he says. Then he walks on ahead of me. "Don't ever hit me again!" he yells back over his shoulder. Fob lopes after him. Fob turns back and gives me a bad look, like he's mad at me, too.

After a while, I nearly lose sight of them. They don't slow down. They don't check to see if I'm following. My arms and legs feel stiff. "Go on, then," I yell. "See if I care!" They continue walking. That's fine by me. Let him go. Darn old Eustace. He'll probably get lost. He has no idea where he's going.

I look around and up and down the lanes of New Bedford. Every building is covered in the same soot and mold and is constructed like a plain old rectangle with a lot of small windows, each of which is made up of twelve smaller windows. Some buildings are painted blue. Some are painted gray. Some are painted white but have now turned gray with grime and soot. Every space is crammed with crates of wool or dippers or candles. From the way it smells, people empty their chamber pots in the lanes.

Everything has changed. I'm not sure where I'm going. I turn back to the last place I spotted Eustace and run to catch up to him.

As I fall in step with him, he turns his head to me, shakes it a bit, and then grins. Just like that, we're not mad anymore. We walk on with Fob ambling alongside us.

In between the churches are alehouses that sell spirits to sailors. Shops are tucked in between those. People stand outside selling their hooks, fruits, fish, biscuits, boots, and ointments. Lots of other people buy those items. We walk for a long, long time in silence, simply watching the hustle and bustle of the New Bedford citizens.

Finally, Eustace talks to me. "All these folks are their own boss?" he asks.

"Yes," I say. "They don't have slavery here." It makes me feel good to say that because I know for sure it's one thing that makes New Bedford better than Tolerone. Eustace could never walk around Kansas and call himself a freeman.

As if reading my mind, Eustace says, "This is a nice place, even if it is dirty. Even if it smells bad, I can take a full breath."

I try to feel what Eustace is feeling right now. I'm sure he misses his ma. I know he does. But if he had stayed in Tolerone, he'd probably have been separated from her anyway. He'd probably have been shipped off to work all day, every day, for mean old slave owners who would never appreciate a single thing he did or knew. They'd probably never realize how smart Eustace is. They'd probably never appreciate how loyal he is. They'd probably never see how strong and courageous he is. Or how forgiving he is. Even if he is a mama's boy and hits girls.

I wonder now if he's looking around and thinking about all the possibilities he has. All those things he had hoped for his life, about being a cowboy or a scientist, are suddenly possible. I feel happy for him. But I feel a bit of unhappiness, too. I know that at some point, our journey, successful or not, will be over, and Eustace and I will have to separate. I feel real bad we had such a bad fight. I reach out and pat him on the back nicely.

"It didn't hurt," he says. "When you punched me. I hardly felt it."

I can't decide if I should be mad about that comment or not. I decide not to, even though it does sound like an insult to me. Eustace is my friend, and sometimes you have to forgive and forget.

"My ears are still ringing," I say. "You didn't have to hit me so hard."

"I didn't mean to," says Eustace. "Sometimes I just get tired of you, Hallelujah Wonder."

I didn't really ever know before that Eustace could get so mad. I guess it's good for me to know.

"Well," I say. "I concede that I may have been a little bit bumptious and a know-it-all at times. But that was too hard a hit you did on my head. Especially if my hit didn't even hurt you."

"It hurt a little," he says. "I lied before. I am sorry about that."

I worry that I may be leading Eustace to all kinds of bad behaviors, shouting, hitting, and lying, to name a few. I commit to being a better friend for the rest of this journey. Because at the end of all this, I'll have to go back to Kansas to be with my family and Ruby. Eustace won't be able to come.

I don't want to think about that now. It makes me too

sad. It's difficult losing people, even when you're losing them to a good life. I intend to make sure that my remaining time with Eustace puts him in the best position to live his happiest life. I can do that. And I hope one day he'll say, "That Hallelujah Wonder was a good and true friend."

✦ CHAPTER 22 ✦

The port is abuzz with activity and shouting. Men haul huge barrels up ramps onto the decks of enormous ships. Sea captains stand on the decks and yell down for more fresh water, more flour, more oil, all the supplies they'll need to be at sea for the duration of the whale hunt. Women bustle around selling dried fish from baskets. Children tag along behind them with the fish heads, which they sell for practically nothing. No one gives my Medicine Head's crate a second glance, so I walk a little easier.

Eustace finds a girl who is selling fish heads, and he gives her a coin for three. He offers me one. The fish head was silver but has been smoked to a coppery color. If it weren't for the blackened eyes, it might look appetizing, I suppose. "No, thanks," I say.

He gives one to Fob, who swallows it in one gulp. Then Eustace chews on his own fish head and eats the eyes and all. He's about to start on the other one, too, but instead he reaches it toward me.

"You sure you don't want some?" His breath is horrible.

"It's all yours." I look around for something I could buy to eat. In this part of New Bedford, the peddlers sell lots and lots of trinkets from all over the world, items the whalers have brought back from their travels. One stall sells monkey paws. One sells something called tiger serum. Another hawker sells scrimshaw, which is whalebone and whale teeth carved and stenciled with dramatic scenes. One peddler has an entire row of shrunken heads, ones much smaller than mine. I walk past them and clutch my crate close.

Then I buy a biscuit and a shriveled old orange.

Eustace smacks his lips and wipes them with the back of his hand. "Are you going to eat the rind?" he wants to know.

"No," I say.

"Can I have it?" he asks.

"Sure."

He slides the pieces of rind into his mouth. His stomach must be made of stone. He will eat anything, like I already said.

We continue along the seaside. There's a group of men sitting under the shade of a sail they've set up as a makeshift tent. They are sharpening long lances. They are harpooners, a fearsome passel of tattooed men, the most respected men on board a whaling ship.

We come alongside a ship where men are rolling huge barrels down a ramp and onto the dock, where they line them up.

"Those barrels look just like the one you have in your barn," Eustace says. At least his breath smells better now, like orange instead of fish eye.

"Whale oil," I say. "Spermaceti. Practically the whole world is lit by it. You couldn't see a thing after dark if it weren't for whalers."

"People in Kansas can see, and they don't use whale oil," Eustace says. He rubs his stomach like he's real satisfied with his meal.

"Well, they can't see as well as the people in New

Bedford can," I say. Even as I say that, I know it's not entirely true. Before the fires started, I remember many Kansas nights when the moon was full and glowing like nothing man could make. Beautiful was what it was. Just a tiny bit, I miss dumb old Kansas when I think about it.

"I heard that some people were testing to see if pig oil would work as good as whale oil," Eustace says.

"They were probably from Kansas," I say. "Without even testing it for myself, I can tell you right now that pig oil doesn't compare favorably to whale oil, so don't buy it if someone tries to sell you some."

"I don't know," says Eustace. "Pigs got a lot of good qualities. How do you know their oil won't light as good as whales'?"

"I just do, all right?" I say. I know I said I was going to try to be a better friend, but sometimes Eustace really wears on my patience.

Up and down the port, dozens of ships with masts spiking the sky cast grave shadows on the docks and the people who work there. Some of the ships are small fishing boats that stay close to the shore. Some are enormous and house more than a hundred men. Some are new, with fresh paint and sharp white sails.

We're walking side-by-side, Eustace and me, with Fob

trailing behind us. Our eyes are up and sky-wise, studying all those rippling sails, when someone steps in front of me. A woman dressed all in black, with a black bonnet and a black veil over her entire face, grabs my arm.

"Hey," I say. I try to pull away from her, but she holds on tight. Her long nails dig into my muscle.

"It's not proper," she sputters. She talks as though she doesn't have any teeth in her mouth. "A disgrace."

"Let go of me," I say.

"Why are you dressed up like a boy?" she says. She points a short, fat finger at Eustace. "Is this Negro boy bothering you?" She stands so close to me that she breathes into my nose. Her breath smells like the dead snake from Kansas.

"Pew!" I say. "What do you want?" I gulp and try not to inhale.

She won't let me go. "You come with me, child," she says. She's small, but she's awfully strong.

I yank my arm out of her grip.

"I'm getting the constable." She loosens the strings of a small pouch she has dangling from her arm. "Don't you move, Negro boy," she says to Eustace. "Walking in broad daylight with a white child. Shame on you."

Eustace droops his shoulders and hangs his head.

The lady pulls a whistle from her pouch. She's muttering things like "I know a runaway when I see one" and "Nice reward on this one." She lifts her veil and puts the whistle between her lips.

Quick as a lick, I reach forward and wrench that whistle from her mouth. I draw my arm far back and launch the whistle toward the ocean. It soars above all the people and flutters like a glittering fish breaching the water.

The lady croaks "No!" and opens her mouth in what will be a scream. I shove her hard in the chest and she falls back into a cart full of sausages.

"Run, Eustace!" I shout at him. He straightens his back up and shuffles along as though he's not sure if he should run or not. "Go!" I yell. He goes.

Then I lean over the lady in black. I shake my finger in her face. "Shame on *you*!" I yell. I spin on my heels and dash away from her. People in the lane stop what they're doing and tell me to watch out and slow down because it's slippery. I don't listen. I keep running.

I catch up to Eustace and Fob, who are standing in the shadow between two buildings. I reach for Eustace's hand and pull him out of the dark.

"Let's go, Eustace." I slap my thigh. "Come on, Fob."

They come, but Eustace has a hang-dog posture. I

try to think of something good to say to him, but nothing comes out. Instead I reach up and put my arm around him. I squeeze his shoulder.

"Hey," I say.

"Hay is for horses," he says as quietly as possible.

"You know what today is?" I ask.

He shakes his head.

I fumble around in my satchel until I feel what I need. Then I pull out my closed fist and put it in front of Eustace's nose.

"Happy birthday," I say. I open my hand and reveal the beautiful thunder egg.

Eustace gasps. "Huh?" he says. Then he smiles, and I can see that his eyes are getting watery.

"Take it," I say. I push it toward him again. "Go on."

Eustace lifts his hand slowly and takes hold of the thunder egg. He rubs his thumb over its surface. Then he lifts it to his face and places the smooth part against his cheek.

"This is the nicest thing anyone has ever given me," he says. "Thank you."

We keep going, and very slowly, Eustace stands up a little taller. He's deep in his Eustace thoughts. He rubs his chin.

"We could cut your hair," he says.

I touch my bun, full of hair that is dry and scratchy. "What for?"

"Make you look like a boy," says Eustace. "We stand out. Me and a white girl. You'd probably have a better chance at getting on a ship, too."

I look at him, skeptical. "I don't think so," I say. "Nah."

Eustace purses his lips. "Even if this Captain Abbot remembers your father," he says, "he's not going to want to take a girl on a long whaling expedition. We'll have better luck if he thinks you're a boy. You could say you're Captain Wonder's son."

I'm mad that so many people think boys are better than girls. But I also don't want to do anything that would make it more difficult to finish this journey. One thing about me is that I've never been fussy about girl stuff—dresses, hair, and whatnot. So I don't even mind about my hair having to get cut. It's dishwater color and coarse and has never meant much to me anyway. Lots of times, my hair has felt like a big cocklebur patch. I usually batch it all up in a ball, tie a string around it, poke in some hairpins, and move on with my day.

"Fine," I say. We find a grimy alley to duck into. I sit down on a barrel. Eustace picks up a swath of my hair and inspects it. Then he pulls a pocket-knife from a little pouch he has tied to his belt. The only other things I've ever seen him pull out of there are seeds, nuts, and random edibles he's found on the ground.

I sit down, and Eustace picks up chunks of my hair and chops them off.

"Are you sure that's the way you're supposed to do it?" I ask. "Doesn't it seem like you should take a more scientific approach to cutting it? Maybe you should take some measurements or something?"

Long strands of hair fall into my lap and all around me. I know some girls would get real sad about their hair coming off like this. Not me. All I feel is free.

When he finishes, I turn my head from side to side and feel air on my neck. My head feels lighter, and I think there's one more reason it's easier to be a boy in this world. If boys only knew how much weight was on a girl's head, understood how tightly the buns yank their temples and how the prickly pins stick their scalps, then they'd see why girls sometimes get disagreeable.

"Perfect," he says. "You look a lot like Captain Wonder, I mean. I can't believe it. You look just like a younger version of your father."

I'm certain he is overstating it, but I get filled up with pride.

"Let's go," I say. "Come on."

The port is huge, with wooden walks running up and down for at least a mile. The endless splashing of the sea water makes the dock slippery, and I think about holding on to Eustace so I don't lose my footing. But I don't, mostly because I'm afraid it will give me away as a girl. I hope I can soon walk on solid ground again. Little shops bustle with activity, selling boots, coats, tobacco, ropes, rat-traps, liquor, hair-brushes, tattooing tools, flour, knives, whips, shackles, and handkerchiefs.

Behind them, on an upper street, sit the homes of the ships' captains. They are big and beautiful, with large windows facing the ocean so that the wives and children can look out and see the ships coming into port. I used to live in a house up there, but it's been so long and things have changed so much that I don't recognize my own house. I remember that it was yellow, but I don't see a yellow house.

I think back to my farmhouse in Tolerone, and to Mother and Priss and Ruby. Even though I haven't started the most difficult part of this adventure, I'm already missing home and pining to stand on Kansas dirt and to hug my Kansas people. But to get back there, I've got to take care of my responsibility as quickly as possible. And that starts with finding Captain Abbot.

I stop a hunched-over man who is barefoot. "Do you know where I can find Captain Abbot?" I ask. I stare at the man's feet, gnarled like tree roots and dirty as bark.

"Who?" he shouts. He cups a hand around his ear and leans close.

"Captain Abbot," I shout. "The man going to the Southern Ocean."

"Who wants to know?" the man shouts at me. Most of his mouth is brown and juicy. His lips puff with blisters and pustules. Before I have a chance to answer, he goes on, "Them grounds is empty of whales. Only a few gigantics left. Not worth the cost." He puts his head back down and shuffles forward, but then he turns around and says, "Captain Abbot! He's a madman. Steer clear of him, you young-uns." The man turns around again and walks down the boardwalk. "He stays on his ship—the one at the end of the port. You can find him there, night and day. But steer clear of him, I say!"

We follow the man's directions and walk on. Way down at the end is an old ship with black wood and patched sails.

Its ropes dangle with seaweed. The name *Xerxes* fades on the prow of the ship.

"That's got to be it," I say to Eustace. A tingle rushes up my spine. I shudder and try to swallow down a metallic taste in my mouth. But my throat is too thick. I cough, and up come smoke and ash from Kansas. Then the Medicine Head, quiet for so long, seems to awaken with a chuckle. I stop walking. I wait and listen. Nothing else comes from the crate. One thing it is not easy to do is carry around a disembodied head with peculiar features. The crate weighs on me.

I point to the *Xerxes*. "That's it," I say to Eustace.

Eustace shields his eyes. He sighs. "I was afraid you were going to say that." Fob whines a little. "But how do you know? Are you sure? Maybe it's one of these newer ships. One that looks more . . . sturdy. That ship looks to be a thousand years old."

"That's not even possible, Eustace," I say. "Or very scientific. That's Captain Abbot's ship. I'm sure. Let's go." I tug at his arms.

Eustace pulls back. "Didn't you hear that man?" He looks at me as though I've said something dim-witted.

"I heard him," I say. My face feels hot. "Darn you, Eustace! I'm going with or without you." I try to press my lips together firmly so he knows I mean business. I remember my haircut and boy clothes and the Medicine Head's crate I'm carrying and suppose I must look quite ridiculous. But Eustace simply blows a big puff of air out of his mouth and says, "All right, let's go."

Honestly, you couldn't find a more loyal friend than Eustace if you searched the whole world over four times.

✦ CHAPTER 23 ✦

We ask around about Captain Abbot, and most people give us sideways faces.

"Why?" they want to know.

"I'm going to sign on with him," Eustace tells them. He points to me, "Him, too."

Some of them ask us if we've lost our wits. They tell us there are all kinds of ships and ship captains hiring on, and that we should be careful to pick a ship and ship captain that can bring us safely back home again. I want to keep walking, but Eustace likes to stop and drink up all that these know-it-alls have to say. Fob runs into fourteen people every fourteen feet. He's walking his crooked walk, but he's also got his nose in the sky, sniffing the new smells and watching the flapping sails of the ships that hover over us.

Finally, we're standing in the shadow of the *Xerxes*. The dock is wet and slimy. Fob's four legs slip out in four different directions. He lands on his belly and scrambles to stand up again. Eustace leans over, grabs him around his stomach, and helps him. I walk like a penguin, sliding my feet forward rather than picking them up. I can't remember ever feeling this unsteady. I wonder when the ground beneath me will be solid again. The ocean slaps against the dock, sending spray onto us and everyone and everything else.

The air is cool off the ocean. But the Medicine Head is whining. It should be still and quiet, but it's calling, even if the cry is soft. I feel a little gut-sick. Is Captain Greeney near? I decide to keep moving forward. *Get on the ship*, I tell myself. *You'll be safe once you're on the ship.*

The *Xerxes* is ancient. Barnacles cling to its hull. The sails are rolled tidily, but they are gray with age and wear. Carpenters lean over the side of the ship and pound new boards over cracks and holes. A long plank joins the dock where we stand to the deck.

When we get to the ramp, a woman sitting on the deck eyes me—a very black, very muscular woman with the shortest hair possible and the least clothing I have ever seen on a person. I have to admit that I'm a bit shocked to see any woman on a ship, especially a black woman. And then I notice what she is doing.

"Hey!" she yells at us. She's sharpening the end of her harpoon with a stone.

Fob whimpers. He slinks behind Eustace's legs.

"Not you!" she snaps at Fob. She stands.

She's tall, much taller than Father was. She's the tallest person I've ever seen, maybe over six feet. The muscles in her arm bulge like pears. The tendons in her forearms quiver like piano strings. She's got raised scars over her stomach that make the forms of circles with eyes and triangles with snakes and one that's an X made out of two harpoons. She's also got a scar pattern in the middle of her chest. That one looks like a baby's handprint.

She purses her lips at us. "Why you kids stare at me that way? Where you think you will go?" she says. She eyes my crate. "What's in that?" She turns her ear to it.

Fob acts real nervous. He puts down his ears and peeks from behind Eustace's legs.

Eustace clears his throat. "We were going to sign on with this whaling expedition, ma'am. Do you do the hiring?" His voice is steady and calm, as though he's not scared of the lady, who looks like she could bust him in half with one punch to the stomach.

"I'm Nova," she says. "I do nearly everything. First mate. Chief harpoonist." Nova rights herself, steps back from me and the Medicine Head. She glances at it nervously. Then she turns her glower to Eustace. "You want to work on *Xerxes*? With Captain Abbot?" She spits on the ground. "Maybe you kids don't have sense. Go home to your mothers. Go." She waves us off and goes back to sharpening her harpoon. Sparks fly off the tip. But she lifts her eyes to the crate and then to my eyes.

I'm scared of her, but I clear my throat. "Listen here," I say. I clear my throat again. "I need to get on that ship."

She studies my eyes, unblinking, for half a minute. Her eyes shimmer green and amber.

"With Captain Abbot," I add.

Then she blinks slowly. All the muscles in her face soften, and she says, "Ah!" as though she's just recognized something in me. "Oh, yes?" she says. "This ship sails to the roughest seas, to the coldest ends of the earth." She uses the harpoon to point to the *Xerxes*. "This ship hunts the biggest leviathans in the ocean, with killer flukes and giant jaws." She raises her brow, as if she's questioning whether or not I understand the perils that might lie ahead. "Captain Abbot is a fierce one."

I shake my head back and forth and adjust the Medicine Head's crate on my hip. "I don't care if it's the devil himself steering it," I say. "I have to get on this voyage."

Nova takes her harpoon and slaps the handle against her chest. She leans over me. This close, I can see she's very beautiful, or used to be. Her big eyes look as old as the world. They are ringed with long, lovely lashes. Her brows are thin and arched. "You don't fool me," she whispers in my ear. I catch my breath and hold it. "I know you, girl. I know who you are."

She turns her head toward the Medicine Head's crate as though she's listening to it. I listen, too. But it's quiet. She taps the top of the crate with the tip of her harpoon, then straightens up again. "All right, young ones. Nova will get you on ship, but you been warned. Storms blow over Captain Abbot once in a while. Don't know what will happen. Or to whom." She looks at me curiously. "You be careful," she says. She flits her gaze to the crate again and sighs a doomed sigh.

I exhale.

Fob begins to growl, and he curls up his top lip. The Medicine Head whispers. *Hold me.* I startle. A tingling sensation, the one that runs through my body when something is about to happen, rushes from my fingertips to my face. I look up to Nova. Is it calling for her? For me? Will it never give up?

"Stop that, Fob," Eustace scolds. But Fob won't stop. He's whimpering and barking and trembling and fidgety. He's looking down the boardwalk. The hair on the back of his neck stands up.

From behind me, someone shouts. I hear a commotion of boxes being tipped over and people shouting "Watch it!"

"Girl!" a voice booms. "Child Wonder, you stop right there! Don't *move!*"

I whirl around. The crowd has parted. One man walks rapidly down the middle of the boardwalk. My sweat turns cold. My ears ring. My hands go numb. I'm scared. I wish I could close my eyes and instantly be back in Kansas with Priss and Mother. I clutch the Medicine Head to my chest. I hold my breath, try to regain control over my fears, over everything. The air gets muggy suddenly, and my shirt clings to my hot back. The Medicine Head grows louder and more desperate. *Hold me!*

I look at Nova, and she is looking at the crate. She must hear it! I look at Eustace, but he's looking at the man coming toward us. Eustace's face is tight, and his body looks as though it will leap into action at any moment. He looks like a cat about to pounce.

Within seconds, Captain Greeney's a few feet from us, and he's boring into me with fiery eyes. He's clearly seen the crate and is probably no longer afraid that it might be a snake. I'm still holding my breath, and my head starts to feel light. The ground beneath me feels unsteady, like I might fall. Then he's there. And he's reaching for the Medicine Head. In a flash, Nova fixes her harpoon on him. Eustace pushes me behind him. Fob snarls like a mad dog.

"Put down the harpoon, Nova," Captain Greeney says. *How do they know each other?* I wonder.

"You step back," she says to Captain Greeney. "You better get away from the captain's ship."

Captain Greeney's lips curl, but they don't make a smile. It's more like the closed mouth of a snake. "That old man? Is he around here?" Greeney looks up to the deck of the ship. "I didn't think he ever came out of there. Or at least that's what I heard."

Nova jabs the tip of her harpoon at him, but she doesn't poke him. "I mean it. I've got nothing to lose."

There's a lot of movement behind me. The crew of the *Xerxes* gathers around us slowly. They all carry the tools of a whaler. Harpoons, mincing knives, toggles, chains, ropes, and hooks. They look like a ragtag bunch of misfits, but I'm glad they're on Nova's side. My side.

Captain Greeney loosens the silk cravat from his neck. "Well, you and I both know that's not true," he says. "You kill me, you'll spend all of eternity in a prison cell."

Nova jabs at him again. "Don't make trouble. Get on out of here."

Captain Greeney lifts his hands, palms up. He slaps them together and wrings them. "Tell you what," he says. "Give me the girl, that little brat I've just chased across the country, along with her baggage, and I'll outfit you with a new ship. Your own ship. You won't be under the thumb of that madman you work for anymore. You can spend the rest of your very, very, very long life as captain of your own vessel."

Eustace curls his arm around me, as though he's afraid Nova might do it. I wonder myself if she'll turn me over to Captain Greeney. She doesn't even know me. Why would she care? Why would she protect me?

By now, all the whalers are surrounding us in a semi-circle. Though most of them are grimy, pale, stinky, fearsome, toothless, and hairless, I'm filled with a sensation of safety. They close in. Captain Greeney takes a few steps backward.

Nova walks toward him with her harpoon aimed exactly at his heart.

"You won't have it," she says to him.

"I will," he says. "Maybe not right this moment, but as long as it's on this planet, I will find it, and I will have it."

Then he leans in a little, looks me right in the eye, and says, "Good day to you, Hallelujah Wonder. We will meet again, I assure you." He turns on his boot heels and leaves.

The deck begins to spin. I exhale finally. Then it feels like I fall into a deep, black hole.

CHAPTER 24

When I wake, I am rocking to and fro in a hammock. It's dark and stinky, but it's warm and cozy. I blink and blink until my sight focuses. Creaking wooden planks make up the ceiling above me. Pale green, spongy moss grows on them.

Moss is a very interesting type of plant, from a scientific point of view. It doesn't have roots. Instead, it gets its water from its leaves. Also, and this is very interesting, I think: Moss grows best on the north side of trees. And you'll be surprised how I know that. It's not because of Father this time. Eustace told me. Moss likes to grow in cool, damp places, and the sun shines too hard on the south sides of trees, so moss mostly grows on the north. Slaves escaping their masters and running north use the moss on the trees as guidance to get where it's safe. That's what Eustace says, anyway.

Above me and all around me, hundreds of ropes, many pairs of pants, blankets, coats, boots, dried meat, and shovels and knives and scythes hang from the rafters and from ropes tied between the rafters. They swing back and forth. We're moving.

I wonder where Eustace and Fob are. I try to sit up, but the hammock closes around me and tilts.

"Rest," says Nova. I see her there, as if she appeared out of the dark. She puts her hand on my chest, and I lie back down. She's wearing some kind of animal skin, and the edges of her garment are jagged, like the person who made it didn't bother to cut it into proper shapes before stitching it together.

"Where's Eustace?" I say to her. "Where's my crate? I need it."

"Calm down," Nova says. "It's beneath your hammock. Rest, I say." She pats my chest like a mother might.

Every muscle in my body contracts. My jaw is clenched. I want the Medicine Head. I have to protect it.

"Captain Greeney!" I say. "Is he gone?"

Nova doesn't answer right away. I hold my breath and wait for her to speak. The ocean splashes the side of the ship, and its boards moan under the strain of the water's pressure.

"Yes," she says. "For now." She unwraps a piece of dried bread from a cloth. "Eat this."

My stomach flops like a fish on land. I take the bread and bite into a corner. It's hard and tasteless. But after the first swallow, my stomach's acrobatics stop, even though my mouth is left dry. "Thanks," I say to Nova. "I need my crate," I add.

She ignores me. "Eat it all," she says. "Will calm the seasickness." She brings her fingers to her own neck and rubs, then crosses her arms. "How do you know him?" she asks. She leans close to me. I can smell salt and sweat and smoke on her. "I know him, too. He's a bad man. He brings bad luck on ships." She watches me out of the sides of her eyes.

Her eyes have a knowing to them that doesn't seem possible. Her pupils are deep and dark, like a cave going back to the beginning of time. Her irises remind me a little of a turtle's eye, which might not seem like a compliment. But it is. All you have to do is get close to a turtle and see for yourself how interesting and beautiful a turtle eye can be.

Something else about Nova's turtle eyes is how they entice a person to look closer and, well, trust her, I guess.

I try to think of what to say. Where do I begin? Do I tell her how Greeney and my father once sailed together in the navy? Do I tell her that Captain Greeney grew jealous of my father and that he was upset when my father sent him home from the Antarctica expedition? That he wanted the artifacts my father collected and credit for my father's discoveries? That he wanted, in particular, the Medicine Head? That his lies destroyed my father's career and forced him to move his family across the country?

"He killed my father," I say.

"Captain Wonder?" she asks. "He was your father, then." She nods. "Hmmm."

My neck tightens. I'm awash with longing and memory, but my heart leaps. The mention of my father's name jolts me like a breaking branch startles a hare. I want to talk about him. I want other people to talk about him.

"Yes!" I say. "Captain Charles Wonder, the greatest scientist in the world." I pronounce every one of those words with crisp tongue and sharp lip. I want each of those words to be perfectly understood.

"I see," she says. She exhales. "Oh, girl, I am sorry for your pain." She smooths my hair. She's tender, like a mother. She looks tough and fierce, but I wish I could curl up into her like a child might. "Captain Wonder was a good man," she whispers. "I knew it when I looked at you. You have the look of him. He was a smart man." Her voice sounds like velvet to me.

I get excited that someone knows of him, remembers him. *Keep talking*, I think. *Keep talking about him.* Every word related to my father makes me know he was alive. That might seem silly to you, but sometimes I wonder if I was dreaming it all. Sometimes the memories of him are so distant that I worry I made it all up and then forgot that I made it up.

"Yes." I bite on the dry bread and choke down a nibble. "He was. I miss him. You knew him? You remember him?" It's hard to talk. But I want to. I want Nova to keep talking. "Tell me how you knew him," I say. I don't want to cry in front of Nova or anyone. I swallow again to try to relieve my neck.

"Yes," she says. "Of course I remember him. I met him after he was in the cannibal islands, where he got a powerful object." She eyes me sideways. "The one I think you got. Do you got what I think you got?" Her voice is very low and serious. "I can hear it, I think."

Should I tell her? I worry that maybe she's saying nice things about my father so that she can get the Medicine Head. Maybe she wants it for herself. Maybe she'll take it from me. I look away from her.

"Girl?" she says. "What's the matter?" She takes my chin in her palm and turns my face back toward hers. Her rich eyes pull me in.

"I do have it," I say.

She nods at me. "Your father came to me with it. He wanted to understand its powers." She shakes her head back and forth as though she is remembering something sad. "I told him I could help him take care of it. But he said he could take care of it." She sighs and slaps her hands on her thighs. "We mustn't let Captain Greeney get it," she says. "He would use it in bad ways. Be greedy. Hurt people."

Father came to Nova? Why would he do that? Why would she be able to answer questions about the Medicine Head? "I know," I say.

She shifts her feet on the floor. "But," she says, "it's not a plaything for children, either." She pinches her lips together. "Do you want me to keep it safe for you? I wouldn't ever open it or hold it again. Nova, you can trust."

Again? What does she mean by that? I think about her offer. She has saved me from Captain Greeney and somehow has gotten me onto this ship. She is here, watching over me while I sleep, comforting me, feeding me. Father came to her. He trusted her enough to confide in her about the Medicine Head. Maybe I should, too. But, I remember, he didn't give it to her.

"No," I decide. "I've got to put it somewhere no one will get it."

She drums her fingers on her lap and shakes her head again. "Just like your father," she says. "But you might be making the same mistake, too. Did you ever think of that?"

I turn my face away from her and stare out a small porthole. All I see is blue sky. It's quiet for a moment between Nova and me. I don't want to answer her, but I don't want to insult her, either. I don't want to think about Father's mistakes.

"That's fine," she says finally. "I don't want it, anyway. It's full of black magic."

"I don't believe in magic," I whisper. "There's a scientific explanation for everything." That's what I say, but I'm not sure I believe it anymore. And I want to know what she knows about the Medicine Head's power. I've known all this time that I've had to keep it away from Captain Greeney. What I want to know is what he'd do with it. "What does Captain Greeney want to do with it?" I look back at Nova's face and study her intently.

She raises one eyebrow at me, as if she's surprised I don't already know. "He wants to destroy it," she says.

I gasp. "Destroy it? Why? Why would he kill my father and chase me across the country only to destroy it?"

She rubs something off my forehead, ash or soot, probably. Then she stands, goes to the porthole, and looks out at the ocean and the sky. She runs a small cloth on the window until it squeaks, cleaning it like Priss cleans our Kansas windows. Then she turns to me and locks my gaze with her own.

"Because," she says, "whoever destroys the Medicine Head gains everlasting life."

Time seems to stop. The natural noises of the creaking ship and splashing waves go away. The sky through the porthole seems to open up to the outer edges of the universe. I see black beyond the white. I see comets, stars, and celestial rings. I blink. And then everything is the same again. The world returns to its ordinary noises and sights.

"Everlasting life?" I say. My ears are ringing, and

my stomach goes topsy-turvy again. "That's impossible. There's no such thing." I scan the sky again, looking for what I saw an instant ago. But there's nothing.

Nova looks out the porthole, too, as though she knows what I saw and what I'm looking for. Then she slowly turns toward me and smiles gently. "That's what I thought, too." She leans back now and pulls a pipe from a wooden box next to the hammock. She lights it and puffs on the end. I have never seen a woman smoke a pipe before. A sickly-sweet scent fills the hold, and my stomach feels worse than ever. I curl over it.

"Your stomach flopping?" she asks.

"A little," I say.

She pushes the pipe toward me. "Here," she says. "Take a puff. It will help."

"No," I say. "I mean, thank you, but no, thanks."

"It's the rocking of the ship," she says. "It makes people sick until they get used to it. It took me decades."

Decades? I think. Nova doesn't look more than thirty years old. How could she have already spent decades on ships? My stomach lurches again. I think I'll never get used to it. I remember good old Kansas, where everywhere was flat and steady. Where the only thing I ever had to worry about was a jackrabbit hole.

"How do you know?" I ask. "About everlasting life."

She shakes her head. "That's the longest story." Then she stands up. "I have to get back to work."

"Wait," I say. "I want to know. I lost my father for the Medicine Head. I left my sister and mother and my home. I want to know why I'm taking it so far away. I want to know if I'm doing the right thing. I want to know if I should keep going on this crazy journey to the ends of the earth, where no one can ever touch it again!" I'm practically shouting, but Nova doesn't seem fazed by it.

"Where?" she asks. She blows whitish-blue smoke from her nose and stares wistfully up at the coils. "People are spread all over the world. Where can you put it where no people get it? It is a big problem for a little girl."

"I'm not a little girl," I say. I sigh. I'm afraid that what I'm about to say will sound ridiculous. I'm afraid it will make her think I am a little girl with a wild imagination. But I tell her anyway. "Antarctica," I whisper, but so softly that Nova doesn't hear me.

She tilts her ear toward me. "Speak louder, girl," she says. "What did you say?"

"Antarctica," I say more loudly.

She leans back and taps ashes onto the floor. Then she smiles. "Antarctica!" she shouts. She shakes her head and

252

starts to laugh a laugh that comes from deep within her belly and shakes her chest. It grows and grows, fuller and louder. She laughs so hard she gets teary and begins coughing. Remnant smoke escapes her lungs.

I don't know what to think. Is she laughing at me? Does she think I'm a silly child? I put my head down and feel my cheeks burn red with embarrassment. Maybe she's right. Maybe this is all foolish. I'm too young. I'm not smart enough for this responsibility. I should never have come to New Bedford. I should have stayed in Tolerone and let whatever would have happened, happen. I'm just a kid. What do I know?

Then Nova's laugh calms into a series of lighter chuckles and coughs. She breathes a few full breaths. Finally she speaks. "Why didn't I think of that?" she whispers.

I wait. I wonder if I heard her right and hold my breath.

"All these years," Nova says, "and I never thought of that." I look up at her. She nods and nods. "You are a very bright girl."

She's not laughing at me. She's laughing at herself. She thinks I have a good idea.

"Yes," I say. "Antarctica." I clear my throat. My neck muscles have relaxed and my tongue moves easier now, so my words come out clear and strong. "My father discovered it for America. I want to see it the way he did. I want to leave the head there. It was given to him, and it should be in a place that belongs to him."

"Stubborn," she says. She points at me. "Like I remember your father. He was persistent. You like that, too, yes?"

"Yes," I say. "I am." I smile. I can't help it. I am like my father. Even though he's as far away from me as one human can be from another, I feel him near me now. I feel like he'd be proud of me, like he'd know that the Medicine Head is safe with me.

The Medicine Head. Where is it?

"Don't worry," Nova says, as if she's reading my mind. "It's safe beneath your hammock." She puts her hand on my arm and helps me out of the hammock and onto the slippery floor. "Careful. You got no sea legs yet."

I kneel down on the slimy floor and look beneath the hammock. There it is, safe and silent.

"You leave it in there," she says.

I don't respond, but I do stand up and go to her.

Nova helps me up the ladder, which is tricky because it's slippery, like everything else. A glossy layer of fat sits on the rungs. I lift my hand, and it glistens.

"Whale oil," Nova says. "Everywhere. Get used to it. You'll be sweating and spitting it before the voyage is through, just like the rest of us. The oil means money for the captain, the crew, for all of us."

I keep climbing.

When my head emerges, I see dozens and dozens of pairs of feet, some with boots and some not. I see many of the same men here who surrounded us on the dock. They don't pay any mind to me. I also see hooves of goats and pigs and pads of dogs and cats. Mostly, I see ropes, wood, coal, buckets, barrels, and all the other things you can think of to make life work. It's like the ship is a city unto itself.

Nova pushes on my bottom. "Up!" she says.

I go up.

✦ CHAPTER 25 ✦

When I stand, I have to adjust my eyes to the sunlight and the bright sky and the flapping white sails. I'm surprised to see we're not very far from the shore. I can still see New Bedford. I look around and spy Eustace and Fob mid-ship. Eustace has part of a huge rope slung over his shoulder and the rest of it coiling in neat circles on the deck. And he seems to be grinning. I turn as though I will go and talk to him, but before I can, Nova spins me in another direction.

"No," she says. "Him later. Captain now." She pushes my shoulder toward the bow of the ship, but my knees don't work correctly. They keep wanting to bend too deeply, and I have trouble walking in a straight line. I look for something to hold on to, a railing or rope, but Nova says, "No. You must learn to walk on the deck."

Not only is the deck unsteady because it rocks back and forth and up and down on the ocean, but it is slick with water and fat. Up and down, side to side go my legs. I raise my arms to balance, which doesn't help much.

All the parts of my body move in separate directions, like my hands aren't attached to my arms, my arms aren't attached to my shoulders, or my head to my neck. I try to walk; my feet seem briefly suspended in air when the ship dips. I straighten my knees to keep my feet attached to the deck. But as soon as I do that, the ship pops up again.

"Whoa!" My knees buckle.

Nova grabs me and holds on. "You will learn," she says. I wonder if I will.

She clutches my arm tightly, but her firm grip doesn't hurt. I feel secure.

Nova points toward the opposite end of the deck. Sailors there roll sails and coil ropes. Some of them are gathered around another man, much older than the rest of them. "There he is," she says.

I cock my head and gawp at a man not more than five feet tall, although he probably used to be taller, since he's now hunched over something terrible. His white beard dangles nearly to the deck, and he holds a wad of leaves to his cheek, which is swollen so much that his eye is nearly closed. He peers at me with his good eye.

"Who's that?" he yells, loud and raspy. I startle and jump back. He points at me. "I didn't hire him!"

That reminds me that I'm supposed to be a boy. I clear my throat and slouch my shoulders like boys do. I try to creep behind Nova.

She pushes me forward, in front of her. "Do not be afraid," she says.

"I don't need any more of them wet-behind-the-ears ones in my crew," he growls. "They cry for their mamas too much." He points at one of the whaleboats tethered to the ship. "Nova, prepare a whaleboat and take him back."

Take me back? No! I think. I can't go back. I have to stay on this stinky, rocking ship. I have to get to Antarctica. I can't have left my family, escaped the fires of Tolerone, hidden in a smelly train, fooled Captain Greeney, and landed in New Bedford only to be turned around and sent home before I get the Medicine Head where it needs to go.

"No!" I say. I lower my voice. "No, please. I'm smart. And I'm a good worker, too."

"Get off my ship!" the captain shouts. "No babies on my ship." He cups his cheek and groans, "Ow, ow, ow."

Does a baby get herself from Kansas to Massachusetts? Does a baby out-think a murdering madman? Does a baby have the enormous responsibility that I do?

"*Nova!*" the captain roars. Then he leans forward and grimaces. He holds both his hands around his face. "Oh, this abominable tooth!" He looks at me and he looks at Nova. "You're making my tooth hurt worse. Get him off here."

"No, no," I say. "Wait. I can do things." I search my mind for things I can do. "I can identify birds. And fish. And I can identify edible plants."

The captain's one good eye rolls around as though he's not impressed. "Oh, blimey!" he yells at me. "I know every plant, bird, and fish on the earth, you dummy! Everything! Nothing is new to me!" He groans and holds his face. "Get off my ship!" he screams, so loud that everyone stops what they're doing and looks at me.

"I can make knots!" I say. "I can make all kinds of

knots. Stopper knots and bends and hitches and loops, too." I look him in his good eye. Then I look at his swollen cheek, puffed up to nearly cover his eye.

His tooth. His tooth! Like the rotten pig's tooth back home. "I can help your tooth," I say. "I know what to do. But you have to let me stay on."

The captain comes in close to my face. He's very short, so he doesn't have to lean far. Some of his stray whiskers tickle my cheek, but I don't dare move.

"Is that so?" he says. "And how did you come to know knots and teeth, you barnacle?" He tosses the wad of tobacco he's been holding against his cheek into the ocean. "Cabin boy!" he yells. "I need a fresh wad of them leaves or the pain's like to kill me." Then he laughs a grotesque laugh. "Kill me!" he repeats, as though it's the funniest thing in the world.

"My father taught me, sir," I say. "He taught me lots of things. And my friend Eustace taught me lots of things, too."

"Hmm." The captain's cheek seems blown up like a puffer fish.

"Yes, sir," I say. "For instance, those tobacco leaves aren't going to help your tooth, sir. That tooth is simply going to have to come out if you want the pain to stop."

He lowers his eyebrow at me. It's gray and scraggly and some of the hairs in it reach below his eye.

"*Ah-hem.* Also, sir," I go on, "some say that an infected tooth is what killed Queen Elizabeth." I wait a second or two. "You'd better have that thing removed as quickly as possible." I feel Nova's hand rest on my shoulder, and she gives me an encouraging squeeze. "I know how. I've done it before."

"So," says the captain. "You can twist knots, can you? And you've got some wise ideas about teeth, do you?" He nods, then reaches inside his shirt and scratches his belly. "Well, tell me one thing, and then I'll let you stay on my ship. Is that a deal?"

"Yes, sir," I say.

"One," he says as he rubs his beard, "what've you got in mind to do on this ship? And two, why are you dressed like a boy?"

I reach for where my bun used to be and touch nothing but shorn stubs. I clear my throat again. "Uh," I say. "That's two questions, sir. Not one."

From behind me, Nova speaks. "Captain, this is the daughter of Captain Wonder." She pushes me forward.

Captain Abbot steps back. He squints his one good eye at me, looks me all the way up and down. "The seaweed you say!" he says. He lurches forward, howling like an animal in a trap, and then he's on his knees, holding his head in his hands.

I decide this is my moment to prove myself. "Get a pliers," I yell. "Someone get a pliers. And get Eustace, too."

Nova seems surprised to hear me boss a bunch of people I've never even met. But she reiterates my requests. "Go!" she shouts at the cabin boy. "And bring the rum, too." She looks at me then to see if that's all right, and I nod to say that it is.

I kneel down and put my hand on the captain's back. "We'll get the tooth out. You'll feel better." His back is knotted with lumps, like the surface of a turtle shell.

Eustace comes running with Fob at his heels. Fob sits down beside me. He's got a squirming mouse hanging out one side of his jaw, so I guess he may have already earned his right to be on this ship.

The cabin boy brings the pliers to me. Then he pulls the bottle of rum from the inside of his shirt and gives it to the captain, who pulls the cork and takes a long drink.

Nova asks, "Have you two done this before?"

Without looking at Eustace, I say, "Sure we have. We know what to do." I pat the captain on the back again. "You ought to take another big drink or two," I tell him.

Then I stand up, and I pull Eustace and Nova in close to me.

"Now," I say, "this is going to hurt quite a bit, so I need both of you to hold him down hard. Legs, arms, all that. Hold him while I pull the tooth out. Once I get the pliers on it, I'm not going to stop pulling until it pops out like that rum cork."

Eustace sits on the deck. I tell the captain to sit and lean back into Eustace. To my surprise, he does what I say. He moans the whole time, as if every small movement hurts.

"Just relax, sir," I say. "Look up at the sky and the sails."

I guess maybe people in pain will do just about anything you tell them to if they believe it'll relieve them.

He pushes the cork in the bottle and lies back with the bottle on top of his chest. He's drunk almost half of it, so I don't have to worry about cleaning out his mouth before I start pulling.

"Is this clean?" I ask Nova. I turn the pliers around and around. She shrugs. "I need a match, then." The cabin boy fetches one and brings it. He lights it, and I pass the pinching end of the pliers through the flame. The cabin boy looks afraid of me, like I'm a torturer. "I'm cleaning it," I say.

When I'm sure it's clean, I tell Nova to sit on the captain's legs.

I kneel down and use my fingers to pinch open his mouth. He's good and drunk and isn't so complaining anymore. I look inside, and I can see the gums swollen nearly all the way over a tooth at the back. I point and wave for Eustace to come in closer and get a good look.

"There it is," I say. "See it, Eustace?"

He peers in. "Yes," he says. "Better get it quick before the rum wears off."

I work the pliers into the captain's mouth. The captain groans. Then I close the pliers around the tooth. He shifts and tries to shake loose from Eustace and Nova. "Hold him down!" I say. I pull as steady as I can in a sure but slow tug, so I don't break off a root.

The captain makes a high crying noise. But then there's no resistance, and I fall back with a tooth on the end of the pliers. Blood drips from the captain's mouth, and his eyes are beet red. He starts coughing and blood spews out of his mouth.

"Thar she blows!" says the cabin boy, laughing. I glower at him.

Nova stands up and grabs the boy by the shirt. She drags him to the side of the ship, reaches down, and lifts him up above her head. Then she heaves him into the ocean below.

Everyone races to the ship's rail. Someone throws him a rope. Now I know why they all seem to respect Nova so much. I decide I'd better get back to fixing up the captain so she doesn't get ideas about tossing me overboard.

"Turn him over," I say. "So he doesn't choke on blood."

Nova comes back to where Eustace and I sit with Captain Abbot. She kneels down and turns his head to the side. "He won't choke on anything," she says. The captain coughs and spits and takes another swig of rum. He swishes it around and spits it out and drinks some more, then sighs.

"Could that boy swim?" I ask Nova.

"I doubt it," Nova says. "Few of us can swim." Then she grins. "Someone threw him a rope. Don't worry. He can climb back up."

I smile, too.

By the time the captain sits up and is feeling better, we're far away from shore and well on our way to the South Atlantic and to Antarctica.

✦ CHAPTER 26 ✦

𝒞aptain 𝒜bbot lets me stay on the ship as long as, he says, I don't cry for my mama all day, which I haven't done once in the weeks I've been aboard the *Xerxes*. I guess Captain Abbot doesn't know that Eustace is a lot more likely to cry for his mama. But he hasn't, either. In fact, he's not even mentioned Ruby to me once. Sometimes the names of Priss and Ruby and Mother are on the tip of my tongue when I'm with Eustace, but I haven't talked about them or home, either. For some reason, our lives in Tolerone don't seem real. Or maybe it's more that talking about our old lives would somehow distract us from the work we need to do here.

And there's a lot of it. From sunup to sundown, everyone aboard the *Xerxes* works. I rarely even see Eustace, much less talk to him the way we used to. The captain has taken a real liking to him. He gives him fun jobs like climbing up the mainmast and standing lookout for any sign of whales.

I cup my hands around my mouth and point my face up into the rigging. "How are you faring up there, Eustace?" I yell.

He's standing, balanced, on a circular platform about the size of a dinner plate way up on the mainmast. Around his waist is a bar to hang on to. When he sees a whale come up for air, he's supposed to shout "Thar she blows!"

Whales are mammals, did you know? That means they breathe air. They don't have gills like fish do. That's because, like I already said, whales used to live on land. They can hold their breath a long, long time, hours even, but they do have to come up to the surface to breathe. When they do, they blow sea water out of their blowholes, and it goes high into the air. That's how whalers know where whales are.

That, and the ships follow the regular whale routes. Whales migrate from one part of an ocean to another all year round. Sometimes they even travel to other oceans. A whale can live a long life and see a lot of interesting places in that time. A whale doesn't stay in one place for long, so if it gets bored with a territory, maybe a sea territory that's like Kansas, it can simply swim away from there and wander somewhere more interesting, warmer or colder, a place with more squid or a place with more interesting whales to talk to. But we haven't seen head or tail of a whale since I've been on the *Xerxes*.

Nova walks by me. "Don't talk to him. He needs to concentrate. One distraction and..." She gestures to the deck, closes her eyes, and hangs out her tongue. "Splat," she says.

Even at night, a lookout stands on the perch. Falling asleep at the post is a deadly mistake. I look up at Eustace again. He's got his eyes peeled on the sea. He's absentmindedly picking things off the mast and putting them in his mouth. If I know Eustace, he's probably eating barnacles or snails that get stuck on there.

"Now, get you to the galley," Nova barks at me.

"All right, all right," I say. I hate the galley. "I don't know the first thing about cooking, I already told you."

"You will learn better," Nova says. "The captain says a woman's place is in the galley."

"I've been trying for weeks," I argue, "but nothing tastes good to me."

"Just cook," she says.

"What about you?" I ask. "You're a woman. Why don't you have to cook?"

"I'm different," she says. "Very different."

"Well, so am I," I say. I've been a bit sassy with Nova, but she likes it. I mean, she likes me. I think my sass reminds her of someone: herself.

"We'll see," she says. "Now get to the galley and put the coffee on."

I slide my way to the galley, which is mid-ship and out in the open except for a makeshift canopy draped over it. The cookstove is small and rusty, and it looks to be from the 1400s. I clank a couple of pots around. In one of them, I dump a bag of beans. In another, I throw in a sack of potatoes, skins and all. I pour some clean water into the coffee pot and scoop in a generous helping of coffee. I sure do wish I had paid more attention to Priss's work in the kitchen in Kansas. I sure do wish I could talk to her.

I enjoy dinnertime because it's the one time of day I get to see Eustace for more than a minute or two. He's taken to the whaling and sailing life mighty quickly. He's got his sea legs.

When he comes for dinner, he says, "Hmm. Good beans," at me and then uses his fingers to shovel them into his mouth. All the sailors use their hands to eat. They reach over onto each other's plates and steal food. Sometimes they wrestle over hard biscuits or a piece of salt horse. I guess if they fight over my food, at least I know it's edible. But if Priss saw what I'm serving, I think she'd die of embarrassment.

Eustace doesn't seem to mind the food, and he also doesn't seem to mind the cramped quarters and smelly sailors who snore. I don't think I've had a good night's sleep since I got on this ship. It's stinky, noisy, lurching, and damp everywhere. It's crowded, and no one's got a moment of privacy except for Captain Abbot, who rarely comes out of his cabin. When I think of the wide-open spaces of Kansas, I sometimes have to stop myself from jumping overboard and swimming the long way back.

I'd like to complain about all of this to Eustace, but he's enjoying himself. I don't want to ruin his grand time. He walks and talks in a way that makes him look and sound free. The crew is an assortment of skin colors and languages. Hierarchy is based on experience and hard work, and that's all. The whole country ought to come and see how folks get along on a whaling ship if they want to learn how to get along on land instead of starting fires and practically starting wars.

In the first weeks, the air at sea whips cool and breezy. I work all day, cleaning things that will never be clean, much less produce a Priss-clean squeak, and preparing food that Priss wouldn't feed to the hogs, so that by nightfall I collapse in my hammock and lie there fitfully. I'm always tired, but I can't sleep. Sometimes I think about holding the Medicine Head in the hopes of catching a glimpse of my family or home, even if it's a terrible moment. At least I'd get to see them. But I never have any privacy. And the Medicine Head has been stone still and silent.

In the beginning of this voyage, my stomach was sick every day, but it's getting a little better. I thought I'd acclimate to sea life more quickly, since I was born next to the ocean. But to be honest, there's not much about it that I like. Sometimes I get that hot rock feeling in my neck like I'm about to cry. Then I try to focus on the matter at hand, which is getting the Medicine Head to Antarctica and leaving it there. I swallow down that hot rock in my neck and try to be strong and courageous like my father was.

Sometimes I wonder if he ever thought about us

longingly when he was out here on the ocean. On days like today, when the sun doesn't shine, the sky stays gray, the ocean lurches and bobs us to and fro, and Nova and Eustace and even Fob act like they're too busy to be with me for five minutes, bad feelings wash over me. I get an angry feeling toward everyone. My heart feels empty and hollow. That's when I wonder about Father. That's when I start to think maybe he liked the ocean better than he liked us. That's when I start to wonder if his scientific explorations were more important to him than his family. I feel angry that he left the Medicine Head. I get mad that I'm the one who has to clean up the mess he created.

On days like today, I go down into the hold and lie in the hammock and close my eyes until a new day comes.

✦ ✦ ✦

One morning, before dawn, I open my eyes to someone yelling, "Thar she blows!"

Thar she blows, I think. *Thar she blows*. I blink. I hear feet racing and ropes dropping and noisy commotion above. Over all that racket, Nova is shouting instructions to the men. "Prepare the whaleboats!" she shouts. "Start the fire!" she yells. "Eustace, you're with me," she calls. "Let's bring the beast in!" she roars. The men cheer.

A whale. That's what it means. We've finally spotted a whale. To be honest, I forgot about whale hunting. All I've been thinking about is Antarctica, and it's escaped me that the *Xerxes* and its crew have a job to do.

I roll out of my hammock and go up the hatch to see what's happening. All the crew, twenty men plus Nova, have sprung to life. I try to stay out of the way. I stand next to my cookstove and watch. I see Fob scrambling here and there and call to him and slap my thigh. He lies down at my feet and whimpers a little. He's scared of all the commotion.

"Ready the whaleboats!" Nova shouts. She gestures for Eustace to follow her to the harpoons. She grabs one and tosses it to Eustace, who catches it expertly, like he's used to having razor-sharp weapons thrown at him.

While the seamen work the pulleys to lower the whale-boats, Nova and Eustace stand at the ship's rail and look out to where the whale was spotted. Suddenly, Eustace is pointing and shaking his head. Nova is listening to him as though he's saying something important. Then she's nodding. She takes Eustace's harpoon and puts it, along with hers, back in the harpoon rack.

"Boats back up!" she shouts. "Boats back up!" She gestures with her arms in the motion of boats rising.

The men yell at her. "What?" "No!" "An easy kill!" "Oil!"

Nova points out at the whale. "She's got a calf," she says. "We won't take her."

I squint out into the ocean. I see the huge spray of a whale breathing, and then next to it, a softer spray. A baby whale. The men look, too.

"So what?" some of them say. "We'll take them both!" they argue.

"No, we won't," says Nova. "Get back to your regular work. *Now!*" The men scatter like rats and return to their posts.

Eustace sees me, and he comes over. I'm happy he's paying attention to me for once. He scratches Fob behind the ear.

"You got coffee?" he asks, as though I'm in charge of feeding him.

"Uh," I say. "I guess. From yesterday, there's still some." I point to the pot I didn't wash last night.

"You should make some more," he says. "The men will want it with breakfast." He takes the cold pot and pours himself a tin cup full of old coffee. He drinks it.

I sure don't like the way he's bossing me and acting like he knows my job better than I do, so I take the pot back from him.

"What was that all about?" I ask. I pour fresh water into the pot. Then I scoop a bunch of coffee into it. I spoon in a little molasses, too, for flavor.

"The whale wasn't that big, for one," says Eustace, who must have been learning all about whales and whaling from his crew mates. "Also, she's nursing a calf. It's not a good idea to kill mothers and calves. The whole whale population could be wiped out if whalers keep that up."

"And you told Nova that?" I ask.

"Yes," he says.

"There'll be others. Older ones without needy calves."

I admit I'm a little disappointed that the action was over before it started. The days go by so slowly on the ship. Having something else to do would have been interesting. I would have been able to study something scientific again. I would have been able to see that whale leg bone Father told me about. Maybe I would even have been allowed to keep one. But I understand that Eustace is right. Letting the mother whale and her calf go so the calf could grow was right. That Eustace. He sure has a good knot in his skull.

I begin to prepare other things for breakfast besides the coffee. Eustace is right again. The seamen will be hungry soon. Suddenly, Eustace seems so much older to me. All the other men and Nova respect him. Even the white men, of which there are about ten.

Only about half the men speak any kind of English I can understand. When they're hungry, they might say a number of words to me to let me know: "eat," "food," "grub," "spuds," "hurk," "slop," "glob," "num," "bobo," "suya," "sush," "pack," or "hack." Some of them do little more than grunt at me. Eustace acts a little bit like the rest of them right now and dunks his finger into my tub of molasses, then licks it off his finger. "Mm," he says. Then he drinks his coffee.

"That was good thinking, Eustace," I say. And I mean it. "My father would have liked that." I mean that, too.

"Thanks, Lu," he says. He grins. "And thanks for the coffee. It's good."

I know it isn't, but I appreciate that he said it was. Then he's off again, doing the work of a whaler on a whaling ship, as though he's been doing it his whole life. Fob sticks with me for the rest of the day.

✦ ✦ ✦

That night, I wake from a bad dream about a cyclone to Eustace shaking my foot.

"Lu," he's whispering. "Lu, come on." Fob licks my cheek.

I'm warm and cozy in my hammock, and I don't want to move. I know as soon as I do, I'll feel cold. "Stop that, Fob," I say.

Eustace shakes my foot again. "Come on," he says.

My eyelids are heavy. I'm still thinking about the dream I was having. A big brown tornado was whipping across Kansas. I was on the road trying to run home to warn Priss and Mother. I was lifting my arms and telling the tornado to stop. I don't know why.

"Leave me alone, Eustace," I whisper. "I'm tired."

"You have to come with me," he says. "You must see this."

All the remnants of my dream are gone now. I remember them, but I'm not seeing the dream visions anymore. Did you know that dreams and even nightmares are good for you? Well, they are. Father said so. He said the reason we dream is because our mind prepares us for all kinds of outlandish situations in our sleep so that someday, if we encounter such a situation in our waking life, we're better able to deal with it. Dreams are like practice for life. I don't remember ever having a dream about getting chased by Captain Greeney or the Medicine Head or meeting a strange old ship captain, but maybe I did. Maybe that's why I've survived this hare-brained adventure so far.

I try to sit up but practically fall out of my hammock instead. Eustace steadies it for me and helps me up.

"Where are we going?" I ask. I'm groggy and cold now. All I want to do is curl back up under the blanket in my hammock. "What's going on?" I ask. I wipe crust from my eyes and stretch my arms.

"Just be quiet and come on," he insists. "You'll want to see this."

I listen and go along because even though he's waking me up from a dream that could maybe one day save my life, I am happy to see him. Maybe he misses me, too, and he wants to talk. Maybe he realizes he should be paying more attention to me. Maybe he remembers that the only reason he's out here on a whaling ship in the middle of the ocean where he seems to be having a bully time is because of me.

We're already drifting away from each other, even though we're closer in proximity than we've ever been. It's strange how that happens. In the past few weeks, Eustace has grown up. His muscles have sharpened. His jaw line has grown taut. He's even grown the beginnings of a beard. I wonder if I look more grown-up, too. I wonder if Mother and Priss and Ruby will recognize me when I get back home. I touch the back of my head. My hair's grown a little. It doesn't poke out quite so cockeyed anymore.

We climb the ladder and emerge through the hatch onto the deck. It's still dark, but the sky is lighted with moon glow and its reflection off the water. Eustace leads me over to the rail of the ship. I don't see anything but waves and sky and stars and clouds and moon. The air is cool, but not cold. Still, I shiver. There's something eerie out there on the water.

"Look," he says. He points way out.

"What?" I squint. "I don't see anything."

"It's coming," says Eustace. "You'll see. Be quiet."

I wait and look and wipe my eyes some more. Then I do see: A shadowy figure floats on the water, far, far away. I tilt my head and lean over the ship's side and stare. Whatever it is makes me want to crawl back into the hold and pull the covers over my head. My spine tingles and my gut feels sick, as though it might unload overboard whatever is in it. "What is that?" I say.

Eustace won't answer. He leans on the rail of the ship and watches. Fob sits and stands and fidgets around.

For a half hour, as the sky gets even lighter, the figure floats closer, until I can see that it's another ship. "Another whaling ship?" I ask.

"No," says Eustace. He bites his nails. "I don't think so. Listen."

I do. And then I hear it. It's the saddest sound I've ever heard. From the ship comes a deep, mournful cry that's made up of hundreds of separate wails of misery.

Fob howls softly. Eustace reaches down and strokes his nose.

"What is that?" I ask. Even though I don't believe in ghosts, the sensation I have is just like the feeling you'd get if you thought you saw one. I can hear my own heartbeat thudding. My breathing races. I put my hand on my chest.

"It's a slave ship," he says. "We're just south of the West Indies, where they'll bring the people that survive the passage from Africa."

Slaves, I think. *People*. People like Ruby and like Eustace. This is where they've come from. This is how they get to America. "Goodness," I say. "You mean that's slaves making those noises?"

Eustace nods. "It's illegal. The slave trade to the Americas. But it's still happening." He sets his jaw and straightens his back. "They're all chained up in the hold of that ship, stuffed and packed like the rocks we fit together for that pig fence."

I think about that fence we made. I remember how we pieced it together so the stones fit each other tightly.

The wailing and crying get louder and clearer.

"Sounds like a brew of all the misery I've ever heard," I say.

Eustace stands up straight and crosses his arms. "It's sorrow and pain and hunger and sickness and broken hearts," he says. "Separation and loneliness and hopelessness and death and grief is what that sound is made of." He glares at the ship. His chin points up, and his jaw is clenched.

The ship is still far away, but I can hear the gutwrenching wails as though they were right next to me or even surging through me. Again, my spine shivers. My mouth is dry. "We've got to do something," I say.

"Like what?" Eustace says. He grips the rail of the ship. "There's nothing we can do for them. Not these ones. Except to know how bad it is. That's all we can do for now. Not look away. Not stop listening."

"I don't know if I can bear it." The crying from the slave ship makes my hair stand on end, and so does Fob's. He whimpers. I reach down and scratch his head. He coils around my legs.

"You have to," says Eustace. "So that when you go back, you remember every second of what you saw and heard. And you can tell people."

"Then what?" I ask. "How does that help?"

He faces me. "And then they can tell people," he says. "And then the people who know how rotten this slave trade is will outnumber the people who don't." Eustace says this as though he's thought about it a long time. He sounds like he's been waiting for someone to ask.

I wonder if Mother knew about the slave ships. I wonder if this is why she became an abolitionist. If every person heard what I heard, they'd all be abolitionists. I think that after I get home to Kansas, I'll be an abolitionist, too.

The ship comes ever closer and eventually passes behind us. Eustace and Fob and I watch it the whole way. In its wake, dozens of sharks follow, and I remember what Father told me.

✦ CHAPTER 27 ✦

$\mathcal{M}$*ore weeks and then* months pass. But we are still in the warm waters. We see whales sometimes, but now Nova won't allow the whaleboats to chase them without permission from Captain Abbot. Anytime the lookout shouts, "Thar she blows!" the captain emerges from his cabin, takes out his spyglass, peers into it, and then shakes his head.

"Sail south," he always says. "Farther south."

This makes the crew angry. Like Eustace and me,

most of them are on their first voyage with Captain Abbot. They've heard rumors about him. And they all signed on because he always comes back with the fullest hold, the most tons of whale oil, the purest, too. But they weren't expecting to be sailing for months and months without a pursuit. A lot of them are just plain bored and ready for something to do.

Nova tries to keep them busy so they don't get grumpy. "Patch the sail," she orders. "Scrub the deck," she barks. "Sharpen the spear tips. Empty the latrines. Catch that turtle for supper." The men spy her through slitted eyes and slink away to carry out the orders. Some nights, she allows them to share a bottle of rum. Still, they are dissatisfied. When they come to the galley for their meals, I hear the word "mutiny" more than once.

They are eager to get whales, render the fat, make money, and get back home. Captain Abbot doesn't seem to be interested in those things. Nova becomes more and more nervous as she runs out of jobs for the men to do. Some of them even take to defying her. Yesterday she ordered a man up to untangle a rope on the mizzenmast, and he told her to do it herself. She had him tied to that same mast and whipped him ten times. Eustace and I watched from separate sides of the ship, and I wondered what he thought about a black woman whipping a white man, but I didn't ask him. After the whipping, the men fell back into order and were more agreeable.

Despite her fearsome approach with the crew, Nova remains kind to me. More and more, she spends time with me in the galley. She sits on the stool and plucks feathers from the seabirds we sometimes catch for eating. She smokes.

"Nova," I ask. "Why don't we ever catch any whales?"

She blows out a huge plume of smoke. "He's waiting for the big ones," she explains. "The giants no one else can get, in the coldest, darkest places."

"Yes," I say. I'm careful. I don't want to make her mad. But I also don't want to be on a ship that gets seized by its own crew and takes me off the course of my journey. "But wouldn't the crew settle down if we just caught a couple of smaller ones in the meanwhile?"

"Hmm," she says. She puffs on her pipe. "He has his reasons." She stares off toward Captain Abbot's cabin. After a while, she walks across the deck to it, knocks, then enters.

I tinker around in the galley. I throw a huge pail of rancid shrimp into a pot of boiling water. I add salt and a rotten onion after I pick out a pocket of tiny white worms. I add the moldy potatoes I found in a corner of the forecastle of the ship. I've got a slop bucket full of chicken feet. Those go in, too. I put in a spoonful of lard and woody turnip, then turn up the heat on the stove. The blacksmith took my stirring spoon and melted it down to make a hook, so now all I've got to stir with is an old whalebone.

Today it's hot but breezy. The spray off the ocean hits me in the face whichever way I turn. I haven't seen myself in a mirror in months. I'll bet Priss would faint if she saw how red my cheeks must be. The heat, the cooking, the salt water, all of it makes me angry. And all day I've been listening to that darn Medicine Head. Sometimes it's real, real difficult not to kick it into the Atlantic Ocean. But I can't do that because some doltish animal might come along and destroy it accidentally.

Even though Nova talks to me some and Eustace does once in a while, I spend a lot of my time alone. I'm as lonely as I've ever been in my life. But one good thing about loneliness is that it gives a girl plenty of time to sort through problems. I've been remembering my dreams, and I've been remembering the visions with the Medicine Head. Sometimes it whispers *Hold me* as I lie on my hammock with my hands behind my head. I lean over and look under my hammock at the crate. But I don't open it. I don't hold the Medicine Head. Even though I want to.

I want to hold it in the hopes that it will show me my father again. Or show me Mother and Priss. Sometimes I want to hold it just to get a glimpse of dumb old Kansas. Sometimes I tell myself that the Medicine Head isn't evil, that maybe its purpose is to prepare me for challenges, like dreams can. Once in a while, I have to admit, I think about keeping the Medicine Head forever, until I die. Sometimes I even think about living forever. I imagine all the wonderful things I could do if I had enough time.

Then the lookout shouts, "Thar she blows!"

These days, the men hardly move when the lookout shouts. They only expect to be sent back to their boring work. This time, though, I hear the voice of Captain Abbot.

"Well!" he shouts. "Get your blasted bones moving!" I hurry to watch. I sit next to my stove. Captain Abbot stretches his back and smooths his beard. He walks to the ship's rail and stares out to where the lookout points. Then he shouts, "Go get him, men!"

The men leap to their posts. Even I get a little excited. I try to remember all I know about whaling, which, I have to admit, is quite a bit.

A couple of years ago I read a book on whaling by a

man whose name I forget. It was a very long book about whales and whalers. Hardly anybody liked it because they thought the book was too dull in some parts, talking about cetology all the livelong day, boring readers to death with information about bones and blowholes and flukes. I bet a lot of those people put the book down before the best part, when a big, mad white whale wrecks the whaling ship by ramming its big head into it. But my father read the whole thing, and I did, too. And my father liked it, and I did, too. Father said there's nothing better in the whole world than a big, bold adventure story mixed up with good information to learn.

"Lower the boats!" shouts Nova.

The men head to the pulleys and yank the ropes so that the whaleboats come down and can be guided into the ocean. Nova heads to the harpoons. Again, she gestures for Eustace and hands one to him. I am suddenly struck with the desire to go, too. I want to get as close as I can to the adventure.

"You come with me," Nova says to Eustace.

"Hey!" I shout. "I want to come! I want to come, too!" I drop the whalebone spoon into the stew I made and rush over to Nova. "Take me," I say.

Nova ignores me.

"Get back to the galley, Lu," says Eustace. "This is dangerous."

"Don't you talk to me that way, Eustace!" I say.

He reaches above me and puts his hands on the bottom of the whaleboat, which is being lowered, lurching, out of the davits above our heads.

"Lu, you've got to move," he says.

I duck.

"You're going to get hurt," he says. The whaleboat swings a bit on its ropes and smacks me on the back of the head.

"Ouch!" I shout at Eustace. "You did that on purpose!" I rub my head where it smarts.

"Get back to the galley, Lu!" says Nova. "Now! This is dangerous."

I slide back to the galley. I sit down on a small stool. Fob curls around my feet and I pat him on the head. I pout out my lip and glower at Eustace, who ignores me.

Six men climb into each of the two whaleboats. Then the other crew lower them onto the ocean's surface. Everyone on board grabs an oar and begins stroking the water. Nova's boat takes off toward the whale first. She rows as strongly as Eustace and the other men. The other boat follows. The whaleboats veer headlong into waves and weave their way toward the breaching whale, whose long, curved back breaks the water's surface every few minutes so that the whale can breathe.

The boats look tiny in the huge expanse of water, against the high waves, under the endless sky, and next to the whale.

I've read that whales can grow to a hundred feet long. This one's not *that* enormous. But it is big. At least half the size of the *Xerxes*, maybe fifty feet long. I squint. I see Nova stand at the prow of the boat, brace herself, and then hurl her harpoon at the whale. The harpoon misses its target, so she pulls it back in. The harpooner on the other boat throws his spear. But it, too, lands short of the whale and sinks into the water.

Eustace is stationed just behind Nova. He helps her ready her harpoon. Then she braces herself again, reaches way back with her harpoon, brings it forward, and releases it in a perfect throw. The harpoon pierces the whale behind its head. Eustace lets out the rope that's attached to the harpoon.

The whale's body glides into the depths of the water. Its fluke seems to wave good-bye at all of us as it goes down and disappears.

Nova and Eustace and all the men in the whaleboats

lean over the side, looking, seeking their catch. The ocean seems to go very still. Maybe I was wrong. Maybe Nova missed again. Maybe the harpoon broke off and the whale swam away.

Then, very near Nova and Eustace's whaleboat, the water seems to flutter and bubble as though it's boiling. Suddenly the whale rises up and out of the water. Its enormous head is blue and gray and covered with discolored patches of white and yellow. The mouth is curved and strange. The animal looks as though it is from a prehistoric age. The whale flies so high that its fins break the surface and look like wings about to take flight. Then the weight of the animal draws it back to the water's surface, raising a fantastic column of foam and water. The men hurl spears and lances. More and more and more. So many that I cry out "Stop!" and "That's enough!"—though no one hears me.

The whale lingers near the surface now, thrashing and flapping its tail. It's angry. It's in pain. It's fighting for its very life. I worry for Eustace. What if the tail hits the boat? What if he's thrown into the water? But the men in the whaleboats seem to relax, as if they're waiting for the whale to do something.

And then it does. The whale begins to swim. With the

harpoon attached to Nova and Eustace's boat. The whale-boat and all in it are tugged behind. The sleigh ride. This is what whalers call this part of the hunt. They'll allow the whale to pull the boat until it tires. For twenty minutes or more, it swims around and around. The drag from the boat slows the whale's journey, tugs at its energy, depletes its life. Blood from the whale's wounds has made the water a swirling pink canvas, beautiful and gory at the same time.

Finally, the whale stops. From its blowhole a sad blast of red water rises into the air. The whale's last exhalation. I hold my own breath. In another minute, the animal rolls over onto its side and floats. It bobs. Lances and spears and the harpoon and ropes all over its body poke up like fence stakes. The whale is claimed.

Then the whalers begin the long tow back to the *Xerxes*.

I exhale. I gasp. And then I cry. I cry real hard.

I run back down into the hold to hide. I don't want anyone to see that I'm a sensitive child who can't handle the realities of whaling, the realities of the price of the light I live by.

CHAPTER 28

Hours later, the dead whale is attached to the side of the *Xerxes*. Nova and the men climb all over it with giant cutting tools, which strip the animal of its blubber. The slices of blubber look like slabs of bacon for a giant. The blacksmith has started a fire beneath the try-pot in a large brick oven in the center of the ship. The cooper hauls barrels from the hold to the deck. The men use hooks and cutting spades to chop the blubber slices into pieces they can toss into the try-pot and boil to liquid.

The entire deck is slick with blood, sea water, blubber, and slabs of fat. Men slip and slide and fall. Fob dares not move from my feet lest his paws skate in four directions. I am disgusted, but I cannot look away.

The stew I've made for the sailors has congealed into a slimy mess, and it's long forgotten. I decide to empty the contents of my pot overboard. I skid my way to the rail and dump it into the ocean. When I look down, I find a frenzy of sharks. Sharp triangular dorsal fins everywhere. They jab and jab with their pointed snouts and terrible teeth into the jelly-like carcass of the whale. I step back. Catch my breath. But all I inhale is sooty, stinky smoke from the rendering. I inhale again. And again. I feel like I can't get enough air. My ears only hear muffled noises.

I turn my face away from the fire and smoke. I look for Eustace and see him in the middle of the deck, pitching slabs of blubber into the try-pot. He's been through so much today, but he doesn't look fatigued. He looks strong and capable, is what he looks.

I decide to go below into the forecastle and curl up in my hammock. I whistle for Fob, but he won't come. He's scared to walk on the greasy deck. I slide over to him, pick him up, and carry him down the hatch with me.

As soon as I set Fob down, he scrambles back up the ladder. I lie back in my hammock and stare up at the ceiling. I think for a while about all I saw today. I think about that cask of spermaceti sitting in our barn. I think about the lamps in our Kansas home. One thing about people is that a lot of them don't like to know where the goods that make their life easier come from. They prefer not to think about it. That's a way to never feel guilty about how other people risk their lives at their jobs or about the horrific deaths of the animals that provide the goods.

But just maybe they should, and then maybe people wouldn't be so wasteful. You should think about that for a long time. I know I will.

✦ ✦ ✦

The commotion on deck goes on for a long time. Finally, long after dark, I hear the last sounds of a broom and a mop being wiped along the deck. Only after that does the *Xerxes* go quietly to sleep. I try to sleep, too, but I can't. One thing about living on a whaling ship is that you're likely to see things that might give you bad dreams. You have to be very brave to live on a whaling ship. Father was.

But I'm not sure I am.

I don't want to close my eyes, even though I know that a bad dream can be good practice for the many hard times I have ahead of me.

I tell myself to sleep, so that a dream may come to prepare me. But I toss and turn and can't get comfortable. I'm roasting, and I feel like I can't get a full breath. It's stuffy down here. The air is thick and stale in our quarters. We're just south of the equator. Sweat beads on my forehead and upper lip.

I'm turned toward the ship's wall when I hear Fob's four paws tripping and scratching down the ladder. I sit up in the dark. Then I hear solid footsteps creaking down the ladder after him. Fob taps toward my hammock. I reach out and feel his head. He's greasy, but I don't mind. I pet him anyway and pat for him to jump up on my legs. He does and curls up.

"Lu?" I hear.

"Yes," I whisper. "I'm here."

I hear a match and then watch as a lamp is lit. Eustace's face glows behind it.

"You must be tired," I say. "You'd better get to sleep."

He kneels next to my hammock. Eustace has the beginnings of furrows in his brow, like a grown man might. "I brought you something," he says. He lifts his hand in front of the lamp. He's holding what looks like a crooked white stick.

"A bone?" I ask. I reach out and touch it. It's slick with oil. "You want me to stir the beans with this or what?" I say.

"Look at it," he says. He's grinning now. Then he pinches his lips together to stop himself from smiling.

"You sure are behaving strange," I say. I hold the bone and feel its shape, like a relaxed boomerang, but thicker on one end than the other. "Hold that lamp up higher for me."

He does, and he's grinning again.

"What?" I ask.

"Nothing," he says. "Nothing at all." But he doesn't stop smiling.

I rub my thumb over the bone's surface and think hard about where this bone came from and why Eustace is behaving like a dog that's cornered a coon. I hold the bone so that the thicker part is toward me and the thin part is facing away. "It sort of looks like a dog's back leg, without the knee joint, of course."

Eustace nods.

"It sort of looks like a femur," I say again. I turn it around and around. "It sort of looks like a leg that's withered." My heart starts to pound. I talk louder. "It sort of looks like a leg bone that's never been used." My voice is shaking. I run my hand over the outline of the bone. "It sort of looks like what a whale's leg bone might look like if the whale never grew the leg." Now I'm shouting. "It sort of looks like a remnant leg bone of a whale, which proves that whales used to have legs, which might prove that they used to walk on land!"

From somewhere in the dark, someone yells at me to quit yammering. Then someone else threatens to come over and shut my mouth for me.

Then, from the pitch black behind me, Nova shouts, "She has suffered your snoring and gases for months! You be quiet, or I will put you on the overnight watch!" I hadn't even known she was there.

Eustace pats my arm. "I thought you'd like it," he whispers. "Good night." He blows out the lamp and disappears into the dark. Fob leaps off my legs and scrambles after him.

I lie back. This bone is the very first part of my own collection.

I drift off for a while, dreaming of a whole whale skeleton hanging from a ceiling, with the leg bones dangling right below it.

I wake with a start. I open my eyes, but it is still dark.

The Medicine Head moans. I cover my ears, but nothing stifles the noise. Finally, I put my feet on the floor. I wiggle my toes. It wouldn't hurt just to look.

Nova breathes deeply. She must be completely exhausted. I don't want to wake her. I don't want the Medicine Head to wake her. I worry that the head might be calling Captain Greeney. Maybe he's right on my tail. Maybe the Medicine Head is trying to warn me.

I gingerly stand and then crouch down to reach beneath my hammock. I pull the Medicine Head's crate toward me and hold it. I stop and listen, but no one is moving at all. Then I stand and climb up onto the deck. The smoke is gone. All that's left is the fatty scent of the whale's burned blubber.

I tiptoe across the deck toward the rail of the ship, where I sit down and hold the Medicine Head's crate on my lap. It's cooler up here, and I think the colder air will maybe calm it. Maybe I won't have to open the crate after all.

I sit for a while and think. The waves slap against the side of the ship. The sharks splash and fight and tear at what's left of the whale, set to drift by the sailors.

But then I hear it again. *Hold me.* The Medicine Head won't rest. I untie the rope and let it drop. I peel away the top and peer inside. The Medicine Head has an expectant look, one that begs me to pick it up. The forehead is uncreased. The eyebrows seem lifted and waiting. *What harm could it do?* I wonder. *What's the worst that could happen?* Perhaps I'll get a glimpse of home. Perhaps I'll see my family again. What I wouldn't give for one glance at Priss's face! Or Mother's. Or Ruby's. And even if the Medicine Head gives me a terrible vision, I might need it for the future. *Yes*, I think. *I have to pick it up.*

I reach in slowly and stretch my fingers around it. I touch it. I lift it.

The wind blasts my face. I hear many voices, but the loudest is Captain Greeney's. Visions speed past my eyes, so fast I can hardly grasp any of them. I see Eustace hiding behind a barrel and shooting a gun. I see Nova shouting up at the men in the rigging. I see all my shipmates gathered at the hull, pointing at the sea. I look, too. Out there is another ship, American flags waving. But then I hear a boom, and I see black smoke rising. A cannonball explodes in front of me! When the smoke clears, Captain Greeney is standing on the deck of the *Xerxes*. He has his sword through Captain Abbot's heart.

I let go of the head. It falls back into the crate. I breathe carefully in and out. My heart is thumping. Was that a premonition? A warning? What am I supposed to think? That Captain Greeney is out here on the ocean searching for me? Chasing me? That he is planning to kill Captain Abbot? I wanted a vision of my mother or my sister or Ruby or a memory of my father.

I feel very angry. I wanted to see someone I miss, someone I love. I don't even care if it's a sad memory. I just want to see something from Kansas.

"Show me something from home!" I shout at the Medicine Head. I snatch it up again.

A blast of air. A flurry of memories. And then I'm back in my Kansas home.

I'm wandering around, moving from room to room. *What is this pain in my chest?* I put my hand there, but I don't feel anything wrong. *Why can't I see well?* I put my hands to my eyes and feel them swollen and sore. From crying. From wailing in a bottomless, endless ocean of despair.

Oh, of course.

It's the first night after Father's death. I cannot be consoled. Nothing eases the pain. My heart feels as though it's been collapsed in a vise. I walk and walk around. I try to sit and lie down. No matter which way I turn or move, the pain will not be relieved. Now I go from room to room and

I bash my head against the doorframes. Hard on this one. Harder on the next one. Until I see stars on the third.

Ruby is here. She's following me, telling me to stop it. She's telling me to lie down and close my eyes. She's telling me to drink water. *No, no, no!* I shout at her. *Get away from me!* I scream. *Leave!* I yell. Finally, Ruby grabs my arm and drags me up the stairs to my room and puts me in my bed. I scream and yell and kick at her. *I hate you*, I say.

Ruby slaps my cheek and holds my chin. "Hallelujah Wonder!" she says. "I know you got big pain in your heart."

I cry hard and snot comes out of my nose.

"You've got to get ahold of yourself. Think what your father would want. Take a big breath." She breathes in to show me. "Now breathe out slowly." She blows out long.

I try to take a big breath, but it's choppy. I can't. I gasp again. I feel like I can't get enough air. My fingertips are numb.

"No, no," she says. "Exhale slow." She blows out to show me.

I exhale, slowly.

"It's the breathing out that's the important part," she says.

I put down the head. And I'm back on the *Xerxes*.

I stare up at the sky. All the stars in it would make you

woozy. And the moon with its half-smile would, too. But they can't stop me from remembering the rest of that horrible night on my own, without the head. I remember what happened next. I remember every moment of my father's death and the days that followed.

I breathed out slow like Ruby showed me. I drooled on her hand.

She didn't wipe it away.

"That's a good girl," she said to me, letting go of my chin. She tucked me in like I was a baby and sat on the edge of my bed. She rubbed my back as I curled up like a seashell and cried softly. Then my cries turned into hiccups. Then I fell asleep for sixteen straight hours. When I woke up, she was still sitting there with me. Her eyes were closed as though she were sleeping upright. I'll never forget that.

After my father's death, I was afflicted with dyspnea. Do you know what that is? Dyspnea is when you start to pant like a dog does after he's been out running. But instead of getting filled up with oxygen, you get filled up with carbon dioxide because you're not exhaling long enough. Too much makes you dizzy and makes your ears ring and fingers tingle. That's what was happening to me.

I close the top of the Medicine Head's crate. I suddenly

realize that I really didn't need to hold the Medicine Head to know what to do. My own brain works just fine. My own imagination is vast. My own dreams can do the rest.

"I don't need you," I say to the Medicine Head.

"Whatchee got there?"

I jump, scared. I was certain I was alone. "Nothing!" I say. I turn around and try to hide the Medicine Head's crate behind a coil of rope.

Captain Abbot stands behind me. "I said, whatchee got there?" he says.

I foolishly try to move the crate farther with my boot heel. It scrapes along the deck. The only light is from the moon. I can see Captain Abbot clearly. He is holding a pistol in his hand.

I slowly stand up.

"I can hear it," he says. "Like you. I've been hearing it all night. It's the heat what gets to it."

My breath comes short and shallow. "I know," I whisper. "About the heat, I mean." A big wave hits the side of the ship, and I lose my balance a little. But I quickly right myself.

"You don't have your sea legs yet," Captain Abbot says. "Like your father. He never got his, either. But it didn't keep him off the ships."

I'm quiet. I'm scared, but I'm also mesmerized. I want him to keep talking about Father.

"Yes, I knew him," Captain Abbot says. He inches closer to me. His face is ancient, almost as wrinkled as the sea. "He found me."

Now the Medicine Head is thrumming *Hold me, hold me* again.

I look at the pistol. Captain Abbot clenches and unclenches it. " 'For what?' you might ask," he says. " 'Why did he find you?' You must want to know." He uses the pistol to point at the crate, which is settled directly at my feet.

"Don't!" I say. I move in front of the Medicine Head.

"Easy," he says. "Your father, he came to ask me about those," he says.

What does he mean?

"Medicine Heads," he says, as if reading my mind. "That's what you've got, correct?" He eyes me a long while.

I wonder what he means by "heads." Are there more?

"You don't have to tell me," he says. "I know. I hear it. I can't get it out of my head. Those things will drive you to do evil. They will drive you mad. They will drive you to want to destroy them." He directs the pistol at the Medicine Head again.

At that, my body lunges forward, toward him, toward a madman holding a pistol. "No!" I shout.

Captain Abbot opens his mouth and steps back. I've surprised him.

"I can't destroy it," I say. My voice is shaking.

Captain Abbot lowers the pistol to his side.

"That's correct," he says. "You shouldn't."

He walks to the rail of the ship and stares out at the ocean for a long while. Then he raises the pistol to his own chest.

He cocks the hammer.

"No!" I shout. I put my hands out. "Don't!"

He pulls the trigger. A blast breaks the calm air.

Captain Abbot collapses onto the deck.

As I rush to him, I kick over the Medicine Head's crate, and the head rolls out. I leave it. The deck is slippery and the ship bobs up and down, and I nearly fall twice, but I finally reach the captain.

"What have you done?" I say. "Why?" I push to turn him over on his back and he rolls easily. I realize that he's frail as a withered tree branch. Any bulk he has comes from layers of clothing.

I look for the wound to put pressure on it. I feel his chest, but there's no blood, no hole. Nothing. I wait.

Nothing happens. I look to where the Medicine Head rolls around on the deck at the whim of the waves. I'm angry at it. I'm angry at myself. I look up at the night sky, all the stars, the moon. I'm angry at the sky. I'm angry at my father.

I look down at Captain Abbot, dead on the deck. I'm about to shout at him. But the words catch in my mouth.

Captain Abbot opens his eyes.

I jerk back but then lean close again. "Captain?" I say.

He coughs. He lifts his fist to his chest and pounds on it. Then he struggles to sit up. I help him, but I'm confused. Did he miss? He couldn't have. The pistol was pointed against his chest. Did the pistol misfire? After he sits up, a bullet falls to the deck. I pick it up and turn it over and over. It's hot and wet with blood.

He blinks. His eyes are watery and red and prehistoric.

"I don't understand," I say. The Medicine Head seems to be laughing. I look at it, lying cockeyed on the deck. "Be quiet!" I demand. "Shut your mouth!"

Then Captain Abbot chuckles, too. He alternately coughs and laughs and clears his throat.

I shake my head back and forth. "I don't understand what's happening," I repeat. I despise not understanding. I want to understand everything. Life used to seem so rational, with simple explanations. But there's no explanation for this. There's no explanation for so many things. Did Father ever feel uncertain, like I do now? Is that what led him to science? Did he use his study and his travels and his reading to search for answers to the never-ending questions?

"Just a demonstration for you, child," Captain Abbot says. "You see, I had one." He thumps his chest some more and spits out a gelatinous glob. "I had a Medicine Head. Like yours. I had one." He puts his hand on my shoulder and uses it as a crutch to stand up. He dusts off the front of his coat. "Given to me by the same tribe that gave one to your father."

I hold my breath. Again, I can hear the Medicine Head calling to me. It's getting louder and louder.

"Be quiet!" I say. I hold on to Captain Abbot's arm. "Not you," I say to him.

"I know," he says. "I know what you're hearing. It got so that the head kept me up at night with its shrieking and whining. It would show me things sometimes. But the more I held it, the more I got trapped in the past, or trapped in the future."

"You had one, and I have one," I say. "Are there more?"

"There were three," he says. "What you have there is the last one. The tribe is wiped out now. Disease."

"Well—well—" I have so many questions. My thoughts race, and my mouth won't cooperate. "Well, where's yours?"

He grabs my chin hard with his hand.

"I destroyed it," he says.

I gaze deep into his eyes. Like rings in a tree, I can see his life, the impossible years of it.

"You couldn't have," I say. "That would mean…"

"Yes," he says. "I am, this year, one hundred seventy-nine years old." The Medicine Head rolls to Captain Abbot. He tosses it into the crate and slaps on the lid.

From the confines of its crate, the Medicine Head howls like a Kansas tornado.

I slap my hands to my ears.

Captain Abbot laughs like a madman.

CHAPTER 29

My ears are hot, as though they've been burned with a fire poker. The Medicine Head screeches.

"Make it stop!" I shout. "How do you get it to stop?"

Captain Abbot pats me on the back. "Bring it to my cabin," he says. "We'll put the crate in the cooling hole. That'll calm it."

I scramble to the Medicine Head's crate, pick it up, and follow Captain Abbot to his cabin. He opens the door, then slides away a green velvet curtain. As soon as we enter, he kneels down, pulls up a trapdoor, and reaches for the crate. I lean over and look in. It's dark and cold. The smell of salt meets my face.

"Come. Come," he says. "I don't want to steal your head. Frankly, I wish I had never seen another one. But give it here. It'll be quiet down here."

I hand it to him, and he carefully places it in the icy hole. I stand up and listen. The voice quiets. In a few seconds, I can't hear it at all. Relief washes over me.

I look around at Captain Abbot's cabin. Oil lamps made of gold and silver burn brightly inside. On a dark mahogany desk sit a cask of wine and crystal glasses fit for the finest table in the finest castle. Maps of the oceans and landmasses of the world lie out, the corners held down by red, blue, green, and orange gems, big as my hand. Above a small but ornate fireplace hangs an enormous painting of a whaling ship crashing into an iceberg. It's beautiful and tragic. On a shelf above the captain's neat cot sit a jar with what looks like a human heart preserved in alcohol, a Revolutionary War medal, and a diploma from Harvard University.

My mouth drops open in awe. This place reminds me of Father's collection. It makes me feel at home, a little.

"I've lived long enough to have many great adventures and collect many fine things," Captain Abbot says.

"What's that?" I ask, gesturing to a tall stuffed bird standing in the corner.

"The elephant bird," Captain Abbot says. "I shot it."

I know something about the elephant bird. What? *Think. Think*, I tell myself. Then I remember. "That's impossible," I say. "The elephant bird went extinct in the early seventeen hundreds."

"Impressive intellect," says Captain Abbot. He pours himself a generous glass of wine. "Your father was impressed with that bird, too. And, like you, he doubted that I shot this one. But shoot it I did." He takes an appreciative swallow of his wine. "I wish now I hadn't, of course. I was young then. Brash. Didn't understand how the ends of things can come so suddenly." He drinks again. "You look like your father, I suppose you know." He gazes at the bird forlornly, as though he's sorry. Then his face changes to something else, anger or jealousy, maybe. "I admire that bird," he says.

What does that mean? I wonder. I pinch my lips together and will Captain Abbot to keep talking.

"And your father," Captain Abbot continues, "asleep now for the long duration. How I admire him for that." He drinks again and settles into his chair.

I clear my throat. "How did you know him?" My voice

sounds soft. I'm afraid to talk, but I want to know about my father.

The chair groans with the captain's every movement. "Well," he says, "that is an interesting story. And I have to admit, I wasn't too pleased to meet him at first."

I don't want to do anything that would interrupt a story about my father.

"Despite my reputation as a reckless lunatic, your father came looking for me once the head was in his possession. It had begun to drive him mad. Showed him treasures all over the world. Again and again he'd sail, leave your mother and you girls behind. Always searching for the next great discovery. The boys, your brothers, died and died again. But still he sailed. After the third boy was gone, he came to me with the head."

I'm stunned Captain Abbot knows so much about my family. How much of our lives did Father share with him? And the bad thoughts I've had about Father lately. Were they correct? Did Father crave treasures and discoveries more than us? More than me?

"You'd better settle in. This is a long story." Captain Abbot scratches his chest. "Itches afterward," he says with a faint smile, referring to where he shot himself. "Now, let's begin. The cannibal tribe had told your father the same story they told me."

"Which was what?" I ask.

"I'm getting to that part," he says. "Patience." He removes his boot and shakes out dust. He removes a holey sock and shakes it out. "Can you darn?" he asks me.

I shake my head.

He slaps the sock onto his leg a couple of times, and then he stretches it back over his foot. His leg runs with red and purple veins like I've only ever seen on very old women. I think I might die of old age myself before he ever finishes this story.

Captain Abbot replaces his boot and begins his story again. "They told me, and told your father, that once a child with three heads was born unto them. The child had one body but three minds. It grew and became a witch doctor with the powers of prophecy and healing. But the minds began to disagree and argue, each thinking it was more powerful than the others. The heads bickered and fought late into the night and early every morning. The body of the three heads grew weary. One day, the heads argued so violently that the body threw itself off a cliff to silence the voices. When the rest of the tribe discovered the witch doctor, body broken at every bone, the mouths of the

314

heads were still moving. They carried the body back to the camp, cut off the heads, shrunk them, and stitched closed the eyes and mouths. But as you know, that didn't silence them."

Captain Abbot pours himself another glass of wine. He drinks.

Keep talking, I think. *Tell me all of it.*

"The tribe kept the heads for a time. They revered them as sacred objects. Why they gave away each of them is a mystery to me. I can only speculate that the heads' howling drove them mad, the way it drives you mad. But you've done well not to obliterate it. I was not so wise."

"What happened?"

"At first, I rarely used it, rarely held it. But the Medicine Head increased its calling. Eventually, I was holding it daily. I began to misuse its magic. Peered into the past too often. Looked into the future too much. Used it to find riches, exploit people. Ruined my family. The more I held it, the more I wanted to hold it. Finally, its cries drove me senseless, and I threw it into a fiery volcano. And then I became as I am."

I look at him. I think I know what he means. But I want to ask anyway. "What do you mean, 'as I am'?"

"Infinite," he says. "On and on. Forever." He holds the glass in his hands and swirls the wine.

I swallow. "Where's the other head?" I ask. "You said three. I have one. You had one. Where's the last?"

"Destroyed as well," he says. He drinks. "By me."

Those words seem to slap me in the temple. "Well," I say, "then you can destroy mine, too!" I'm practically shouting. "I mean, as long as you're already suffering the consequence of destroying the first, you may as well destroy mine."

He smirks, but then his face falls deadly serious. "That's what we thought, too," he says. He coughs. "But the head doesn't work that way." He drinks again. "I could, but the consequences for you would be the same as the other."

"What do you mean?" I ask. "Who had the other head? What happened to him?"

"Not him," Captain Abbot says. "Her. Nova had the second head, given to her by the tribe while she was aboard a different whaling expedition."

"Nova?" I ask. "You mean she's like you? Forever?"

"Yes," he says. "Yes, sadly. Yes." He groans. "She's not as old as me, of course, but she's beyond a century. I've lost track myself." He strokes his long beard. "The head chose her and she used it. Once she held it, the head claimed her. So it didn't matter that she gave it to me to destroy. She was its target regardless. I imagine the same would apply to you, even if I or Nova destroyed it for you."

Poor Nova.

"She's watched her husband, her children, all age and die." He sighs.

I think about the handprint on Nova's chest.

"When your father found me," he says, "and told me of his encounter with the cannibal tribe and the gift of the head, I told him the same. And before we could determine what to do with it, he was running for his life to Kansas. So you see, I could destroy yours, but you would pay a terrible price."

I think about Mother and Priss. And then I wonder about Greeney. "But how does Greeney know about the head?" I ask.

"Why, don't you know?" asks Captain Abbot. "Greeney was your father's apprentice. He was there when the tribe gave your father the head. Half as intelligent, half as good, he thought that if the head was his, he could surpass all your father's great discoveries."

"He killed my father," I say.

"I know that," says Captain Abbot. It seems as though

his face grows smooth and soft. "But what I wouldn't give to have the gift of death. I know it's hard, Miss Wonder, for you and your family. But death is that looming event that makes every experience before that point sweet and urgent."

My neck is tight again. Like I might cry. I gulp the tightness down.

"Be happy for your father," he says. "Look at me."

I do. I take in his ancient face, lined with misery and apathy.

"Would you have wanted this for him?" he asks. "I've got no curiosity left. No wonder for the world. Every day I am only weary. Each day, I can think of nothing more than driving myself to the deadliest places and chases. What have I got to lose? But still, nothing, no one excites me. Life without death is a dreary, endless tedium. Do not destroy the head."

I shake my head. "I wasn't going to," I say. "I mean, I've thought about it, but I wouldn't. I've got a different idea."

He nods. "I assume you're thinking about the coldest, loneliest place in the world," he says.

"Yes," I say. "Antarctica."

"Now, why didn't your father think of that?" He leans back and pats his stomach.

"He did, but he ran out of time," I say.

"I see," says Captain Abbot. "He left a great responsibility for you, Miss Wonder, but also a powerful mind with which to conquer it."

✦ CHAPTER 30 ✦

We sail on toward the cold waters. Months—
I've lost count of them—pass. The whales we take become
bigger with each catch, and I grow used to the violence of
it. I participate in the butchering and rendering. I work.
I receive approving nods from Nova. Forevermore, I
will appreciate the oil I use, the light I need. Now I know
the animals' sacrifice. I understand the workers' toil. But the
men seem happy in their work. They grin, pleased, at the
stacks of oil barrels in the hold. Still, they want more. They

want every barrel filled to its brim. Every drop means another coin.

The captain hasn't spoken to me again. Eustace is busy, growing up and growing away from me. He follows in Nova's shadow wherever she goes and learns much from her. I miss him. But I understand. I am changing, too. The patience I once yearned for has grown ripe in me. Most of the time, anyway.

One morning, I wake and can see my breath. It's freezing aboard the *Xerxes*. From somewhere in the deep recesses of the ship, Nova has found and issued everyone a variety of coats, capes, hats, mittens, and shawls collected from anywhere and everywhere to keep the crew warm. Some of the men are dressed so that they look ready for field work in Kansas, in short cotton coats, plain in color. Other sailors look as though they are ready for dinner and the theater, with long woolen tailcoats and top hats made of silk. Others are wearing women's lacy shawls tied around their heads like scarves. One man is wearing a woman's layered skirt over his own pants. Nova has given me a simple cotton bonnet, which makes me think of Priss. I put it on without back-talking. Then Nova pulls a long, hairy white fur from a trunk.

"What is that?" I ask.

"Yak fur," she says. "Very warm." She ties it around the bonnet and winds it around my neck.

When I ascend the hatch, everyone seems agitated. We are hundreds of miles off the coast of South America. Nova begins scrubbing the insides and outsides of the rendering cauldrons. She nods toward where Captain Abbot stands, with his hands clasped behind his back, staring out at the sea.

"He's close!" Captain Abbot keeps repeating.

The ocean appears still and silent. *Who's close?* But I, too, have that strange tingly feeling, as though something's about to happen. Just as I did all that time ago, before I found the dead snake, before I found Father hanging from the tree. Something is about to happen. I remind myself to breathe calmly. But my breaths are short, and soon my ears ring and my fingers tingle. *Stay calm.* I walk the deck to find Eustace, who is near a whaleboat, stringing harpoons. A heavy buffalo cape hangs over his shoulders and down his back. He's wearing some kind of animal fur on his head. He's beginning to look a bit feral, a bit like Nova in that way.

My fingertips tingle, and not just from the cold. I'm not breathing right. *Exhale slowly*, I tell myself. And I do.

"Hey," I say to Eustace.

"Hay is for horses," he says. Then he adds in a whisper, "The captain's been pacing back and forth all day and all night, I think. I haven't seen him go into or come out of his quarters in days." Fob appears from behind Eustace's legs. I lean over and give his nose a scratch. Fob moans. He's got his tail tucked between his legs. He's fearful of something.

"Keep your eye out!" Captain Abbot shouts.

I look out, but I can't see a thing. The air is so full of ice crystals that I can't even see the horizon. It's as though the ocean and the sky are one.

Eustace points out to where I'm looking. "What's that?" he says.

"Where?" I say.

"There," he says. "Way out. It looks like another ship."

I stare and stare. "I don't see anything. Maybe your eyes are playing tricks on you."

Eustace ignores me. His cheeks go tight. His jaw clenches.

But then, above us, the lookout on the mast shouts down, "Captain! Captain! Thar he blows!" He's pointing far out over the other side of the ship.

All morning the clouds have spun gray and wispy, and now they are building black and threatening. Captain Abbot and the rest of the crew run to the rail and cup their hands around their eyes. We rush over, too. I look. Still, I see nothing. But Eustace says, "I see it. I see it! A whale!" When he says that, Nova springs into action. She runs to the whaleboats, and she reaches in to check her harpoon.

Captain Abbot calls, "He's a sperm! Let's get him! Bring plenty of ropes and spears. He'll put up a fight, the old son of a gun. He will!"

"Eustace," Nova calls, and he goes to her.

I squint again. I don't see anything except the waves, the horizon, and the angry sky. I'm sick to death of that scene. But something must be out there, because the whole ship is pulsing with action. I search and search to see what everyone else sees.

And then there he is.

A plume of white water blasts into the air. A smooth gray back breaks the waves. Without the water spout, you might never know that it's the back of a whale. You might think it's only another rolling wave, so beautifully does it blend in.

"I'm coming, too!" I say. This time, no one objects. I feel pride swell up in my chest. I go to the whaleboats, which are being lowered by ropes and pulleys into the roiling water below. I think about the sharks I saw and the miles of water beneath us, but I still climb into the whale-boat with Eustace and Fob and Nova.

Eustace hands me an oar, a much smaller one than any of the others. Only months ago, I would have shouted at him. Not this time. This time, I take it and trust that he's given me the responsibility I can handle. I dip the oar into the water and row in time with the other sailors.

Nova sets her oar aside. She perches at the bow with her harpoon in hand.

Once out of the shadow of the *Xerxes*, we loosen the ropes that held us to the ship, and the men above pull them up. Now it's just us, this boat, the ocean, and that whale out there. Then the rain starts. Soft at first, but it quickly falls in thick sheets. The wind picks up, too.

"Row," orders Nova. The other whaleboat is near us, and as we approach where we last saw the whale, Nova directs the crew. I look over the side into the water and wonder if he's below us. It occurs to me that he could be right there, under me, and I get scared a little.

Then I feel a tremor beneath my feet.

"Did you feel that?" I ask. They all ignore me, but Nova touches the bottom of the boat and stares over the side. The ocean has gone strangely quiet. The waves that once rocked us to and fro have calmed. The rain now falls hard and straight down, like ropes dropping from the sky. It feels like something is about to happen.

The whaleboat begins to rattle. Nova leans over, and her eyes widen.

"Oh no!" she says. *"Hang on!"*

Instead of hanging on to something, I lean over the edge to see what she's seeing.

It's like a white mountain rising from the deep blue depths, surging closer and closer. I bend over farther to get a better look. *What is happening?* The ocean seems to be growing underneath our boat. And the next thing I see is water rushing ahead of it in a great push. Then I see the head of a whale, a leviathan. He's a sperm. With a head like the engine of a train.

Before I can move or speak, I feel a huge crash as the whale rams into our underside. The whole whaleboat is hoisted into the air. I am like a Kansas jackrabbit being tossed around by a wild dog.

"Hang on!" Eustace yells. "Stay with the boat!"

But I lose my grip. I'm flying away from the boat and the crew in it. Time seems to go slowly. I'm in the air. The whale is in the air. He's the size of three or four railway cars. He's beautiful. My yak fur flies away. There, too, goes my bonnet. I am flying and free.

"We've been stove!" Nova shouts. She's watching me. "Mark where she lands!" I am so high, I look down and see the whaleboat. The ocean seems a lifetime away. I am weightless. It seems like I should be able to take in a deep breath, fill my lungs, sprout wings, and fly. But then I am coming down again, coming down quickly. The whale has dipped back into the water. His fluke disappears beneath the surface. And it seems like the ocean is rising up to meet me and swallow me like the giant jaws of a whale.

Then, from my toes to the top of my head, I am shocked by freezing cold water. Stunned still.

I sink. Water fills my boots. My clothes pull me down and down. I do nothing but suffer the cold, like a body full of hornet stings. I hear nothing but water gurgling in my ears. Water rushes up my nose and flows down my throat. The salt burns. I am frozen and on fire at the same time.

In my head I'm saying *I'm overboard. Help.* But no one hears those words because I can't say them aloud. I'm all spun around. I try to calm my thinking. Finally, I kick my legs and doggy-paddle my arms a little. Then a little more, and a little more.

I see a twisting underwater column. It's like a cyclone. It's coming toward me and there's no way to avoid it.

Suddenly, I am spinning and spinning inside it.

A whooshing noise rushes past my ears. The whale has created his own whirling wake and I am in it, twisting. I spin and spin and I am certain that this is how I will die. *I had to come all the way to the ocean to finally see a cyclone*, I think.

That's when I remember my tornado dream.

I put out my arms, and they create resistance against the spinning water. It presses on them, but I feel myself slowing down. I fight to keep holding out my arms. I'm so tired, I think it might be OK to put them down and drown. But then I think of Priss and Mother and Ruby and Eustace and even Fob. I don't stop.

I slow. Finally, I stop spinning in the water. I just hover there. But now I don't know up from down.

I look one way and see black and bubbles.

I look another way and see bubbles and light. The surface. I kick and swim and try to get to it. But the water is freezing and pulling on my clothes, and though I fight to go up, I'm going down. I kick and kick to keep the surface in sight.

I don't know how long I've been in the water, but I'm not feeling panicked yet. I hold my breath like I've been practicing for so many years.

I see a shadow, a bluish-gray looming form moving past me.

I reach for it. *The boat,* I think. *Here, somehow, is the boat. I will grab hold and climb up.* I stretch and reach for it until my fingertips are finally pressed against its side. But when I touch it, I know it is not the wood of a boat. The surface is smooth and firm but supple. Most of all, it is alive. I sense the life in me touching the life in the whale.

I jerk back, afraid. But I reach out again, curious. I stroke the animal's skin as it slips away from me. The body goes on and on, forever it seems. It's at least as long as the *Xerxes.*

Pressure builds in my ears. My chest burns now. I want air. I'm struggling to swim. My lungs urge me to inhale. My head's going light and dreamy. I wonder if I'm drowning. My arms and legs are so tired. *I have to rest,* I think.

I let my body go limp. But I keep a hand on the whale. *Swim away,* I think. *You're too beautiful to kill.*

I see the face of my father after I cut him down from the tree, as though it's right in front of me. I don't want that face to be the last thing I see if I'm going to die. I try to think of Father studying or reading. But I get nothing but the swollen, discolored face of a murdered man. Then his head is replaced by the Medicine Head, and I suck in a big gulp of water.

I remember why I'm here, why I'm in the middle of the

ocean in the first place. I remember the great responsibility I have, and I try to swim again. I reach and reach for the surface, but it seems miles away.

I feel the end of the whale's body. Right here, I know, is where the legs of his ancestors once grew. And then his tail dips down, away from my touch. My last connection to anything alive slips away. I let go. I lean back in the water and let it press me down.

But then a swoosh jerks me up. And then another forceful current pushes me higher. The sky's light becomes bigger and closer. One more time, a surge of water shoves me toward the surface. The whale's fluke passes beneath me. He gives one more flick of his tail, and I'm jolted upward. The whale has heaved me to the surface.

When my head breaks the waves, I gasp. I see the boat. I see Fob with his paws on the boat's rim. He's barking, but I can't hear. I can only see his mouth open and close. The sun has come out, and it's so bright I have to close my eyes. The next thing I know, jaws bite down on my collar, and I'm being tugged through the water.

✦ CHAPTER 31 ✦

Fob snarls and snorts in my ear. His teeth are clenched on my coat and he's circling and circling his legs through the water, pulling me toward the boat. Salt water burns my throat and nose. Every time I take a breath, waves hit my face and more water gets in my mouth.

"Come, Fob!" calls Eustace. "Good boy!" He's leaning over the boat and patting the side of it. "Come!" he keeps saying. The boat and Eustace's arms seem ages away.

Slowly, Fob pulls me toward it. Sometimes his legs get caught in my blouse and we go under for a bit. But he always frees them and swims again.

Finally, we are there, and I try to grab hold of something, but my arms are heavy. I'm too weak. Eustace grabs each of my shoulders and he's got me. Then many more arms are reaching and pulling me up and over the side of the boat, and I fall to the bottom.

I look up at the sky and it's now bright blue. All the gray and black clouds have gone. Where could they have gone so quickly? The faces of the whaleboat crew, Eustace, and Nova lean over and stare at me. Nova turns me over on my side and beats on my back. I cough up water, lots of water, out my nose and mouth. When it's all out, I can breathe normally.

The other whalers have pulled Fob into the boat, too. They cover him with a blanket, which he shakes off. He comes to me and licks my face and curls up right next to me. He whimpers and sighs.

"Did you get the whale?" I whisper.

"Don't worry about that," says Nova.

"Did he get away?" I whisper again.

Eustace nods. I'm very happy the whale got away. I wonder if I should tell them how I touched him, how I held my hand to him, how he pushed me to the surface with his fluke. I wonder if they'd believe me. I wish I had a specimen or something to prove how I was rescued, but I guess some discoveries can't be proved. I decide not to try. I think I'd like to keep that discovery all to myself forever.

I lift my arm and flop it over Fob. It feels heavy as a sack of rocks. "You've very brave," I whisper. He wags his tail.

"And you are a very lucky young lady," says Nova. She takes a big fur cloak off her own shoulders and covers me. "Yes, you are. I see many people fall over and never come back up."

We row back to the *Xerxes*. Captain Abbot is irate. He stomps up and down the deck and demands to know why we let the bastard get away. No one answers him. His eyes bore through me.

Nova helps me down to my hammock. I sit in it while she takes off my coat and boots and clothes. She goes to her trunk and pulls out a long blue dress. "You'll have to wear this," she says, snapping out the wrinkles. "I wore this on my wedding day," she adds. She looks sad, so I don't ask any questions. I let her undress and dress me, and I don't even feel embarrassed.

A thunderclap startles us. Nova looks above. She pats my hand and leaves me to my thoughts.

The ship rocks and bolts, lurches and lunges. The wind whips, and above me, I hear the men shouting and working. Sails are moved. Ropes dropped. The barrels clack against each other. The storm is back and raging.

The Medicine Head whispers to me. I tell myself that the Medicine Head is tucked safely away in Captain Abbot's cabin, cool and quiet. "No," I say out loud. I close my eyes and try to sleep. Chills wrack my body. My teeth chatter. I try to think about home and Mother and Priss. I try to think about my home and the nice, dry, hot, flat lands of Kansas. I can't wait to be back there. Then sleep washes over me.

When I wake, it is still dark. And the Medicine Head is whispering to me again. *How can that be?* I wonder. It's as cold as it's ever been on our voyage. I close my eyes and try to ignore it, but the words are clear and strong. Finally, I get up and creep up the ladder.

All is tranquil on the deck. A dim glow comes from Captain Abbot's cabin. I tiptoe toward it. The door is slightly ajar. I reach my fingers in and pinch the curtain against the door. Then I catch a glance of Captain Abbot sitting near his fireplace with my Medicine Head's crate on his knees.

"I hear you," he says. I startle and catch my breath, but he doesn't turn around. He's not talking to me. He's talking to the head.

"You want to come out of there, don't you? What do you want to show me now?" He picks up the crate and holds it. "I can't. I can't," he mumbles. He loosens the knot at the top of the crate with one hand, like the experienced seaman he is, as though his fingers aren't listening to the words coming from his mouth. The rope falls to the floor. He begins to pry the crate open.

"Oh, yes," he whispers. "There you are. What do you want to show me? The whale, the giant one? Where did he go?"

Captain Abbot reaches in. The straw rustles as he gropes for the Medicine Head. Then he lifts it from the crate and holds it to his face. He and the Medicine Head are practically nose-to-nose. I don't hear a thing. Captain Abbot's eyes are closed. He is motionless. He is smiling a strange grin. I back away and return to my hammock.

✦ CHAPTER 32 ✦

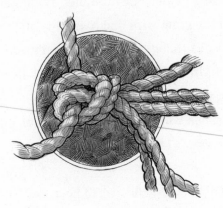

"Antarctica!" the captain roars the next morning. "That's where the monster's headed, and that's where we're going, too!"

He winks at me.

For weeks we sail on in the South Atlantic, trailing a pod of whales that seems to know the clearest way. Wherever they emerge to breathe is where we go. Captain Abbot takes a few for rendering, but not many. He's not satisfied with them and wants to get right back on the trail of the big one that got away because of me. Each day brings us closer and closer to my destination. And each day grows colder and colder. Ice hangs from all the rigging and sails. The deck is slick ice. The sea bobs with icebergs and ice sheets.

I welcome the fire that burns the blubber into oil. Though it smells terrible and is smoky, the heat makes the frigid ride tolerable. I find myself looking forward to the next kill. Belowdecks, ice has formed on the beams of the ceiling. The moisture on the deck has crystallized and is slippery again. Eustace stands watch for icebergs and whales. He keeps flitting his eyes to the north and saying "There's something out there."

"Th-there is something out there," I stutter. "Ice."

"Something else," he says.

Sometimes icebergs appear in the distance. They are so big, they look like islands or mountains. In between are great plates of ice floating on the water. Once in a while, a seal rests on top of one. I saw a seal scratching himself by dragging his body along the ice, like a dog might do in the gravel.

A new but familiar scent is on the air. Land.

"Do you smell that, Eustace?" I ask.

"Yes, I do," he says. "Soil."

"This means we're getting closer, right?" I ask.

"Yes," Nova says. "We're getting there. The *Xerxes* won't be able to take us all the way to the continent, though. We'll have to take a whaleboat. Too much ice. It would shred the ship to pieces."

✦ ✦ ✦

One morning, as I lie in my hammock curled up with Fob to keep warm, I hear a cannon fire. I jolt upright.

"What was that?" I ask.

Nova leaps from her hammock. "Up," she says. "Up the hatch!"

When I get to the deck, she nearly pushes me out of her way and dashes past me.

"Hey," I say. "Watch out!" But she's gone, and I can't see where. A lantern flame flickers in the dark. After my eyes adjust, I see Captain Abbot standing at the bow.

It's pitch black except for stars and lanterns on deck. The air is sharply cold, pinching like needles on my skin wherever it's bare. Captain Abbot smokes a pipe.

He turns to me. "He's here for you, Miss Wonder. Or for the head. Captain Greeney, that is."

"What!" I yell. I run to where they are and look out at the dark ocean. I peer through the icy air. Then I make out the shape of a ship and the dull lights of lanterns. "Is he shooting cannons at us?" I ask. I think about all the people on board our ship. I think about the Medicine Head. If it's destroyed, who will live forever? Me? Captain Greeney? Both of us?

"He is," says Captain Abbot.

"W-well," I stutter. "What are we going to do? We have to do something!"

Captain Abbot puts his hand on my shoulder.

"We're not going to do anything."

Another cannonball zings through the air. It drops in the ocean, only a few feet from the deck of the *Xerxes* this time.

"We're all going to die!" I yell.

"Not all of us," says Captain Abbot. "Only one of us." He laughs and tilts back his head until he begins to cough.

"You're mad," I say. "We've got to run. Tell the men to sail! Or we've got to fight. Tell the men to ready the harpoons! Where are our cannons?"

"Cannons?" he laughs. He coughs. "This is a whaling ship, you nitwit! I am the captain!" He coughs again. "And I say we do nothing."

"Do nothing?" I yell. "You must be mad. We could all lose our lives!"

Captain Abbot leans over and breathes into my face.

His breath is fusty as a pigpen. "Well," he says. "Not *all* of us." He crosses his arms over his chest. "Besides, only one of us will be claimed by the big drink tonight. You can count on that, lassie."

"You're insane," I say. I turn away from him. I've got to get off this ship. I've got to get Eustace and Fob off this ship. I've got to get the Medicine Head off this ship.

Captain Abbot laughs into the night. Then he shouts at me. "The big leviathan is coming back! He's coming back! Hee hee hee!" He laughs like a child.

Maybe he's lost his mind. Another cannonball shoots through the air and lands with a tremendous splash near the *Xerxes*. I look where it landed. Rings of water crash against the side of the boat. And all over are the pointed fins of dread. Sharks. What are they doing in this freezing water? More importantly, what will they do to me if the *Xerxes* goes down?

Nova, I think. *I've got to find Nova.* I rush to one end of the ship and then the other. I look up at the masts. I look in the ropes. I descend to the forecastle and the hold. I can't find her. She's not in the galley. She's not at the try-pot.

The only place I haven't looked is the captain's cabin. I run to it and open the door.

Then a cannonball hits the side of the *Xerxes* and

340

explodes. Wood and sparks shoot into the air and into the water.

"Water!" a crewman shouts. "Planks and nails!" shouts another. The cooper races past me to the damage with his tools. "Don't worry, Barnacle," he says to me. "It's more smoke than fire!"

In the captain's cabin, I find Nova leaning over my Medicine Head's crate, rocking back and forth on her knees and chanting. She's smoking her pipe, and the room is thick with its strange scent.

"What are you doing?" I say to her. "I need that!"

She ignores me and sings more of her song over the Medicine Head. She takes her pipe and waves it over and around the crate.

"Nova!" I shout.

She leans back and raises her face to the ceiling. She blows out an impressive plume of smoke, which rises in rings.

"Now you are ready," she says softly. She stands with the Medicine Head's crate and hands it to me. "You must go. Now is the time." She takes the buffalo robe from her shoulders and wraps it around mine. "You'll need this."

"Come with me," I beg her. I want to cling to her and tell her that I love her. "I'm scared."

She puts her hands on my cheeks. Then she pulls me into a tight embrace and strokes the top of my head. "Hallelujah Wonder. I wish you were my own child. You are very brave and strong and smart."

I can hear her heart beating. I hug her back hard.

"Eustace can row you in," she says. "I must stay and protect the captain and the ship." She softens her eyes in a way I've rarely seen her do. "You're braver than you know." Then she leans into my forehead and kisses it. "Now go!" She points to the door.

Another cannon blast rocks the ship. I exit the captain's cabin. The whole deck is full of smoke.

"Eustace?" I call. "Eustace?" I can't see. My eyes sting.

From the haze appears Fob, dirty and scared and shivering. Icicles dangle from his jaw and whiskers. He tries to sit down on my feet.

"Come on, boy," I say. My mouth barely works, it's so cold. "Come on. Show me where Eustace is." Fob stands up, but his whole body is shaking. He walks gingerly across the deck to where the whaleboats hang. Eustace is at the pulley.

"Lu, are you all right?" he asks. "Do you have it?"

"Yes," I say. I lift the crate for him to see.

"Get in," he says. He nods to the boat. "I'll lower you and then jump in."

I step onto a keg. Another cannonball blasts the *Xerxes*. I get into the boat and hold the Medicine Head's crate. The head is dead quiet.

Eustace heaves Fob in next to me.

"He's been with us all along," Eustace says, as if to explain why we're bringing the dog. But he doesn't have to explain to me. Fob is welcome wherever in the world I go. Even if it might be to my frozen tomb.

"Sit, Fob," I say, even though he's already sitting. Eustace guides the whaleboat, lurching, over the side of the *Xerxes* and slowly lowers it onto the surface of the slate-gray ocean. Chunks of ice slap against the whaleboat. I grab the rope that moors us to the *Xerxes* and try to hold us steady. My teeth chatter. The joints in my fingers don't want to work. Even my bones are cold. Eustace climbs down the rope and lands in the whaleboat. He unties us, takes the oars, and we're off.

"This is it," he says. "Hold on."

I hold tight to the Medicine Head's crate. I smell Nova's smoke coming up off the wood. It reminds me to be brave.

Eustace rows us away from the *Xerxes*, away from the cannon fire. Away from Captain Greeney's ship. Away from Captain Greeney.

I lean over the whaleboat. Long, eerie shadows glide beneath us. First this way, then that. Sharks. Sometimes they rise close enough to the surface to cut the water with their fins, like a scalpel opening skin. Wherever they swim, the ice chunks curtsy above them. Ice floes rise out of the ocean like floating hills. Some people could be tricked into thinking that those blocks of ice are land, are solid rock with bases settled into solid ground. But not me. I know we have to go farther. I know we're close. But we haven't reached Antarctica yet.

The air is thin, so thin it's impossible to breathe deeply. Short breath in. Short breath out. Each one is like a steel knife in my neck. Eustace, Fob, and I shiver from head to toe. The cold is otherworldly. When I open my lips the slightest bit, I worry the cold is going to break my teeth or snap off my tongue.

The sky is magic, with auras of orange and blue and pink and purple and cream that arc and bend above the horizon.

"Eustace?" I whisper. I raise my finger, shaking like an old woman's, to the sky.

He nods. "It looks like the thunder egg," he says. "I know it."

As Eustace rows, the water on the leeward side of the

whaleboat flutters and spits, just like it did before the giant whale breached and leapt into the air, tossing me into the ocean. We watch. Then the water calms down and ripples normally.

"What was that?" I ask.

"Don't know," says Eustace. He rows and rows, pulling at the water with more strength than I've seen in any human before.

I look back toward the *Xerxes* and Captain Greeney's ship. Smoke rises from the *Xerxes*, but it is afloat. I squint, and out of the smoke, I see the shape of another small whaleboat coming toward us.

"No," I whisper. Saliva falls from my lip and freezes to my chin in a second. It's him. It's Captain Greeney following us in his own whaleboat.

"Row, Eustace!" I say. My mouth is frozen. It's difficult to make the words. "He's coming."

Eustace heaves the oars through the water. Greeney's boat gets nearer and nearer until his body and then his eyes are in view. He sets down his oars. He's reaching for something in the bottom of his boat. And then a harpoon flies past us and lands in the water and ice beyond.

"He's trying to catch us," I say.

Eustace doesn't respond to me. He's working so hard,

fighting the cold and the ice and the water and the weight of the boat and me and Fob. He strokes and strokes the oars. He's breathing heavily but evenly.

Another harpoon flies at us, and this time it penetrates the side of our boat. The rope attached to it goes taut. Our boat lurches. Waves lap up and over it all around. Then Greeney pulls on the rope, yanks himself toward us.

"Pull the harpoon out, Lu," says Eustace. He continues to stroke, though we go nowhere. He keeps tension in the rope. "You have to pull the harpoon out! I can't stop rowing!"

I'm so cold that I don't feel like I can move. I'm not sure my body works.

"Do it," pleads Eustace.

I put down the crate. Every movement hurts. I shake my arms and my fingers to life.

Greeney is slowly yanking himself closer to us even as Eustace rows and rows to get away from him.

I grab hold of the harpoon. Its arrow tip is deep in the wood. I push it down and then up again. It barely budges.

"Resign yourself!" Greeney shouts across the water. "I will have the head!"

You won't, I think. I shake the arrow tip back and forth

and up and down. *Come on*, I think. Fob barks at Greeney. It's a sad, hoarse bark.

"You'll die like my father did," I say. It's so quiet I don't know if he's heard. "You must die," I say louder. "Like all of us do."

Then the ocean beneath me turns from grayish white to black. The water moves with whatever glides beneath us. I work and work at the harpoon tip. Eustace stops rowing and fighting against the pull of Greeney's harpoon to watch the shadow slide away. Whatever it is, it's big. One hundred feet or more.

To get tossed into this water, this bitter cold water, means certain death.

I tug at the harpoon, slow and steady, as I once did with Captain Abbot's tooth. Finally, I wrench it free from our boat.

I hold it high. My arms shake. But my body fills with vigor. I rear back and throw it at Greeney's boat. The harpoon wobbles through the air and lands in his bow.

"I am free of you, Captain Greeney!" I shout, my voice strong now.

He scrambles to pick it up and stands.

"I'll follow you right to the South Pole!" he shouts at me. "I will have it."

"You won't," I say, shaking my head. "You weren't brave enough to get there last time. And you're not now, either." My words fly straight and sure.

He leans back and prepares to throw the harpoon at us again. His face contorts into something snakelike. His eyes widen and his lips sneer.

A strange wave rolls across the water, ominous. The wake pitches our boat up and down.

"What is that?" I ask. I watch a long shadow creep through the water. The wave it creates grows bigger and crushes any ice in its way.

"Hang on," says Eustace. He holds on to the sides of the boat. "It's your whale. It's got to be your whale. Watch."

I do.

The ocean seems to rise up and then fall away like the earth descending into a sinkhole. Only this time, the curved back of a giant rises from where the water falls. The whale gains speed, and the wake grows larger. When he's within feet of Captain Greeney's boat, the whale dives. His enormous fluke pops above the water and then slips down quiet as a ghost. The water goes silent and still.

Captain Greeney has seen the whale, too. He's watching the water. He sits and grabs hold of the sides of his boat. He looks over one way and then the other.

Very slowly, Eustace takes up the oars and calmly pulls us farther away from Captain Greeney. "We have to keep going," he says.

I put the Medicine Head's crate on my lap. Eustace rows and I watch behind us, at the scene of Greeney on his whaleboat.

Then the water all around Captain Greeney flutters and bubbles and froths. His boat looks as though it sits on top of a boiling pot of soup.

The nose of the whale bursts out of the water and pushes Greeney's boat into the air. The boat rises and rises, balanced on the boxlike nose of the sperm whale, my sperm whale.

Water sprays all around until the whale's two fins are out of the water, his hump is out of the water. He rises until his own weight tips him forward and he dives, sending Greeney's boat sailing through the air. Greeney is thrown from his boat. He's aloft and flying. The whale falls back into the sea with a mighty splash. Then Greeney's boat, and Greeney, too, land in the water. The waves roil. Frothing water bubbles and spurts.

Fob barks. I pat his head and tell him, "Shh."

The whale thrashes and splashes and ruins the boat. Wood and ice chunks fly in every direction. Our boat rocks but remains upright in the violence. Eustace pulls and pulls the oars through the water and ice.

The whale shows no mercy. When he finally stops, parts of the boat float here and there, oars, boots, a cap, and harpoons bobbing on the water. For a while, the whale hovers on the surface. I can hear him heaving, as though he has exhausted himself. He blows a long spray of water and air into the sky. Then the whale curves his back and dives. Eustace and I wait. But nothing happens. There's no sign of the whale or of the man who murdered my father.

Captain Greeney has succumbed to the ocean. That's what Captain Abbot meant when he said "only one of us." The Medicine Head showed him all this.

He's not insane at all.

The ocean calms down like a lion does after he eats. Small tears gather in the corners of my eyes, which freeze and hurt like glass shards. Even after all he put my father and my family through, my heart is heavy for Captain Greeney. "Death is a gift," I whisper, for my own sake, mostly.

✦ CHAPTER 33 ✦

Our whaleboat is encased in ice. It creaks and cracks. The ice hunks crumble and squeak against each other and the side of the boat.

"We have to keep going," I say.

The ocean is slushy. Eustace rows us through the last field of ice. He leans over and smashes us through big chunks. He works hard. Sweat on his forehead and in his hairline has frozen. Ice crystals cover his entire face.

I smell the air. Dirt. Rock. A scent that's elemental and dry.

From underneath the boat comes a flittering and swooshing noise. Short, squat shadows buzz under the water all around us.

"Not again," I say. I'm afraid the whale has returned to destroy us, too. But these shadows are too fast, too short. "What are those?"

"Penguins," says Eustace. "They're penguins."

A black-and-white body pops up on a sheet of ice and stares at us as we glide by. We watch it. It means we are close to land.

"I told you they're nothing like chickens," I say to Eustace.

Eustace chuckles. "You were right about that," he says. "They don't look a bit like chickens." He speaks slowly and quietly. His lips quiver and his voice shakes.

"They probably taste the same," I say. I giggle and shiver at the same time, and so does Eustace. My body warms a bit with the laugh.

Eustace pokes away slabs of ice as he strokes us through the water. I can hear what sounds like waves splashing against a shore. We keep going. My whole body shakes. When I lick my lips, the moisture freezes.

Eustace slows in his rowing. He closes his eyes and leans back a bit. Then he stops moving altogether and appears to be sleeping upright.

"Eustace?" I say. "Hey. Eustace. Are you all right?" I breathe into my hands.

He doesn't answer. His face is stone still. He's not shivering or shaking the way I am. I'm so cold, I can barely move, but I get to my knees. I crawl to him. "Come, Fob," I say.

Fob whines but creeps toward Eustace, too.

I grab Eustace's arm and peel the oar out of his hand, which is curled like a claw. I remove the fur mitten Nova gave him. I pull his hand to my mouth and blow warm air on his fingers.

"Sit, Fob," I say, and he settles on top of Eustace's feet. "Don't move, boy." Fob curls around Eustace's legs. He whines.

"You've got to clench and unclench your fingers and toes," I say to Eustace, even though I'm not sure he can hear me. I'm not sure I'm really saying the words. I know I'm thinking them, but I have a strange sense of being outside myself. "Or you'll lose them."

I move his fingers back and forth. I blow on them. Finally, he opens his eyes and says, "Ow, that hurts." He closes his eyes again.

I slap his hands on his own thigh. Again and again.

"Ow," he says more forcefully. "Stop that."

"Stay awake," I say. "You can't fall asleep." I smack him on one cheek and then the other. He tries to grab my hand, but he's too slow.

"You better stop hitting me," he says.

"Wake up," I say, "and I'll stop hitting you."

Eustace sits up straight. He puts his mitten back on and takes the oar in hand again.

I am fumbling around in the whaleboat, thinking to find an extra blanket or something, when I discover a lantern and matches.

I lift them and try to smile, but my mouth is frozen.

"Not yet," says Eustace. "Not until we get rid of that thing." He gazes at the Medicine Head. "No heat," he says.

"Right," I say.

Pretty soon, Eustace is rowing steadily again. I drum my fingers on top of the Medicine Head's crate. It's absolutely quiet.

Ice mountains rise into the sky. White hills roll beyond. Between them are patches of black. Nothing seems alive out there except the land itself. And then there's a place before us where the ocean slopes up onto a shore with dirt. Dirt. The continent of Antarctica. This is where my father was. This is where I am. Wonder's Land. Our namesake at the edge of the world.

Eustace stares up at the white cliffs. "Wow," he says. "It's beautiful." He pulls the oars through the ice and water.

Suddenly, the boat stops. Eustace jabs at the ice with his oars. He pokes at it with a harpoon. Then he says, "We're stuck solid. We won't get in any closer. I think I can throw it from here."

He turns to me. I hold the crate tight. I'm not sure I can give it up. What if I can never see my father again? What if holding the head is the only way?

"Give it to me," Eustace says. "Lu, give it to me."

And then I see an apparition. Father is on the ship *Vivienne*. He's holding his binoculars. I see him pointing and then writing down his discovery. I can hear him, too. He's saying, "I did it! There it is! The continent of Antarctica!" I don't breathe. I want to listen to him forever. I would like to stay right here and have this dream forever. My body is rigid. My heart says, *Hold me. Thump. Thump. Hold me. Thump. Thump. Hold me. Hold me. Thump. Hold me. Hold me. Thump.*

I'm dying, I know. I don't care. I want to be with Father.

"Hallelujah!" shouts Eustace. I exhale. My breath is a white fog, like the ghost of myself. The apparition of my father disappears. "You'll freeze to death if we don't finish this thing now," Eustace says. He drops the oars. He comes to me and rubs his hands on my face.

"We're almost done," he says. "We've almost done it. Let go of the crate."

"I can't," I whisper. I want to close my eyes and sleep.

"Yes, you can," he says, gently. He puts his hands over mine and rubs them until they tingle. I lift one finger at a time from the crate. I open and close my fingers, which resist moving from their crowbar curl. Eustace takes off the top. "Let's do it," he says.

I reach in and pick up the Medicine Head. I wait for something to happen. But nothing does. The Medicine Head has no power here. Its leathery skin feels hard and won't give a bit. The lips sneer at me. The eyes seem closed in frozen concentration.

"Lu!" I hear. "Give it to me."

"Yes," I say. "Take it."

Eustace drops it into the bottom of the boat and begins circling a rope around it.

"I need a good knot," he says. "Can you do it?"

I wiggle my fingers. They are practically frozen solid. "Yes, I can do it."

I kneel down in the bottom of the boat and force my

fingers to make the loops for a simple buntline hitch. When I'm finished, Eustace attaches the other end of the rope to the harpoon. He jabs an oar into the ice on either side of the boat to hold it steady. Then he stands and rears back.

"Wait," I say. "Wait." I stand. "I want to do it."

"What?" he says. "I mean, are you sure?"

"I can," I say. "Remember that lady's whistle I tossed?"

He nods and moves. He helps steady me.

I draw the harpoon back and then, like a whale slapping its fluke, I hurl it forward, flinging it as far as I can, with the Medicine Head attached.

It flies off into the white, through the winter air. It flies and flies away from Captain Abbot and Captain Greeney and Eustace and Nova and Fob. It flies away from Father. It flies and flies away from me, and as soon as I hear the sharp piercing of a steel point into frozen ground, I know it's gone forever. The wind blows and picks up snow. Soon it will be buried.

I will the ice and gales of Antarctica to tether the Medicine Head to it forever. I will the Medicine Head to be covered and encased in a frozen grave.

I work my fingers so that they pinch a match, and I strike it until it's lit. It sparks and then grows very small.

I cup my other hand around the flame until it grows strong. Then I open the lantern and put the flame to the wick.

Fire. A small one, but fire nevertheless. I close the lantern and put it between us at our feet. And I don't know how, but the heat from that small flame makes all the difference.

Eustace sits down next to me and holds me in his arms. Fob tucks himself between us. There's a heat there, too, in the center of us.

I feel free, close to Father. I feel like I can finally go back to Kansas, go back home.

"You did it," Eustace says. "You did it, Hallelujah Wonder." He hugs me tight. Fob barks, a full, hearty, healthy bark. In the distance, I can hear the sounds of hammers putting the *Xerxes* back together. I can hear the strong voice of Nova shouting for the men to lower another whaleboat. She's coming for us.

I hug Eustace back. "We did it, Eustace."

✦ CHAPTER 34 ✦

On days such as today, when the warm winds guide the *Xerxes* over the flat Atlantic Ocean, I like to slide across the deck to a place near the galley where I can sit and think.

"Keep an eye on Fob," I tell Eustace.

Fob pads over to him and lies down. "Another few weeks and you'll be in Kansas, Lu," Eustace says. He smiles. "You're almost home. Big work to be done there."

"Yes," I say. "I'm sure the farm needs tending. And

that Priss could use some help with the hogs. Your ma. My mother." I scratch at dead skin, which has turned white and flaky, on my fingertips. The very same thing has happened to the tips of Eustace's fingers as a result of the temperatures in Antarctica. I scratch and watch that skin float away. "And the abolitionists need me, too."

Eustace picks the skin off his fingertips as well. "Yes," he says. "A lot of big work. I'm proud of you, Hallelujah Wonder."

My chest swells up.

"I'm proud of you, too, Eustace," I say. And I mean it. "I'll tell your ma all about it." I mean that, too.

It'll be difficult to leave Eustace, but leave him I will. For now, anyway. He's safe here with Captain Abbot and Nova. And he likes this work. I like to think that someday, when I'm older, after I've taken care of Father's treasure in a proper museum, I'll come back here for a visit. I still hope to be a scientist, but I think I'll be one who stays on land, mostly. I've had enough of the ocean for a while. A couple of years ago, Father told me some people were digging up bones of what looked like huge lizards in America. I might spend some time seeing what that's all about. I will carry on the Wonder name in my own way.

I think about Kansas, full of terrible problems, lonely

360

acres, cross neighbors, stingy clouds, but it is where I will return. I lie down and hold my breath until a noise like the swooshing of water fills my ears.

Soon I can almost feel the earth rock-solid beneath me. I pretend I'm on the plains. If I squint, the sails of the *Xerxes* are the thin streaming clouds of the Tolerone sky. On the windward side, the gentle waves glisten like waving wheat fields. On the leeward side, the breaching of a sperm whale is the curve of a rocky limestone outcropping. I go on this way for as long as I can, trying to beat however long I held my breath yesterday. Eventually, though, I have to breathe again. And with the oxygen filling my lungs comes back reality, comes back the tail end of my journey, comes back Mother, waiting and rocking, comes back Ruby, comes back Priss, and comes back unsettled Kansas.

I breathe out slowly.

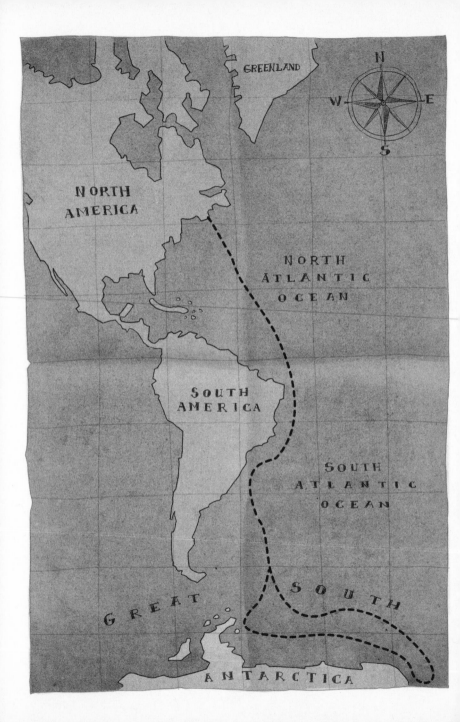

✦ AUTHOR'S NOTE ✦

A number of years ago, a colleague and I were rummaging through the book closet at the school where we taught, looking for novels to teach to our classes. Though boxes of treasures filled the room, we struggled to find a novel with a strong female protagonist.

"Where's the great American adventure book for girls?" I said.

"Maybe you should write it," my colleague responded.

At the time, I laughed. Becoming a writer hadn't even occurred to me. I was a young mother and a recent graduate and a novice teacher, not a writer. More than ten years passed and a lot of life changes occurred, and the number of books featuring bold female characters has grown since then. But the voice of a spirited nineteenth-century girl had sprouted in my mind nonetheless, and I had to tell her story.

Though I am landlocked where I live in southern Minnesota, I am enamored of sea life, ocean travel, and the pioneer spirit, that desire inside people to leave one place in search of other opportunities. And though I am a fiction writer, my favorite genre to read is historical nonfiction. A few years ago, I picked up Nathaniel Philbrick's book *In the Heart of Sea: The Tragedy of the Whaleship Essex*, which won the National Book Award for nonfiction. The book details the lengths to which a group of whalers went to survive when, in 1820, their ship was stove by a whale and sunk. The story of tragedy, endurance, and cannibalism captured the interest of the young nation when it first made American headlines. Herman Melville, too, found the tale irresistible, and out of it grew that great literary touchstone *Moby-Dick*, which I read next. Smitten by descriptions of life at sea, I then read Philbrick's *Sea of Glory: America's Voyage of Discovery, The U.S. Exploring Expedition 1838–1842*, which chronicled the journey to discover Antarctica. It also introduced me to the story of the ship captain, naturalist, botanist, cartographer, possible thief, and sometime tyrant Charles Wilkes, whose collection of artifacts from around the world became the basis for what is now the Smithsonian Institution. Charles Wilkes very loosely morphed into my Charles Wonder, Hallelujah Wonder's father.

The real Charles Wilkes set sail for Antarctica in 1838 to chart new hunting grounds for the whaling industry, to claim the discovery of Antarctica for America, and "to extend the bounds of science and to promote knowledge." In 1840, the Wilkes Expedition did indeed penetrate the frozen waters around Antarctica and claim the discovery of the continent. While the expedition was highly successful in a number of scientific, nautical, and commercial ways, Wilkes rubbed a lot of his crew the wrong way. Some of the survivors of the excursion (twenty-eight of the crew members died) came back intent on ruining his reputation. They charged him with abuse and with stealing precious artifacts. His promotions were delayed, and he was court-martialed. Eventually, he was acquitted of all charges except excessive punishment of his sailors. Wilkes was undeterred. He continued to travel over water and land, pursue scientific endeavors, and participate in the Civil War, nearly starting a war between the United States and the United Kingdom when he ordered shots fired upon the *Trent*, a British steamer. Another court-martial followed. He was an interesting fellow, and

I couldn't shake him from my mind. He spun around up there, becoming fictionalized, until he came out as Hallelujah's father.

I also spent time in New Bedford, Massachusetts, once the whaling capital of the world. Walking the haunt of Herman Melville, with its old streets, buildings, and distinct air, helped me create the New Bedford of Hallelujah's world. At the same time, I was researching the Civil War for one of my adult books, *Stillwater,* and rereading *Adventures of Huckleberry Finn* and *The Narrative of the Life of Frederick Douglass* for classes I was teaching. Mark Twain's penchant for irony and humor emboldened me to tackle serious themes such as slavery, war, violence, and loss. The life of Frederick Douglass, an incredibly intelligent and articulate escaped slave who spent time in New Bedford, helped me round out Eustace, Hallelujah's best and most trusted friend, her match in intelligence and her better in courage.

Hallelujah and Eustace's relationship may seem unlikely, given that she is a white girl and he is a slave, but according to some narratives of the time, slave children played with white children, particularly the children of their masters. Older slave women were often put in charge of the care of the white children of their masters, along with the care of the black children whose parents went to the fields. Children, whose minds aren't always settled on the prejudices and practices of their parents, made friends. I've included other seemingly unusual but nevertheless accurate details—not all slave owners owned enormous plantations, not all slave owners owned a lot of slaves, and not all slaves had quarters on their masters' plantations. The country was spreading west at top speed. Each new state and territory adapted the laws to fit their needs.

Hallelujah and Eustace speak mostly in period-accurate dialect. I did take some liberties with anachronisms here and there, both to be sensitive to modern readers and to capture the essence of childhood in a manner recognizable to today's readers. Many words to describe slaves and black people existed in the 1850s and were used liberally. Most of them are highly offensive. I chose not to use them. I use "Negro" occasionally but selected "black" in most cases, even though it probably wasn't a descriptor widely used at the time. Other anachronisms, such as "kid" to describe a child, I chose because the tone more accurately describes the characters in this stage of their life.

While Tolerone is an invented town, some of the events in this book are based on real events in Lawrence, Kansas, in the mid-1850s. The tensions of the Civil War first manifested in Lawrence, where abolitionists and slave owners squared off to determine whether the territory would become a free or slave state. The conflict was known as "Bleeding Kansas," a phrase coined by Horace Greeley, a prominent abolitionist.

Whaling ships of the period provided America with a wonderful example of how well diversity can work. The challenges of life at sea forced the captains and crewmen to view one another as human beings working together to survive harsh conditions, participate in dangerous employment, and succeed commercially. Skin color didn't matter. Language barriers were overcome. And although it would have been challenging for women and children to be hired for work on a whaling ship, the practice was not unheard of. In fact, some captains chose to bring their wives and children along on voyages. The wives would cook and clean and mend, and the children would help.

Very early in the practice of whaling, some whalers noted what seemed like a leg bone within the bodies of the animals. So while the theory of "vestigial organs" wasn't officially recorded until Darwin's *On the Origin of Species* in 1859, certainly scientists and laymen were speculating about the use and origin and implication of these bones before then. In fact, the seeds of evolutionary theory predate Charles Darwin himself. Darwin's own grandfather,

Erasmus, noted that life-forms change over time, but he couldn't pin down what might be causing these changes. His ideas were published in the 1790s. For these reasons, it didn't seem like too much of a stretch for Hallelujah's father to have a theory about leg bones and the possibility that whales once walked on land.

All of these historical works and events, along with an imaginary but persistent voice of a girl in my head, came together to become *Wonder at the Edge of the World*. The book is a work of fiction, but it is inspired in part by real people, real events, and real books. Many thanks to Ben Davidson at New York University and Brian Fors at South Central College, who offered their insight to help make the book as historically accurate as necessary to tell Lu's story.

✦ ACKNOWLEDGMENTS ✦

Thanks to Faye Bender, Andrea Spooner, Deirdre Jones, Brian Fors, Ben Davidson, the staff of the New Bedford Whaling Museum, Nathaniel Philbrick, L. Frank Baum, Mark Twain, and Herman Melville.

✦ ABOUT THE AUTHOR ✦

Nicole Helget is the author of three adult novels: *The Turtle Catcher*, *The Summer of Ordinary Ways*, and *Stillwater*. She has also coauthored a middle grade novel, *Horse Camp*, with her husband. She lives in Minnesota.